FOGGY

with a Chance of

MURDER

FOGGY
with a Chance of
MURDER

A NOVEL OF SUSPENSE

G. G. VANDAGRIFF

DESERET
BOOK

SALT LAKE CITY, UTAH

Library of Congress Cataloging-in-Publication Data
Vandagriff, G. G. author.
Foggy with a chance of murder / G. G. Vandagriff.
    p.   cm.
    Summary: What should have been a peaceful walk on the beach turns tragic when travel author Chloe Greene tries unsuccessfully to save a ten-year-old boy from drowning.
    ISBN 978-1-60908-014-3 (paperbound)
    1. Terrorism—Fiction. 2. Mormons—Fiction. I. Title.
    PS3572.A427F64 2011
    813.'54—dc22   2011001530

Printed in the United States of America
Malloy Lithographing Incorporated, Ann Arbor, MI

10 9 8 7 6 5 4 3 2 1

*To Alana Lee Tompkins,
my number one fan and dear friend*

ACKNOWLEDGMENTS

To Zina Whetten, who helped me make that rocky climb to the altar of complete submission.

To Lisa Hawkins, a loyal fan long before I knew her and now an ace alpha reader and midnight editor (who knows the law a little better than she should).

To a new fan, Marta Olsen Smith, who answered a Facebook plea and gave me the great title for this book.

To all my friends and to those I don't yet know who work with people to overcome their addictions.

And, as always, to David, my true knight in every respect.

CHAPTER ONE

Chloe sat on the narrow strip of beach staring into the Pacific Ocean off San Clemente. The never-ending crash of the waves calmed her with its constancy. Because it was June, the fog blended with the ocean on the horizon, making the twilight bluish gray and eerie in a way that appealed to her sense of the dramatic. Life would go on. That much was certain. The earth, the moon, and the surf would continue their cycles, no matter how much crazy humans messed up their lives with bad decisions, addictions, and poor judgment.

Behind her, in the elegant beach house, she could hear the noise of the cocktail party in progress. She refused to go back inside and mingle with her mother's friends, who knew nothing about the laws against sexual harassment. Yet there was no way to get to her car unless she went through the house. Its glassed-in porch abutted their neighbor's glassed-in porch on one side, and an ancient bougainvillea-covered fence connected to the opposite neighbor's wall. There was no way out but through.

And through she would not go. Not after Lawrence Samuelson had pinched her and a drunken Otis Lamb had kissed her on the neck. Why hadn't she escaped before the party began? Because her mother had begged her to stay. She never tired of showing off her "brilliant writer" daughter.

Shivering slightly from the breeze, Chloe got to her feet and walked north. The tide was coming in. If she wanted to remain on the beach, she needed to move to a wider strip of sand.

The wind stiffened. The fog crept further inland, and the sun began to go down behind it with a flamingo pink glow. Dressed only in her Speedo swimsuit and white terry cloth robe, Chloe shivered. Her suit was still wet from her dip in the cold sea that wouldn't begin warming up until July. Clutching her arms around herself, she endeavored to coax some warmth into them. The surf crept up to her bare toes, engulfing her to the ankles. Ever since she could remember, she had loved the feel of her toes sinking into the wet sand.

She always paid a price for walking on the beach, however. It was a trigger for emotions she was still running from. Three books ago (*Lucca, Corfu,* and *Cinque Terre*), she had been walking this same stretch with Luke when he told her of his betrayal. She tried to stifle the pain, but, like a dangerous riptide, it lurked just below the surface of her consciousness, waiting to pull her into a dark sea of memory.

Against the sunset, the beach was bare except for a man running towards her. As he came closer, she could see he was no ordinary jogger. His brow was furrowed, and he looked anxiously out at the sea.

"Have you seen a little boy?" he called to her above the sound of the waves.

Chloe's memories vaporized, and she turned her eyes from the man back toward the way she had come. The beach was empty. She stared out into the water behind her.

"How old is he?" she asked as the man drew closer. His brown eyes were stark with worry.

"Only ten. He's in a black wetsuit."

"I've just been watching the ocean back there," she said, indicating the stretch behind her. "I haven't seen anything. Are you sure he's out there?"

"He left the house about half an hour ago, Ginger said. Wearing his wetsuit. I can't imagine why she let him go."

"I'll help you look. Does he have a boogie board?"

"Yes, but it's back at the house. I don't know what he was thinking." The man ran a hand through his light brown hair.

At that moment, Chloe saw a patch of black against the white foam of the surf. Without another thought, she threw off her robe. "There!" she cried and ran through the water toward the waves.

The cold water shocked her, but she didn't stop. Trained as a life-guard, she dived expertly into the ocean.

The black patch disappeared beneath the wave. It was taking too long to resurface. Frantically scanning the water, Chloe swam towards the location where she had seen what she thought was the boy. The man materialized beside her. A new wave broke. She saw the black patch just for a moment and dived towards it. In the churning water, she finally reached the spot. Another new wave was swelling when she felt the slam of the body against her chest. Grabbing hold of a limb, she pulled it up out of the water and saw a small, white-faced child, a blue-lipped replica of the man who was swimming beside her.

Together they dragged the boy to the shore, hauling the dead weight between them. When they reached the sand, they laid his body down, and the man began to administer CPR. Chloe hoped it wasn't too late.

"I'm calling 911," she told him, running towards the nearest beach house.

No one responded to her frenzied knocks at the door. Panicked, she ran down the steps and up to the next house. She pounded on the wide front window while an old man with white hair approached.

"Emergency!" she called through the window, miming a telephone call with her hand.

The old man drew open the sliding door, and Chloe repeated, "Emergency! I need to use your phone!"

The man nodded and stepped aside, pointing in the direction of what looked like the kitchen.

"What house number is this?" she asked.

"Number 35," the owner said, his eyebrows drawn together in concern.

With icy fingers, she dialed the number. "Possible drowning. A ten-year-old boy," she reported. "Number 35 Capistrano Shores. Out on the beach."

As soon as the call was acknowledged, she barely thanked the owner before running back outside.

Chloe could see by the man's frantic efforts that he had made no progress in reviving his son. The little body in the wetsuit lay unmoving, sprawled on the sand.

"Ambulance is on the way," she said.

The father sat back wearily, the pain in his eyes making them nearly black. "It's too late. It's too late." He felt again for a pulse and found none. "He's gone."

Chloe didn't know what to do. She knelt next to the man, who loomed over her even as they crouched. *Football player* floated inconsequentially through her mind as she noted his powerful neck and shoulders. *How helpless he must feel! A parent's worst nightmare.*

"Let me try," she said with an intensity she didn't understand herself. She rolled the body over, pulled it onto her lap so the head was dangling over her leg, and began tapping sharply on the boy's back. Over and over she pelted him, hoping to see salt water spew out of his mouth. Nothing did.

Finally, she heard the scream of the ambulance. Within moments, paramedics swarmed over the beach with their equipment. Chloe stood by helplessly. The man sat by his son like a statue. Someone had draped a blanket over his shoulders. He was fully dressed, his khakis and polo shirt drenched from the attempted rescue. He must have arrived home to find his son missing.

The young paramedics failed in their attempts to resuscitate the child. They stared at one another, and then, controlling their faces, they spoke to the father. The man didn't reply. Head bowed, he followed the stretcher carrying his son to the ambulance. As he passed Chloe, he put a hand on her shoulder but still didn't speak. Left standing on the beach, she felt as though an abyss had opened inside her heart, allowing fresh pain to flood in like the tide. Devastation was never far away. The world was not a safe place.

CHAPTER TWO

Chloe's tiny but unusually self-effacing mother was repentant the next morning. "I'm sorry, sweetie. I guess I got a little tipsy last night. But you didn't need to disappear. All my neighbors wanted to talk with you. It's not every day they can meet a best-selling author."

Chloe looked at her hungover mother. She lay on the couch with a compress over her eyes, carefully arranged so as not to disturb her strawberry blonde hair. What had happened to the lovely Texan beauty queen with the head for business who had accompanied Chloe and Daddy all over the world? Mother had managed both hers and Daddy's creative temperaments with a discipline that could run a small country and still manage to rustle up a dinner fit for royalty. Now her hands weren't even steady enough to put on lipstick.

"Your neighbors include drunken lechers who love to pinch women. Mother, you were supposed to stick to club soda last night."

"I know, honey bunch. I'm sorry. I wanted it to be a good night for you, just back from your book tour and everything. Some of the people who live down here are retired from real influential jobs. They have pull. I thought maybe it would help your sales."

Chloe didn't answer but walked toward the window and looked out at the ocean. The peace of her return was shredded. Not only had her mother gone off the wagon in her absence, but an innocent child had died and the happiness of a father had been destroyed. She was all too familiar with grief. Any comfort she had taken in the success of her tour to promote *Blood and Wine* had vanished, and she knew she was going to have a job of getting it back. Maybe a stint at the shooting range would give her some illusion of power.

Life in Cinque Terre had been good, simple, and restoring, but her writing was not something she was particularly proud of. She wrote only suspense novels that took place in offbeat locales. She had withdrawn from a career as a promising novelist because she couldn't go deeper and show her pain to the world. Light fiction was the only way to control the hurt of Daddy's death and Luke's desertion. Hers was a superficial existence, and she knew it. She despised herself for offering brightly colored alternate worlds full of take-charge women, entertaining her readers instead of tackling the hard questions. Daddy would have called her a coward.

"I'm going down to the corner to get a paper," she told her mother.

After a quick glance in the mirror that showed long, violently wavy red-blonde hair, she shrugged hopelessly at her wild appearance and walked out into the foggy morning. Crossing the railroad tracks, Chloe turned the corner to the 7 Eleven. How she missed Daddy! When he was alive, they used to take morning walks together and then settle down in their beachfront living room to share the Orange County edition of the *Los Angeles Times*. If he were alive, her mother wouldn't be a drunk. Most of all, Chloe could talk to him about last night, about this sense of helplessness she was feeling. She had to get her mojo back. Right now, the world wasn't a place she cared to dwell in. Men were killed in random accidents on freeways, small boys drowned in the charming ocean, and even the strongest of mothers got drunk from grief.

Purchasing a paper and a bottle of orange juice, Chloe wished she had someplace to go besides the beach. She thought suddenly of house number 35. It was 10:00 A.M. Surely the old man whose telephone she had used would be awake by now. She must thank him properly.

The house was trimmed in white and nautical blue. Hesitantly, she unlatched the gate and went to the door. It had a brass knocker and a doorbell. She opted for the doorbell, thinking the occupant might be hard of hearing.

The white-haired man opened the door and smiled at her. The smile made him appear surprisingly youthful. "May I help you?"

"Hello. I'm Chloe Greene. I'm the one who tore through here yesterday and summoned the paramedics. I just wanted to say thank you."

The man opened the door wider. "Come in. I gather the poor boy didn't make it. You couldn't be his mother. If you were, I'm the last one you would be thinking about."

Chloe entered the neat home and noticed the nautical touches had been continued inside. The walls were paneled in teak, and the fixtures were brass. He was either a recreational sailor or a retired Navy man.

"No. I don't know who he was. I just ran into his father on the beach. I helped pull the boy out, that's all."

Gesturing to a white leather, overstuffed chair, the man introduced himself. "I'm Edward Petersen. I'm afraid I can't offer you any coffee."

"That's all right. As a matter of fact, I brought some orange juice." She sat down across from a coffee table littered with maga-zines, books, and a yellow legal tablet filled with notes.

"Don't mind the clutter. I'm working on a project."

Chloe laid her newspaper on the coffee table. "I thought we could find out the identity of the little boy," she said, opening it. "I'd like to do something, but I don't know what."

"Let me get a glass for your juice," Mr. Petersen said. "By the way, are you Chloe Greene, the author?"

"I am," she answered, scanning the paper.

"Well, I'm a great fan," he said, indicating a row of her thrillers on a nearby teak bookshelf. She noticed a row of books beneath hers that seemed to be mostly ecclesiastical in nature—*Jesus the Christ, A Disciple's Life, History of the Church.* What an odd juxtaposition!

Her eyes went back to the newspaper, searching for an article on the drowning. "I'm glad you like my books. Let's see, would it be in the Orange County section?"

Mr. Petersen had picked up that section of the paper. "Here it is," he said, holding it out to her. "No! The boy was Robert Stevens III. Oh, my." He handed the paper to her and shifted his gaze to the ocean outside his window. "I loved that child. If I had guessed it was Robbie, I would have gone out and tried to help. My instinct was to stay out of the way. But his father must be distraught. What does it say?"

Chloe focused on the small photo of the boy that looked like a school picture. He had on a red-and-white striped rugby shirt, his hair blond and carefully combed. Brown eyes looked solemnly at the camera, his face stark, oddly like his father's and not that of a little boy.

"'Son of Local Tech Tycoon Dies in Drowning Accident,'" she read aloud.

"'Robert Stevens III, age 10, succumbed to the incoming tide at approximately 8:30 last night along the beach of the Capistrano Shores development. He had apparently been swimming alone. His father, Robert Stevens Jr., was away at the time the boy went into the water. He returned home to find his child, left in the care of his aunt, Ginger Stevens, missing. Assisted by an unknown good Samaritan, Stevens pulled his boy from the water. Paramedics were called, but efforts to resuscitate the boy failed.

"'Robert Stevens III was a student at San Clemente Elementary School, where he played soccer. His teachers described him as a quiet, serious student who had recently lost his mother to breast cancer. His father, Robert Stevens Jr., is the founder and CEO of Stevens Communications, a manufacturer of circuit boards for handheld electronic devices.'"

Chloe put the paper down and opened her bottle of orange juice. Seeing the emotion-packed facts reduced to black and white disoriented her, as though two different events had occurred. "What do you think? This doesn't tell us much."

"Oh, I think it says a great deal," Mr. Petersen said. "And combined with what I know of the family, it makes a sad story. I wonder where the memorial service will be held. The boy's mother is buried in Pacific View."

"In Newport Beach?"

"That's where Rob Stevens's company is headquartered. The cemetery has a beautiful view of the ocean, but now Rob may not want that. Will you come to the services with me if I can find out where they are?" Mr. Petersen asked.

"I'm sure Mr. Stevens never wants to see me again. And besides, I'm not much of a believer."

"What do you mean?"

She gestured toward the lower row of books. "I guess you'd call me an agnostic."

"You don't believe in an afterlife?"

"I'm not sure. I can't believe there's a God who cares about me." Oddly, it didn't seem strange to be talking so existentially to this man. Somehow the occasion and his quiet serenity warranted it. His snug little house and his calm, accepting smile radiated a tranquility she had thought she would never feel again. She found she wanted to talk.

"Why?" he persisted.

"What about all the tragedy we see here? The boy's mother died of breast cancer. For all we know, he could have committed suicide out of grief."

Chloe remembered the black wetsuit the boy had been wearing and thought suicide unlikely. She frowned. "But what about this aunt? The one who was supposed to be watching him? Where was she when she was needed? Why didn't God use her to protect little Robert?"

Mr. Petersen's brow furrowed, and he began to fold the portion of the newspaper he had retained.

"What?" Chloe demanded. "What is it you know?"

"She has an affliction," he said. "I doubt if she realized he was gone."

"What kind of affliction? I mean, my heart is breaking here. Please tell me what you know. Help me understand."

"Between the two of us?"

"Of course."

"Ms. Stevens is an alcoholic, I'm afraid."

The news hit Chloe with the impact of a Mack truck. Suddenly, it was just too personal, too much. Tears stung her eyes. "Now I really don't believe God cares."

Mr. Petersen sighed, and his bright blue eyes sought hers. "We don't know the whole story, Chloe Greene. There may be a reason we can't see."

"And what was the reason my father was killed in a random multicar crash on the Santa Ana freeway?"

His eyes softened, and he handed her a clean handkerchief from his trouser pocket.

"How long ago was that?"

"Five years ago. My mother's become an alcoholic, too." Chloe stood defiantly. "I'm sorry, Mr. Petersen. It's just too much."

He stood beside her. "I know this is hard for you to hear, but death isn't the end. It's part of life. Part of a vast continuum. There's a bigger picture."

"Even if I believed that, can you explain why it had to happen so tragically? Breast cancer, a car accident, a drowning?"

"Only God knows why. And He does know. I can imagine that it must be hard for you to trust Him, but He's crying along with us now. He doesn't like to see us drenched in grief like this. But it's part of mortality. It's the price we pay for coming to this earth."

"How can you possibly know that? How can you trust such a whimsical being?"

"I've lived a lot of years, Chloe Greene. I've learned a lot in that time about eternal perspective."

Chloe sat again, as though her legs had given out. Mr. Petersen reseated himself.

"I trust God," he told her. "Ultimately, He is the only being who is trustworthy. There is hope for a better world."

Chloe blew her nose into the handkerchief. "You sound so sure."

"I've seen the hand of the Lord work over the years, not just in isolated events. It was part of my job."

"You're a minister?"

"No. A missionary. Before my wife died, she and I went to Russia on a mission for The Church of Jesus Christ of Latter-day Saints."

"I've never heard of it."

"A lot of people call us Mormons."

"Oh. I know about Mormons. I had a friend in school who was a Mormon. She didn't smoke or drink or have sex or even swear. As a matter of fact, she almost got me to believe in God. We had a lot of interesting discussions. But she committed suicide. Your religion must not have brought her much comfort or hope."

"Well, they're finding out a lot of new things about depression these days. It's an illness, as real as cancer."

"And it kills."

"Yes, I'm afraid so, in some cases. Where did you go to school?"

"Stanford. I graduated about ten years ago."

"And you've been writing ever since?"

"I worked for my father for a while in order to get the money to travel to Prague. Then I wrote a novel set just before and after the fall of the Berlin Wall. But after Daddy died, I'm afraid I hadn't much left in me for serious fiction. So I started writing my offbeat thrillers. Ironically, they were a success."

"So your whole life hasn't been a tragedy."

"No. But I'd give up my career to have Daddy back." She sniffed. "I don't know why I'm telling you this. Do you still work for your church? Are you trying to convert me?"

He smiled. "I'm just trying to offer you a little comfort. And it's a comfort for me to talk about these things at a time like this. But, no, I'm retired now. I write a little myself, as a matter of fact." He indicated the mess on the coffee table.

"What do you write?"

"Well, right now I'm writing a book on hope."

"Hope? How can anyone possibly write a book on hope?"

"Like I said, I've been around long enough to have more of an eternal perspective. I think that in this troubled world I can bring a message about what is important about living to people's hearts."

Chloe digested this. Finally, she asked, "Do you have a family?"

"My Rachel died about five years ago. I have four sons living and twenty-four grandchildren."

"Good grief! That's a lot of grandchildren. You said four sons living. Have you had other children?"

"A daughter who died of polio when she was ten and another son who was killed by a drunk driver five years ago."

"The same year as your wife! That must have been a rough year. And you can still write about hope?"

He gave her his calm smile. "Oh, yes. I have mighty hope. It's what keeps me going."

"Don't you get lonely here by yourself?"

"The grandchildren are all in college now. They like to visit the beach. It's one of the reasons I live here. I'm also an old sea dog. The smell of the ocean is a tonic for my soul."

Chloe realized that she'd been uncharacteristically nosy. "I'm sorry to give you the third degree. It's just that you were so emphatic about the hope thing . . ."

"It's all right. The reason I'm writing about hope is that people need it so badly. No one knows that more than I. I don't say I don't hurt. But hoping helps."

"I can see that." She stood again. "So you know the Stevens family. You're going to the funeral?"

"I think I'll try. Are you sure you wouldn't like to come with me?"

"No. I really don't think Mr. Stevens would like it. But I'll send flowers if you let me know the name of the funeral home."

"If I might suggest something—I know at his wife's funeral Rob requested no flowers. He wanted the money to go to breast cancer research instead. This time he may have a similar request. Shall I let you know?"

"Yes, please. Here. I'll write down my telephone number."

CHAPTER THREE

Rob Stevens stood by the pathetically small casket, listening to the empty words of the minister he had found through the mortuary. Well, not really listening. To be fair, he was sure the man was doing his best with the help of some kind of prayer book.

His mind wandered, ascending to the clouds and, like a camera making a film, it looked down on the small crowd surrounding the hole in the green carpet of lawn. Ginger, weeping into a handkerchief, full of guilt and self-hatred. A handful of his employees, shifting uncomfortably on their feet, ill at ease in the circumstances. His neighbor, Edward Petersen, who was also the world's most persistent home teacher.

Coming down from the clouds abruptly, he felt eyes on the back of his neck. Who was staring at him? Turning just enough to capture the person in his peripheral vision, he discovered that it was a stranger about his own age. He was tall and blond, with the still-toned body of a former athlete. Who was he and what was he doing here? Dressed casually, he obviously wasn't attached to the funeral home. He looked as if he had strayed off a golf course somewhere.

The minister cleared his throat, and Rob looked at him, surprised he had let his mind wander at such a time. Denial, shock— his old friends from the time of Pamela's death. He knew that when they left, the pain would be nearly unbearable. Now the minister was staring at him, as though Rob were supposed to do something.

"Let us pray," the man said, and Rob realized with some guilt that the clergyman had been waiting until he had Rob's full attention.

But instead of listening to the prayer, instead of looking at the smooth, burnished walnut of the casket, instead of thinking of his dead son, his mind settled on the stranger behind him. Who would come uninvited to a funeral? It was all that Rob himself could do to be there, and it was for his own son. *My son. My son who is dead. When will the feeling come back to my body? My heart?*

"Who the devil is Chloe Greene?" Rob wondered aloud the next day as he sorted through the donation cards. How was he to thank her for a thousand dollar donation, for heaven's sake? How had she known about the breast cancer fund? Rob tapped the edge of the card on the tabletop, wondering what he should do.

Ginger came into the room. Rob clenched his teeth. He could scarcely bear the sight of his sister. He was taking her to rehab that very afternoon. If he'd done it years ago, Robbie might still be alive. Of course, he should have known better than to leave his son in her care, even for thirty minutes. Rob knew he was ultimately to blame. The crater in his chest ached. It had opened during the night as he had paced the empty beach in the moonlight. This time his period of denial had been regrettably short.

Robbie. The light of his life had gone out. There was no one left now of his happy little family. Just eighteen months ago, there had been three of them. Now that family was gone.

"Have you heard of a Chloe Greene?" he asked Ginger.

"The writer? Yes, of course. I have her books."

Writer? "Do you know her?"

"Heavens, no. I'd like to, though. She's been all over the world. I'll bet she has some exciting stories to tell. Even more exciting than the ones she writes about."

Ginger's mind was incomprehensible to him, so he didn't bother asking what she meant. "Do you happen to know where I can find one of her books?"

"As a matter of fact, I was just packing up her most recent one to take into rehab with me. Would you like to see it?"

For some reason, he felt compelled. "Yes, please."

Moments later, he was staring at the photograph of the woman he had hoped he would never see again. She had been a brave soul and had tried like a madwoman to save Robbie, but the memory of those moments was too much. She'd been there. She'd held Robbie in her arms and on her lap. He should have been grateful to her for her help, but all he felt when he looked at the photo was anguish. She was beautiful, now that he could study her properly. A face with high cheekbones, full lips, and large golden eyes, surrounded by a cloud of red-gold hair. *Very Botticelli.* She might have been the model for *The Birth of Venus.*

He had no wish to see her ever again; however, he had to acknowledge her obviously heartfelt donation. Taking out his pen, he made a note of the publisher's name. He would have his assistant look up the address and send a thank-you note care of her publisher.

"You all ready to leave then, Ginger?"

"Are you sure about this, Rob? This place costs an arm and a leg."

"You need help. You've needed it for years."

"You blame me for Robbie's death."

"If I blame anyone, I blame myself for thinking you could watch him."

"You blame me," she insisted. "And you're right. I'm just telling you I don't know if I can get sober. I don't think I even want to."

"As of now, you have no choice. You're signed up to stay six months."

"I'm only going because I owe it to you and Robbie. It's my penance. But I don't think it'll work. You're wasting your money."

They were cruising the freeway at seventy-five miles an hour when Ginger continued her lament. "I'll never forgive myself, Rob. But I don't even deserve the anesthetic of alcohol at this point. Maybe if I feel the pain, full on, it will change me, but I have regrets you know nothing about. And I think Robbie's death may be just one too many to live with."

Before he could reply, they heard a loud report, and suddenly his Porsche was spinning out of control across the busy freeway. Horns blared as Rob tried to steer the car out of the skid, but the move was too sharp, and in a moment he felt himself hanging upside down as the car rolled. Once it had spun completely around, it tumbled over and over, finally stopping on its roof inside a strong, six-foot barrier of oleanders. He and his sister were hanging by their seat belts. As far as he could tell, they were both uninjured, but the roof of the car was partially crushed. Rob and Ginger were pinned inside.

Wouldn't you know it? Just when he wanted to die, a miracle happened, and for some strange reason, he was spared.

Suddenly, Ginger started to scream. Rob was unable even to mumble a word.

Out of nowhere there were sirens, and soon two highway patrolmen were standing outside the window.

"I need a drink. Oh, man, do I need a drink," Ginger whined.

The officers leaned in the upside-down window.

"There was nothing wrong with my tires," Rob found himself repeating.

"Any injuries?"

"No, believe it or not. Until today, I've always hated oleanders," Rob said, realizing only dimly how idiotic he sounded.

"Well, they saved your life today," a short California Highway Patrol officer informed him. "If you'd flipped onto the other side of the freeway, you'd have been killed for certain. The paramedics will be here soon. We'll get you out in no time."

"Look at my tire, can you?" Rob asked as he struggled with the airbag. "There was a loud noise before it went. I know it sounds nuts, but I think the driver next to me must have shot it out."

The paramedics arrived while the CHP officers were doing their investigation. The emergency workers began the time-consuming task of extracting Rob and Ginger from the Porsche. By the time they were free, the paramedics had determined that Ginger's right arm was broken. Rob was only shaken up, and he refused a tranquilizing shot to steady him.

"We'll take your tire and have forensics look at it," one of the patrolmen said.

They asked Rob to come with them to file an incident report, while Ginger went by ambulance to the emergency room to have her arm set. "Don't let her go until I come for her," Rob said to one of the EMTs privately. "She's on her way to rehab."

"Anyone got it in for you that you know of?" one of the patrolmen asked on the way to police headquarters.

"Just God," Rob replied curtly.

After remaining silent for a while, the patrolman said, "Been having some other troubles, have you?"

"My son drowned a few days ago."

"But no evidence of foul play?"

"No. My sister was in charge, and she was so wasted she didn't even know he was gone from the house. That's why she's finally going into rehab. Pretty much against her will."

When he had given his statement, called for a rental car to be delivered to CHP headquarters, and arranged for a tow of the Porsche, Rob picked Ginger up from the ER. He didn't know if it was good or bad that she was muzzy with tranquilizers, but at least she had stopped asking for a drink.

When they finally reached Renaissance House, Ginger reluctantly checked herself in. Rob watched as she was escorted behind the doors of the lockdown facility. Looking over her shoulder, she gave him one last pleading look, but he steeled himself against it.

He was filling out more admission papers when a tall, professional-looking redhead walked into the room and seated herself across from him at the desk.

"I'm so sorry about your loss, Mr. Stevens."

"Thanks," he said and reapplied himself to the work in front of him.

"I'm the therapist in charge of your sister's care. Sonia Updike." She held out a hand across the table.

"Pleased to meet you."

"I'm afraid I have to bother you with some questions."

Resigned, he laid down his pen.

"First, we normally wouldn't admit someone who'd just been in a car accident and was injured. I called the doctor who treated your sister in the ER, and he assures me that she can start rehab—and we have the medical facilities to see that her arm is healing as it should.

She'll be on suicide watch the first week, anyway, so if there's a concussion or something the ER didn't see, we'll know about it."

Rob ran his hand over his face. "Okay. Because she needs to be here."

Sonia held his eyes with her own for a moment. "I read about your son's death in the newspaper. It's obvious there is some correlation between that and your sister's coming to rehab—and it is somewhat apparent that you want her to be here more than she does. Tell me, do you hold her in any way to blame?"

"I hold myself to blame for thinking she could watch him for half an hour. I should have had her in rehab years ago. Then maybe Robbie would still be alive."

"So you blame yourself?"

"For trusting Ginger."

"How long has she been an alcoholic, Mr. Stevens?"

"Since she was in college. It's been fourteen years since she graduated. She came down from Alaska to live with me eighteen months ago, when my wife died. She did it as a favor to me. She thought she could manage not to drink in the daytime, but it was dusk when this happened, and she had a pretty good buzz on already. Frankly, I don't know if there's much hope of her ever getting sober."

"So you're sending her into treatment as punishment?"

"Let's say there are consequences I should have foreseen but didn't. I truly believe my sister needs to be sober. She needs to get a life."

"And what about you? Are you seeing anyone about your anger?"

"Me?"

"Yes, you. Alcoholics create a flawed family system, Mr. Stevens. Treating the alcoholic isn't enough. The whole family needs a fresh start."

"What am I supposed to do?"

"You could start by going to Al-Anon."

"But I'm not the alcoholic!"

"Al-Anon is for families of alcoholics. Children, spouses, care-givers, anyone who is affected. Will Ms. Stevens be returning to live with you?"

Rob narrowed his eyes. "More than likely. Until she gets a job."

"Then you definitely need some help. Especially under the circumstances."

"You mean Robbie's death."

"You really should consider private counseling, Mr. Stevens."

He rolled the pen between his hands. Private counseling. That would mean digging out all the old pain and regret about Pamela. And Robbie as well. Al-Anon would be less personal, surely.

"I'll try Al-Anon."

"Well, that's a start. Here's a list of meetings near your home. You should plan on going at least once a week to start."

Rob left the treatment center with no place to go. For days he had been focusing on Robbie's funeral and Ginger's rehab. Anything but the pain. Now there was no one to go home to. He couldn't manage the office. Robbie's face wouldn't go away. His cold, dead face. Rob could not block out the sound of those treacherous waves. They had lulled him to sleep after Pamela's death, but now they kept him awake. He felt like he hadn't slept in years.

Rob got into his rented Audi and headed for the cemetery. At least he could be near him. Him and Pamela. His family. He knotted his fist and hit the dashboard. Pain tore through him like wildfire.

How could he go on living at the beach? Or go on living at all, for that matter? What was the point?

His phone rang. The police confirmed that the preliminary forensics reports indicated that the tire had been destroyed by a bullet. Someone else wanted him dead, too.

Battered by the events of the last week, Rob could scarcely concentrate on this surprising fact. Perversely, he decided to stay alive, at least long enough to find out the who and why of this mystery.

CHAPTER FOUR

Thank you so much for your more than generous donation to Breast Cancer Research in my son's name. I will also never be able to adequately express my gratitude for all you did to try to save him on that horrible day. Your generosity and courage speak of a tender heart.

Sincerely,

Robert Stevens Jr.

Chloe looked at the note in her hand. She read it again.

Did she have a tender heart? Chloe searched the deep blue walls of her bedroom, studded with reproductions of her book covers which had been framed by her proud mother. She supposed she might. What there was left of it. There was no other explanation for why she had felt compelled to donate such a large amount of money to this man's cause. But she still felt the gesture was incomplete.

For some reason she couldn't understand, she had a further compulsion to try to help this wounded man. If only to make the world feel safer. Chloe knew she was a raging codependent, according to her best friend, Rosemary. To keep her own pain manageable, Chloe felt she had to take care of everyone else so the world wouldn't fall apart.

Until Daddy died, the world had always seemed safe, even during their trips to out-of-the-way places around the globe. After his death, all that had changed. Anything and anyone could be taken from her by random force at any moment.

Feeling the need for some connection, she decided to call on Mr. Petersen again to see if he had gone to the funeral. This time, she found him sitting on the wooden stairs that led from his patio down to the beach, elbows on his knees, chin in his hands, idly studying the waves. When he saw her, he gave a warm smile of welcome. "I see you brought your own orange juice again."

"Would you mind chatting with me for a few minutes?" Chloe inquired.

"I'd be honored," he said. "Let's go indoors. I'm used to this damp and foggy weather, but you look a little blue with the cold."

She was feeling the cold and appreciated his kind attention. They entered his shipshape, little house.

"I see you're still working on your book," she said, studying the clutter on his coffee table. "Have you ever considered using a word processor?"

"I'm spoiled. I've got a granddaughter who transcribes everything for me. I can't think with a blank computer screen staring me in the face. Have a seat. I'll get a glass for your juice."

Chloe seated herself in the oversized leather armchair she had used on her last visit and unscrewed the top of her juice bottle.

"Here we are," her host said a moment later, handing her a glass.

"Thanks." Pouring her juice, Chloe tried to think of how to

begin. "I got a note from Robert Stevens today. It was forwarded from my publisher in New York."

"About?"

"Well, mostly to thank me for my donation, I think. But he did mention my attempt to help him on the beach."

"That was prompt. He must have mailed it shortly after the funeral if it's been to New York and back again."

"Yes. That's what I thought. Did you go to the funeral?"

"I did, yes," he replied. "It was just a small graveside service."

"How was he?"

"Poker stiff. I don't think he was really there."

"How was the service?"

"Not really too comforting, I'm afraid."

"What do you mean by that?"

"I don't know. I guess I thought it focused too much on the tragedy. Rob was raised a Mormon. I was disappointed that he had a nondenominational minister."

"What would you have focused on if you had been in charge?"

"Oh, I would have mentioned the tragedy. But I would have extended some hope. He can be with his son again. This does not have to be the end of their relationship."

"What do you mean by that?"

Mr. Petersen settled into his chair. "I believe in the Resurrection, Chloe Greene. All men will be resurrected because of Jesus Christ's sacrifice."

"You really believe that?"

"Death is not the end, I promise you."

"My father feels very dead to me," Chloe said, aware of the sour note in her voice.

"Resurrection is a free gift given to us all by the grace of God,"

Mr. Petersen insisted. "Robbie will be resurrected. So will your father. So will you, someday. That's what I believe."

Chloe felt a little jolt. She saw Daddy as she last remembered him, bending over to kiss her cheek, his black hair falling over one eye, reminding her not to overwork to meet her deadline. Was it really possible there could be a life after this one? Every particle of her education had taught her that the only heaven was the one we tried to create here on earth through tolerance and benevolence. God was a myth for weak and lazy people to lean on.

"I'm afraid that sounds like a contrived fairy tale to me. The monks made it up in the Dark Ages to keep people in line and downtrodden, subject to a corrupt, power-hungry church."

"I might agree with you about the monks. But the church was only corrupt because it deviated from Christ's teachings when He was on earth. It had no power or authority to act in His name. Men will always seek power and authority for themselves if they are not fully anchored in Christ." The look in Mr. Petersen's surprisingly blue eyes was steady and stern. "Unfortunately, that is the nature of the natural man. But there is another way." Gently, he placed his hand on the arm of her chair and leaned closer. "I have felt the Savior's love, Chloe Greene. It is real. And it brings peace."

"Excuse my skepticism, but how do you know it isn't a delusion? The natural tendency of man to look for an answer to salve his pain?"

"I can't put it into words, Chloe. But my peace is real. Not delusional. I wish you could feel it, but it obviously goes against everything you have been taught or have felt in your life."

She was silent, studying the papers on the coffee table. So this was the source of his hope. In spite of herself, she could feel it emanating from him with a kind of mellow sweetness that calmed the turbulence inside of her. Fighting against it, she superimposed images of the Holocaust, children starving in Africa, and Daddy's broken body the paramedics had pulled from the senseless, random crash.

"I'm sorry," Chloe said. "I'm glad you have peace. But we live in a wicked and unfathomable world. I don't believe your God would have created such a place."

"Man makes it wicked, Chloe. Not God."

She stood up, determined to hang onto her grief. It was hard and real—not an insipid watercolor of a rainbow with butterflies.

"Think about it. Pray about it. I promise it will bring you peace," Mr. Petersen continued.

"I think only man can make the world a better place. You are a man of peace," Chloe replied. "You have good karma. But all you've convinced me of is that my way of life is a cop-out. I need to help people, not entertain them. Maybe I should look into training for hospice or joining the Peace Corps."

"Those are excellent ideas, Chloe. But I would miss your books. Without realizing it, maybe, you have helped bring happiness into a lot of lives. People like to read about the good guys winning."

"You're kind. Kindness is a good thing. I'm not always kind. You haven't convinced me about God, but you have made me decide to be a kinder person. Thank you." She stood. "I'll visit you again sometime, if you like. Don't you get lonely?"

"Of course I do. I hope you will come again." Mr. Petersen's face was tender and paternal as he walked her to the door. It was hard not to believe he was sincere. Too bad there weren't many of his kind in the world. As she shook his hand, she felt a peculiar sensation of warmth from the crown of her head to the tips of her toes. "I'll always be happy to see you, Chloe Greene," he said.

She almost said *I don't want to deprive you of your false sense of security*, but instead she left the house, taking the sweetness of Mr.

Petersen with her. Perversely, she tried to dissipate it again with scenes of reality's horrors. By the time she arrived home, she had reaffirmed to herself that the only God was nature. The waves, the sun, the moon.

It was just as well she hadn't deceived herself with Mr. Petersen's philosophy. She arrived home to find her mother weeping uncontrollably on the couch in the living room.

"What is it, Mother?"

"I don't know," Martha Greene answered. "I can't seem to get myself together, Chloe. You had better accept me this way. There's no trace of the real me left, sweetie."

"It's the booze. The real you is being destroyed by it. It's poison, Mother. I've been telling you, you need to get back to AA. Let me call your sponsor now. Please?"

"I don't think she can help. I don't think anyone can. I'm ashamed to go back. Look at me. I'm a mess! No one would believe in a month of Sundays that I used to be a beauty queen."

"Where is her number?"

"It's taped above the phone. Amanda Redmond."

Chloe found the number and dialed.

"This is Amanda," a perky voice answered.

"Ms. Redmond, this is Martha Greene's daughter. I'm afraid she's drinking again, and she seems pretty much out of control. Is there anything you can do to help?"

"Does she want me to help?"

"She gave me your number, but she says she doesn't think there's anything anyone can do to help."

"I'll try. But she's going to have to exert some effort. There's an AA meeting tonight. It's not her regular group, but it will help anyway. Tell her I'll come for her at quarter to seven."

"All right. Thank you."

30

"And Ms. Greene?"

"Yes?"

"You might want to try an Al-Anon meeting yourself. I think it would help you to cope. I'll get a list of meetings for you tonight from AA."

Chloe sighed. "I suppose I should. I keep putting it off, hoping she'll get better. She was doing so well before I left on my trip."

"That's one of the reasons you need Al-Anon. You can't do all this caretaking by yourself. You need help."

"Okay. I'll give it a try." It seemed that today was the day for giving things a try.

Chloe spent the rest of the day getting her mother ready for her meeting. She got her into the shower and then fixed her hair. She chose a pair of navy slacks and a cream-colored silk blouse for her to wear.

"Do you think you can do your makeup?"

Martha raised her shaking hands. "I can try, but I'll probably look like a clown."

"Why don't you just do foundation, some blush, and lip gloss?"

"What about my eyes? I'll look like a zombie. I don't have your coloring. My eyes disappear if I don't do something to them."

"Okay. If you do the rest, I'll try to do some eye shadow and mascara for you."

Chloe departed into her own room to change out of her morning sweats. Earlier, she had been for a run along the beach, trying to dissipate unfocused anxiety. The running had helped a little, but sometime during her visit with Mr. Petersen, the anxiety had completely disappeared.

Putting on a sage green gauze skirt with a peach silk peasant blouse, she tied a black Italian scarf around her waist. She never wore makeup, but she spent several minutes calming her mane into a wavy mass corralled at the base of her neck with a tortoiseshell clip.

By the time she was finished, her mother was ready for her. With a great deal of difficulty and after more than one try, Chloe managed the mascara and eye shadow that were so important to her mother. "You're going to have to get rid of these shakes, or I really may poke your eye out," she told her.

Then they went out to lunch—Chloe's treat—at the restaurant down on San Clemente pier. She had a serious craving for mussels.

Sitting out in the foggy mist that shrouded the sun, they watched the children playing beneath them on the sand, running in and out of the chilly water. She thought of little Robert Stevens III.

"Mother, have you ever met Robert Stevens? He lives in the development. His wife died a little while ago."

"Robert Stevens? No. I've never met him. Is he my age?"

"No. I think he's closer to mine. His little boy was killed the other day. Drowning."

"Oh, dear. Why do these awful things have to happen?" Her mother looked ready to weep, and Chloe regretted confiding in her.

"Mr. Stevens is in good hands, but it will be rough for a while." She tried to sound confident. "Someone very nice is looking after him." She knew that Mr. Petersen was keeping an eye on Rob, just as surely as she knew the moon would rise that night and magnify Rob's sorrow.

"Who's that?"

"No one you know." Chloe squirmed in her seat. With a little distance between her and the morning's conversation, she felt slightly uncomfortable with her aggressive agnosticism.

After lunch, she took her mother on a stroll through downtown San Clemente. Tourists, disappointed in the weather, thronged the sidewalks. She convinced her mother to stop for an ice cream and then poked around in the art boutiques. Martha bought a watercolor for her bathroom. It was of a pastel bouquet of flowers in a crystal vase. Chloe thought it rather pedestrian but was glad to see her mother showing interest in something. The whole house was done in pastels, except the midnight blue Chloe had chosen for her room. She had used the warm colors of Tuscany—terra-cotta, golden yellow, and sage green—in her drapes, bedspread, and painted furniture to contrast. Since Daddy's death, she'd meant to get her own place, but it seemed pointless when she spent so little time at home. She was gone at least ten months out of the year on her writing jaunts.

"When do you think you'll take your next trip, honey bun?" her mother asked as they got back into the car and headed for home.

"I haven't even decided where to go yet. I seem to need Italy like other people need food, but my readers are probably ready for a change. I'm thinking a sheep farm in New Zealand maybe. But I'm not going anywhere until I'm certain you're okay. And I mean really okay. You've got to do this, Mother."

Her mother put a knuckle between her teeth. A second later she seemed to draw herself up. "I know I do. Your father would be disgusted with me."

"Now, don't shame yourself. That's no way to get better. You've got to have positive direction, or you'll never get anywhere. Whatever happened to your friend Mary?"

"She remarried. Two months ago. She's very happy."

"You must have other friends. How's your sponsor? Is she anyone you could get close to?"

"I don't know. She's a real modern woman. Career and everything."

"Have you thought about getting a job?"

"A job? What would I do?"

"Or some volunteer work. At the hospital or the library or something like that. You need something to give shape to your days."

Martha sighed. "I can't believe I've come to this. I used to be your daddy's financial advisor, for Pete's sake."

Chloe realized that if she were a praying woman, she would pray for her mother. If anyone needed peace, Martha did. Losing Daddy had been cataclysmic. Chloe knew what she felt, but what would it have been like for the dynamic, intimate relationship her parents had enjoyed to be wiped out in moments?

After getting her mother settled with a stack of magazines and the TV tuned to Oprah, Chloe went out to do some grocery shopping. She was glad of the take-out deli. She got Caesar salad for two, a rotisserie chicken, and a loaf of French bread. With a sudden craving for strawberries, she bought a quart and some crème fraîche to go on top of them. Then she set about shopping for staples. When she was living at home, she paid for the food. Her mother had been left a nice trust fund, although she took little interest in the day-to-day business of life. Perhaps that was one reason she'd taken to drink. It was much easier to fix a drink than to fix a nutritious meal for one.

What am I going to do about my mother? Hopefully, Alcoholics Anonymous would help Martha Greene find some answers.

After dinner, it was simply a matter of keeping her mother sober until Amanda Redmond appeared, which she did at exactly 6:45.

"Hello, Martha! It's good to see you. It's been a long time."

Amanda was a tall woman with long, light brown hair and a

rather plain, snub-nosed face. She looked as though she were in her forties.

"It hasn't been that long, has it?"

"A couple of months at least. Is this your daughter?"

"Yes, I'm sorry. Of course. Amanda, this is Chloe. She's a writer."

"*That* Chloe Greene?" The woman's face lit with a smile that brightened her blunt-featured face. "I'm impressed. I loved your adventure on Corfu. It's my favorite place in the world. You captured it so well."

"Thank you," Chloe said, embarrassed as usual when anyone praised her writing. "It's nice to meet you. Thank you for taking Mother out tonight."

"It's not a problem. Are you ready to go, Martha?"

"As ready as I'll ever be. Good-bye, honey bun," she told Chloe. "I'll only be a little while."

"Don't worry about me. I have some comedies on Netflix. I'll be fine. You go ahead now."

As soon as her mother was out the door, Chloe went back to her bedroom, sat on the floor in the lotus position, and tried to center herself, picturing the clear aquamarine waters at the base of the rough, black cliffs on the island of Corfu.

The telephone rang. It was a sales call. Something like this always happened when she began her meditation.

Then her next-door neighbor came by to borrow a lime. George Kunz probably had actually come to invite her mother over for a drink.

"No. I'm sorry. We're fresh out of limes. Mother's gone for the evening, I'm afraid."

"Oh, well, just tell her George came by. She's welcome to stop by later. I'm having some people in."

"I'll tell her," Chloe lied. No wonder her mother was an alcoholic. The whole development seemed to survive on booze.

Finally she turned off her cell phone and went back to her room to meditate. She thought of Daddy. He had been a big bear of a man, but thankfully, she hadn't inherited his girth. He had been so much fun. Daddy's *joie de vivre* had made growing up a delight. His lucrative retail import business had taken him all over the world to shop, and Chloe had inherited her wanderlust from him. Every summer she and her mother had accompanied him on at least one trip. They had gone to all the major cities of the world, but most of his purchases were made in tiny, almost forgotten villages. Hence, her love for the out-of-the-way places. He had encouraged her writing from the time she was ten. Saying that his death had left a monumental hole in her heart and her life was an understatement. Would she and her mother ever recover?

Her mind strayed to Mr. Petersen. What a spirited argument her Jewish-born father would have had with him! But to Chloe's surprise, she could see the calm, white-haired man confounding Jonah Greene.

Slowly, the mellow sweetness she had felt in Mr. Petersen's living room mitigated her grief somewhat as she played out the imaginary conversation in her head. She ended up sitting in the lotus position, laughing. She couldn't help it. In her mind, she saw Mr. Petersen running rings around Daddy's logic, like ropes that bound him up in his own hubris. She had loved her father more than could be imagined, but she would be the first to admit that he was a self-professed expert on everything from philosophy to cooking. Mr. Petersen's quiet certainty in the face of Daddy's robust arguments would have driven him mad but in the end would have made them the best of friends. Daddy had always loved anyone who could stand up to him.

Imagining Daddy's laughter joining with hers, for a moment she felt as loved as she had when she was a little girl, running to Daddy as he came through the door, his arms wide for her to run into. She could even smell his fancy Italian aftershave.

Chloe clung to the picture of Jonah Greene. The love she felt for him was so overwhelming that her laughter spilled over into grateful sobs. She had crossed a Rubicon in that moment. For the first time since Daddy's death, there was a deep sense of well-being in her breast that overflowed into rare, healing tears. She knew without understanding that Daddy would want her to become fast friends with Mr. Petersen. She could even feel a bit of Jonah's energizing presence in the room with her now. Without a clue to whom she was speaking, she whispered, "Thank you."

After a time, she got up slowly to make herself some hummus with red peppers and pita bread. What an extraordinary experience! Somehow, she felt better than she had felt even when Luke's tenderness had surrounded her.

But that memory confounded her peace, leaving a bitter taste in her mouth. How could she have fallen for such a shallow, narcissistic man?

She abandoned her hummus and raided the freezer for her mother's Extreme Moose Tracks ice cream. Any thoughts of Luke always drove her to take large amounts of chocolate for medicinal purposes.

Carrying the entire carton out to the deck overlooking the rosy orange and indigo sunset, the most brilliant she had seen since the June fog had descended, she forced thoughts of Luke away and concentrated on her mother. Soon, her musings turned in another direction, and she found she was thinking of the as yet unknown Robert Stevens. She wondered if she could teach him to meditate. She had to admit, though, that even she hadn't ever had such a tremendously moving experience from the practice in the past. Maybe Mr. Petersen's God had a sense of humor and had reached through the universe to tickle her funny bone.

Chloe couldn't wait to tell Mr. Petersen about it.

CHAPTER FIVE

A few days later, Rob Stevens emerged from the Al-Anon
meeting with a heavy heart. He could do step one. He could
acknowledge that Ginger was an alcoholic and that, ultimately, once she was out of rehab, he had no power to change her.
But step two—acknowledging that there was a higher power—how
could he possibly do that? To do so would mean there was a God
who had let Pamela and Robbie die tragically and years before their
time. Why would He do that to him? What had Rob done to deserve
a double tragedy?

But, of course, he wasn't exempt from pain. Why should God
make anything different for him than for other people? There was
pain and tragedy everywhere he looked.

It hadn't always been that way, though. He'd drifted away from
his parent's faith long ago, when life was good—an exciting new
business, a lovely wife, and then Robbie.

He raised his eyes from the pavement. And he saw her. Chloe
Greene. Coming out of the meeting. She had seen him and was

headed straight towards him. He couldn't turn away without being unforgivably rude to the woman who had tried to save Robbie's life.

When she reached him, he noticed the concern in her large, golden eyes. He hadn't noticed before, but there was a black ring around her irises. She wore not a shred of makeup, and her hair was curling around the softened angles of her Botticelli face.

"I thought I recognized you," she said.

"I'm sorry. I didn't see you in the meeting," he said. Rob couldn't seem to avoid looking into those extraordinary eyes.

"I kind of stayed towards the back. This is my first time."

"Mine too. I had no idea there would be so many people here."

"There must be a lot of alcoholics in San Clemente."

"Yeah," he said. "I guess you probably know about Ginger."

"Not really."

"My sister. The one I left in charge of Robbie."

"She's the reason you're here?"

He nodded. "She's in rehab now, but I don't know what things will be like when she gets out. The rehab center sort of made me promise I'd try this."

"Did it help?" She looked up at him again, the concern making little lines between her brows.

He shrugged.

"I'm sorry." She sounded sad. Why did she care so much? What difference did it make to her? Clearly, she had her own problems to deal with.

"Did it help you?" he asked.

"Yes. Yes, I think it did. Of course, it takes more than one meeting."

"I suppose so." He shifted his feet and looked vaguely over her shoulder. "So you bought that higher power stuff?"

"Probably not in the traditional sense. I find my God in nature."

He sighed. "Well, it was nice running into you. And thanks again for the donation. And for the other. With Robbie."

A change came over her face, and she smiled. The unexpectedness of it took his breath away. "You suddenly look like a naughty sprite," he said.

"I have this sudden urge to tell you an outrageous story about my father. He died five years ago."

What an unusual creature she was! He was certainly in no hurry to go home. "Let's go across the street to Starbucks, and you can tell me why you have the unmitigated gall to smile at me like that under the circumstances."

Carrying two double lattes to the table where Chloe waited, Rob wondered who the alcoholic was in her life. Before he got past that thought, she thanked him for the latte and leaned across the table, her eyes sparkling. "I don't suppose you do it, because it's really not a man's sort of thing, but I meditate. You know, lotus position and all that."

Somehow he had absolutely no difficulty believing this; however, it did make him slightly uncomfortable. "You're not trying to talk me into sitting down in tights with my legs like a pretzel, are you?"

"Intriguing picture," she said, grinning again. "But the answer is no. I just have to tell someone this extraordinary experience I had. Do you know your neighbor Mr. Petersen?"

What's this? "Edward?"

"Oh, is that his first name? The Mormon with the white hair?"

"Yes, we're acquainted. He's my home teacher, not that I ever make myself available."

"Home teacher?"

"Just something about the church I used to belong to. Go on with the story."

"Okay. Here goes. First, you have to understand that my father, a non-practicing Jew whom I adored with all my heart, died five years ago. I was devoted to him. My mother and I traveled the world with him. I am a writer because of him." Suddenly she sobered completely. "And you have to understand that he was what made my world spin. I have never stopped grieving in five years."

His own grief was so all-encompassing that he couldn't make room for hers, but somehow he didn't think she expected that of him. "I think I have the picture."

"Well, I guess you know this Edward believes in God—a merciful God who loves us."

Suddenly wary, Rob nodded.

"Well, I took rather strong objection to his beliefs, but he wasn't at all offended. In fact, he was sweetness itself. I wish there were more people like him in the world."

Rob had never thought of it that way, but what she said was true. And in his own bitterness he had been cursing the Supreme Being steadily, just in case He existed. Rob needed someone to blame. And Edward Petersen had understood.

The sprite continued, "That day I went home and did my meditation as soon as Mom went to AA. Picture this: my father came whooshing into my mind—he always whooshed—and he was arguing with Mr. Petersen, using all the force of the great philosopher he was. But Mr. Petersen just smiled his sweet smile and gave comforting, carefully reasoned answers to my father, who became enraged. Soon I was picturing my father all tied up in his logic, which was contradicting itself, and his eyes were bulging. Then suddenly, I began to laugh, and I just knew he was laughing with me."

Rob was startled.

"He always laughed when someone bested him, and he just couldn't budge Mr. Petersen from his calm, peaceful beliefs. So he

42

laughed, and they shook hands. Mr. Petersen laughed back. And then, you know what?"

Rob said, "I can't possibly imagine."

"I swear I could see, smell, and feel my father. The laughter released something inside me. I don't know how to explain it, but I knew my father really *was* happy!" Her face lit with delight. For just a second, Rob's sorrows fled, and he smiled at her.

"And look!" she exclaimed holding her hands out as though displaying her sea foam green gauze dress. "No black. Not a shred. Not a scarf, a pin, a shoe, much less a dress."

"And your point is . . . ?"

"Someone—nature or Buddha or Allah or even Mr. Petersen's God—knew exactly how to make me laugh again." Her face once again turned serious. "I don't know if my grief can possibly compare with yours. All I can say is that I was in a black cave, and there was a dirty gray scrim between me and the rest of the world. I felt nothing. No joy. Not even sorrow. Just emptiness."

"Yeah. That describes it pretty well. Except the anger. I'm angry at myself for allowing it to happen and angry at my sister for not watching Robbie for just the few minutes I was gone."

"My point is, Robert—I hope you don't mind my calling you Robert—whoever it is that's in control knew me so well that he or she knew exactly how to make me laugh. And he knew that laughing with my father again would blow away the scrim and bring me out of my cave. I still feel like I'm missing an arm, but I'm going to start writing seriously again, I'm going to start living seriously again, and I'm going to stop enabling my mother and get her the help she needs."

"So you are suggesting I take up yoga, and all my troubles will disappear with one huge chuckle," he said, hearing his own bitterness.

"No. I'm not. I've just learned that each of us is different, and the way down your rocky road will be different according to what you need to heal. That's what I learned from my experience. But it's been five years for me." Pausing, she took her first sip of latte. "For you it may be longer, or it may be shorter, but one day it will be less. I promise you. With all my heart. Even though you don't know me from Adam. Or Eve, I should say."

He didn't know what to say, so he just looked at her. She *was* a sprite. A fairy. Some magical little thing that someone had sent at his lowest ebb. What Edward would call a tender mercy.

"Look, I've got to go," she said, consulting her watch. "It was nice seeing you. I know you probably didn't want to see me, but I'd like to offer my condolences in person. I hope you don't think I'm making light of your grief—I just want you to have some hope." Then, smiling slightly, with a trace of apology, she left him.

He followed her out of the café. Odd. Definitely odd. Edward Petersen? Yoga? Laughter? But the oddest thing of all was that he believed her.

Shrugging, he turned to find his dark green Porsche. Then he remembered his accident. His muscles stiffened. He had a murderer to find. The police had absolutely nothing to go on other than an appeal to the public for witnesses, which had yielded nothing so far. Where should he start?

Perhaps it was just random road rage and jealousy because he drove a vintage Porsche. These days, that would be enough to kindle murder in some deranged person's head. That made far more sense than the idea that someone was targeting him.

And, of course, he had work to do. He should never have wasted his evening like this. He'd gotten too far behind at the office as it was.

Later that night, as he lay awake with his chronic insomnia, he thought of Chloe again. Had he been imagining her concern for him? He didn't think so. The meeting had helped her, she said. All that mumbo jumbo about a higher power. How could he possibly trust a higher power? For the rest of his life, he'd be waiting for the next blow to fall. Maybe he'd be the next one to go. His resolution to find his shooter had vanished, now that he had depersonalized the act. He wouldn't mind dying. Anything was better than this life. Even nothingness.

The next day, he went to the rehab center to see Ginger's therapist. He needed an update. He felt uneasy and guilty about virtually forcing his sister into therapy. Work was his coping mechanism. Perhaps, even if it killed her, Ginger was entitled to her own method of coping.

"I can't really tell you how things are going with Ginger—confidentiality rules, you know," Sonia told him. "But I have some more questions for you. Do you know what started her drinking? I mean, was there something traumatic that happened when she was in college?"

Fourteen years ago. He'd been twenty. A junior at San Diego State. Ginger had been a year ahead of him at Stanford. She had always been the brains in the family. What had she majored in? Anthropology. Something like that. She was planning to go with some program to Africa the summer after graduation, he recalled. Only she hadn't gone. She'd gotten an apartment and lived on her trust fund. It had taken a while for him to find out she was a drunk. She had quit communicating with him. He should have known something was wrong. They'd been close after their parents had died; then suddenly, nothing. It was as if she'd dropped off the face of the earth.

"I don't know. Something must have happened. She had a complete lifestyle change. She used to be really smart, a woman with places to go and people to see. After graduation, she came apart. Went into seclusion."

"Did you ever ask her about it?"

He shrugged. "I was too busy living my own life. I figured if she wanted to take some time off, she was entitled. She'd always worked so hard. I didn't know she was drinking until that following Christmas, when we got together. I never knew what started it, and I guess I felt too awkward to ask. It never occurred to me that there might be a specific reason. I just thought she liked booze."

"Still, you thought it was strange."

"Looking back, definitely. Not in character at all."

"Is there anyone left that you know of from those days whom you could ask?"

"I don't know. I'll check around. Maybe I can turn up something. If I hadn't been so concerned with myself, I'd have done something about this years ago."

"It was Ginger's problem, not yours. She was your older sister, wasn't she? You probably felt you didn't have any right to go nosing around."

"Don't make excuses for me. I've dropped the ball on this one."

"It's not your fault Ginger is an alcoholic, Mr. Stevens. Did you go to Al-Anon?"

"I gave it a try. I can do step one."

"Well, just remember that. There's nothing you can do to make her not drink. It is up to her and her willingness to turn it over to a higher power. All we can do is try to find out what underlies her problem and try to give her some direction in her life."

He started his search by calling the alumni office at Stanford.

"My sister, Ginger Stevens, was in the class of '90. She's sick now, and I'd like to find some of her old friends. How would I go about doing that?"

"You could start with the alumni organization for the class of 1990. Let me see." He heard fingers tapping on a computer. "The president is Gordon Stone. He lives in Columbus, Ohio. Would you like his phone number or his e-mail address?"

"E-mail would be fine."

He entered the address directly onto his computer. "Thanks for your help."

"Good luck with your sister."

Rob pondered how he should word his e-mail. Finally, he began to type.

My name is Rob Stevens. My sister Ginger was in your class
at Stanford. I think she majored in anthropology. She's in the
hospital, very ill, and I'm trying to locate some of her friends.
Did you know her? If not, do you know anyone in her major who
might have known her? She was supposed to go with a group to
Africa after she graduated, but she didn't go. I'd appreciate any
help you could give me.

Thanks,
Rob Stevens

CHAPTER SIX

Chloe had been pleased with the Al-Anon meeting but was somewhat uneasy about her encounter with Rob Stevens. His dark chocolate eyes, weary with pain, haunted her. She had wanted so much to lighten his burden just a little, but now she felt that he had probably taken her for a nut. But she was a nut, wasn't she, with her odd combination of philosophies—yoga, environmentalism, zen, and all her other eclectic tastes and habits collected from years of dabbling in different cultures?

Walking along the beach at low tide, she felt the sand between her toes and recalled her first meeting with Rob. Would she ever be able to walk along here without remembering it? Yet another tragic memory for this strip of beach. She stepped carefully around a mound of gravel that had washed ashore and wondered if Rob would sell his place. How could he go on living here with the memory of what had happened?

Chloe sighed and looked out to sea. Another foggy day.

Al-Anon had been great. After her own Rubicon, she felt sure that somewhere there was a higher power that she could rely on to help her mother. *The main thing is I don't have to make my mother well. It's between my mother and whoever it was who lifted my burden of grief.* What were her mother's beliefs? Would it be too interfering of her to try to get her mother and Mr. Petersen together? He was a kindly man. He would make a good friend, at any rate. She would invite him over for dinner.

Mr. Petersen was delighted with her invitation.

"Now, I'm a pretty good cook. What can I bring?" he inquired from the doorway of his house.

"How about if you bring the ice cream?" she said, laughing.

"I'll do better than that. I'll bring ice cream pie. You like chocolate, I presume?"

"Couldn't live without it. Why don't you come at about six-thirty? My mother's trying to get sober, but I can't promise anything. Don't be shocked if she's a little high."

⌒

"You invited Edward Petersen for dinner?" her mother asked, her voice incredulous.

"You know him?"

"Know of him. He's a Mormon, Chloe! How could you do that? Especially without asking me!"

"What's the big deal?"

"Chloe. Mormonism is a cult. I won't have that man in my house."

Chloe was stunned. "What do you mean, a cult?"

"Mormons are not even Christians."

She didn't know which way to go with that one. "First of all, in case you have forgotten, Daddy wasn't a Christian, and you married him. Second of all, I happen to know they *are* Christians."

Her mother's eyes narrowed in suspicion. "Just what has that man been telling you?"

"Good things. Things that have given me hope."

"I won't have that man in my house," she repeated.

"Then you can leave and go out to dinner by yourself. This is my house, too, and I've invited him."

"Why? Why did you do it?"

Chloe was bowled over by her mother's antagonism. "He's been a good friend to me. I thought he might be good company for you, too."

"Has he been trying to convert you?"

"No. Just trying to give me comfort. And he has. What do you have against Mormons? This is so unlike you."

Her mother's eyes darted around the room as if she were scrambling for an answer. "Did you know they don't drink? What if he comes here and I'm drinking?"

"You'd drink, just to spite him?"

That stopped her mother cold. "No. No, of course not."

"Well, what do you have against Mormons?"

"They participate in a cult, that's all. They have all kinds of weird beliefs."

"And this from a woman who bristles at anti-Semitism?"

Martha Greene slumped in her overstuffed, mauve chair. "I had a friend once. The Mormons converted her. She changed completely. She kept trying to get me to read something called the Book of Mormon. I took it to my preacher, and he said it was the work of the devil. I tried to tell my friend all of this, but she wouldn't believe me. She went to an all-Mormon school in Utah and married a

Mormon in one of those temples. And guess what? They wouldn't let me into the temple to be at her wedding."

Chloe felt as though she'd been hit broadside. Knowing Mr. Petersen, she couldn't believe he was a member of anything as strange as a cult. And there was certainly nothing satanic about him. But it was clear he wasn't going to be able to help her mother. She wondered if she should call and say one of them was sick. No, she couldn't possibly lie to him. Maybe he could set her mother's fears to rest.

"Well, he's coming. I hope you'll be polite to him. He's a very nice man."

Martha went to her room and shut the door.

Chloe decided it was high time she paid her weekly visit to the shooting range. Calling Rosemary, her best friend since fourth grade, she asked, "Anything hot you can't leave for the afternoon?"

"What did you have in mind?" her friend answered in her Texas drawl, far more pronounced than Martha's. She always said it made the clients trust her. Rosemary was a successful real estate agent.

"I need to shoot something," Chloe said, "or I'm going to shoot someone."

"Well, now, we certainly can't have that. How about I meet you at the range in half an hour?"

"I'm leaving my gun at home and renting a Glock."

"That bad?"

"Just accumulated steam. I'm getting awfully close to blowing my stack."

"Okay. See you then."

⌒⌡

Mr. Salinger at the shooting range was always delighted to see Chloe. He'd had a picture of her made into a life-sized poster for his office. All five foot two of her stood next to her target. Holding her gun with both hands like an FBI agent and aiming at the camera, she had one eye closed as though aiming her pistol. The inner ring of her target showed six shots, all in the center ring. Though Rosemary had been her instructor, Mr. Salinger took a lot of pride in Chloe's accomplishments.

Chloe's friend arrived on the dot in her black Escalade, her big red hair tied with a camouflage bandana so it wouldn't blow in her eyes. Chloe stood on her tiptoes, and the six-foot Rosemary bent down so they could exchange air kisses. No one would take this glamorous woman for a black belt or a self-defense instructor. She had insisted that Chloe learn to shoot when she became a crime writer so she'd be correct in her written details. Most of the time, Chloe carried only a Taser gun, as she had no desire to kill anyone. It went against her whole moral grain. But what Rosemary had said was true: "There's nothing like the feel of a gun going off. You have to experience it."

The experience had certainly lent a great deal of verisimilitude to her writing.

"So who's the target going to be today, Miss Chloe?" she asked.

"Alcohol," Chloe answered solemnly, as she put on her protective glasses. Then she put the earphones over her head and ears. The weight of the Glock felt very satisfactory in her hands. Alcohol was going to take quite a beating.

Mr. Petersen arrived promptly at six-thirty, bearing a chocolate ice cream pie in an Oreo crust. Chloe put it in the freezer and invited her guest out to the glassed-in patio where she lighted the grill for the steaks.

She explained to him, "My mother has some really odd ideas about the Mormons. She hasn't been to church in years. I don't even know her religion; her preacher, when she was younger, told her all kinds of wild stories. I don't know if she'll come out of her room."

Her neighbor looked at her with concern. "Are you sure it wouldn't be better if I just left?"

"I don't go along with this anti-stuff. You're my guest, and you're staying. If Mother wants to be childish, she can stay in her room." Poking at the grill, she said, "I wish you could meet the real Martha Greene." She emitted a small sigh. "She's changed since my father died."

"How?"

"Well, aside from the drinking, she seems to have become a very passive person. I'm not used to that. I liked it when she stated her mind. But today wasn't like that. Some kind of weird fear possessed her."

Edward looked thoughtful. "I hope we can make some progress on that front over dinner."

Chloe went inside to get the steaks while her guest remained on the patio in a lounge chair. Clearly, he didn't feel welcome inside.

Putting the steaks on the grill, she said, "She was full of all of this stuff about your temples. She was very upset when they wouldn't let her go in for her friend's wedding."

Mr. Petersen sighed. "A lot of people worry about that. But you can go through any of our temples before they are dedicated and see that they are just beautiful houses built to the Lord. Like Solomon's temple in the Old Testament."

Chloe gave a little chuckle. "I wish Daddy were alive. You two could have a lively discussion about that. He was Jewish."

"Was he? I would like to have met him. Jews and Mormons have a lot in common, believe it or not."

"My mother says you're a cult."

"We have nearly fourteen million members. I think we're past the cult status."

"She said you weren't Christians."

"Yes. That's a popular misconception. That's why we prefer to call ourselves The Church of Jesus Christ of Latter-day Saints rather than the Mormon church."

"But why would she say those things?"

"Well, we're not Protestants, and we're not Catholics, so a lot of people think that means we're not Christians."

Chloe was puzzled. "That doesn't even begin to make sense!"

"I know. But for some reason, that's what people believe. Partly, it's because of the Book of Mormon. They don't think we believe in the Bible, which we do. The Book of Mormon is another testament of Jesus Christ."

"Yes. Mother talked about it. She said her preacher told her it was the work of the devil."

"It's not. Can you trust me on that?"

"I'm not even sure I believe in the devil. Or your version of God. I've chosen a combination of yoga and meditation that works for me. Meditating on nature's beauties and blessings has always put things into perspective for me. But the other day, I had the most amazing experience ever!"

He raised an eyebrow.

Between bouts of laughter, she related her impression of his confrontation with her bellicose father and the result. "Something is unlocked inside me now. I can breathe deeply. I can laugh. I can remember my father with joy and not that awful black hopelessness. I know somehow that he wants me to be happy, not sad. And the weirdest thing of all is that I know he would want you and me to be friends."

"I think you'd better call me Edward, then." He chuckled. "I wish I had known your father. We could very well have had just such a chat. Have you shared this with your mother?"

"No. I thought about telling her tonight, when you were here. I want her to have her own experience with my father, but I don't know how to approach it."

"Sometimes it's better to keep sacred experiences like that to yourself for a while. Until she's ready to hear it. You'll know when the time is right."

"How?"

"Her heart will be softened. It's something you can add to your meditations."

"But I learned at Al-Anon that it's not my responsibility to change her. It's not even possible."

"You're right. It takes an Almighty Power to do that. Meditation *is* powerful. It may not change others, but it changes us. Have you heard what C. S. Lewis said on the subject?"

"I've only read *The Chronicles of Narnia.*"

Edward chuckled. It was a nice sound. "One time C. S. Lewis was being derided for his belief in God when his wife was dying. A colleague asked, 'Do you really expect your prayers to change God?'"

"What did he say?"

"'No, but they change me.'"

Chloe thought for a moment. "That's profound. Really profound."

After a few moments pondering Lewis's words, she turned her attention back to her barbecue. "Well, these steaks are done. I guess it's time to go in and face the music. I'm sorry things have turned out like this. I really wanted my mother to meet you. I thought you could help her."

"Well, just keep meditating. The change in your life may bring about a change in hers."

Martha decided to come out of her room, after all. She nodded curtly when Chloe introduced her guest.

"Please call me Edward," he said to both women. "Mr. Petersen makes me sound like an old man."

Chloe smiled, but her mother maintained a straight face. They sat down at the round table that Chloe had set carefully with an edible fruit centerpiece. Their steaks were already on their plates. Chloe passed the salad and the twice-baked potatoes. Silence reigned. They began to eat.

"So, Edward, are you trying to convert my daughter?" Martha asked.

"I've just been answering some questions for her."

"What kind of questions?"

"Why don't you ask her?"

Martha turned towards Chloe.

Chloe responded. "I was really upset about that boy's death. It was Edward's phone I used to call the paramedics. When I went over to thank him, he was able to give me some comfort." Her mother's brow furrowed. "Don't worry, Mother. I have no intention of becoming a Mormon. But I drew a lot of strength from Edward's serenity. He's suffered far more than we have, and he's learned to have hope in spite of it."

Her mother raised an eyebrow. "You believe in the Resurrection?" she asked their guest.

"Yes, we do."

"Well."

They ate for a while in silence.

"I'm a big fan of your daughter's books," Edward told Martha.

That put a smile on her mother's face. "Yes. She's quite the writer. She's been writing since she was a little girl. Can you believe the first book she tried to publish was a big success? She's a best-selling author now."

"You must be very proud of her."

"I am. The only problem is, she's gone so much of the time. It takes her almost a year to write a book. And she stays on location the whole time. She just comes home between books to do editing and book tours and such."

"So where are you going next, Chloe?"

They spent the rest of dinner discussing New Zealand, where Edward had gone on a mission when he was nineteen and had visited many times since. He knew parts of the country well and suggested the most scenic regions for her to discover a beautiful but authentic sheep operation.

Taking his leave soon after they had eaten his ice cream pie, he shook Martha's hand. "It was nice to meet Chloe's mother. I'm sorry if the religion issue upset you."

"Just don't go trying to convert her," Martha said.

CHAPTER SEVEN

Rob had insomnia again. What could Ginger's secret be? Was it a love affair gone bad? As far as he knew, Ginger had never had much of a love life. Except with the bottle. She was large and overweight now. Untidy. Unkempt. Unlikely to attract anyone. What had happened to that bright, cheerful older sister who had always jollied him out of the sullens?

He turned over. How long had it been since he'd had a good night's sleep? Even before Robbie's death he hadn't been sleeping well. Pamela's last days still tore at his heart. Why did she have to suffer so much? She'd been so patient. But then she'd always been patient. It was one of the things he had appreciated about her. Ever since he'd met her.

Guilt attacked him. *Did I take that patience for granted?* Now that he really thought about it, he knew it couldn't have come without a price. What inner struggles had she overcome that enabled her to be so even-tempered? Had Pamela secretly screamed bloody murder when she was on her solitary runs? Had she written all her hidden unhappinesses in her journal? Would it be wrong of him to look, now that she was gone? He was tempted but afraid of what he would find. Maybe he would see a side of his wife that he didn't know existed. And she was gone, so how could he ever reconcile his own selfish image of her with the real person she had written about every night at her little French provincial writing desk? There had been shelves full of her journals, now packed away in storage with the rest of her things that he couldn't bring himself to discard.

Rob remembered the day they had met. He had gone up to Stanford during his sister's senior year for Big Game weekend. Ginger had actually fixed him up on a blind date with Pamela. That's how he had met her.

He sat up straight in bed. *Met her! How could I forget? I met her through Ginger!* Pamela had been Ginger's friend at Stanford. If only Pamela were alive, she could undoubtedly tell him what the problem was.

Thinking back, he realized that Pamela and Ginger had not remained close. One would think that after marrying Ginger's brother, Pamela would have stayed friends with her. But there had been no individual contact between them that he was aware of. Ginger had come for Christmas every year. Why hadn't he seen it before? They had always acted like virtual strangers. He had even forgotten how close they were during Ginger's senior year. They had been roommates then. Had Pamela kept in touch with any of their friends? He tried to remember. Yes. There was one woman. Brooke something. They had met for lunch a couple of times in Newport, and they used to exchange Christmas cards. The Christmas card list!

Bounding out of bed, Rob went to his computer, pulled up the old Christmas card list, and scrolled through it, trying to find Brooke. If only he could remember her last name. Unfortunately, Pamela's married friends were all listed as Mr. and Mrs. under the husband's name. Pamela had been a bit old-fashioned. And there were no single Brookes. Oh, well. A dead end.

Deciding he might as well try to find something to read, he turned to the bookshelves on the wall behind him in the little study, which contained the fold-out couch Ginger had used as her bed. The house, like all the others in the development, was a converted double-wide manufactured home with only three small bedrooms. One had been Robbie's, one was his, and he had given his forest green study over to Ginger. He'd only moved his computer back in there after she'd gone into rehab.

Some of the books were hers. He found a whole row of books by Chloe Greene. Taking the first one, *Springtime in Prague*, he wandered back to his bedroom, lay down, and turned on his reading lamp. Curious, he read the biography of the author on the inside of the back cover. Chloe Greene had acquired her love of travel during a lifetime of traveling with her parents on business trips to faraway places around the globe. They had visited Prague under Communism, and this book gave an account of the awakening she had found later in a country blooming under freedom. She enjoyed a surprising number of pastimes: swimming (he flinched), rock-climbing, surfing, sailing, shooting (that little scrap of a creature?), browsing street markets, and doing yoga and meditation. She was a passionate member of the Sierra Club and a 1994 graduate of Stanford University. She had gone to Stanford! Doing the math, he realized she had been a freshman when Ginger was a senior. And she had majored in anthropology.

It was too much. First the Al-Anon meeting and now this. He was running into Chloe Greene all over the place. He would have to get in touch with her now. She might know something about Ginger. He studied the photo on the back cover. She was undeniably beautiful in the way of a Renaissance portrait. He wished he wouldn't think of Botticelli's *Birth of Venus* when he looked at her. It was as though he were imagining her naked, and there was something too emphatically pure about her for that. He wondered briefly if she had ever been married. Judging by the number of books on Ginger's shelves, Chloe had been busy traveling in the years since her graduation. Maybe she hadn't had time to get married. Those eyes—he thought he could lose himself there. They were honey-colored, that's what they were. Just looking at them made him feel a bit of the sweetness of honey in the region of his heart. *What am I thinking?*

The story of her "laughing with Daddy" came into his mind, and it must have jolted something loose inside of him, for unexpectedly he found himself weeping. Holding Chloe's book tight against his chest, he felt his bitterness ease a bit with each tear. He'd heard somewhere that tears actually drained negative toxins from one's body. Soon he was asleep.

The following morning, over his Honey Nut Cheerios, he decided on his strategy. He needed to talk to Chloe about Ginger. Chloe knew Edward Petersen. He would know where to find her. He would pay Edward a visit this evening after work. In the meantime, he would check his e-mail.

There was a message waiting for him from the 1990 alumni president.

> Yes, I knew Ginger. She was one of the most popular girls in the senior class. I'm sorry to hear she is ill. I know who several of her friends are. Here are their names and e-mail addresses.

There followed three names: Sandra Thompson, Rick Niebolt, and Brooke Sampson, the one Pamela met for lunch.

Rob printed out the e-mail and took it with him to work. Once there, however, he became involved in a dispute concerning the company's plant in Indonesia and had no time to write his e-mails until late in the afternoon. He wrote the same one to each of Ginger's three friends:

> I understand that you were a friend of Ginger Stevens when she
> was at Stanford. I am her brother. She is very ill, and I would like
> to talk to you about when you were friends in school. It might
> help her recovery. Please give me a call on my cell at 555-762-
> 9882. Thank you very much.

Making sure his phone was on, he left the office and headed for Edward Petersen's house. It probably wasn't necessary to talk to Chloe now that he had contacted Ginger's friends, but just on the off chance . . .

Edward was at home, whittling something on his porch. "Rob! How good it is to see you. Come in, come in, if you don't mind the mess. I'm just doing a little writing."

The man seemed so happy to see him, Rob didn't have the heart to just ask his favor and run. He stepped into the teak-paneled room, admiring it. "I like what you've done with your place."

"Thanks. Would you like some lemonade?" his host inquired.

After the commute from Newport in the afternoon traffic, lemonade sounded good. "Yes, please, if it's not a bother. What are you whittling?"

"Oh, just a sailboat for a five-year-old grandson. I use balsa wood, so it's easy. Plus, it guarantees that it will actually float."

"What's all this? Writing your memoirs?" Rob asked idly, gesturing toward the magazines and legal tablet on the coffee table.

"No. It's a book on hope, as a matter of fact." He left the room to fetch the lemonade.

Hope! How could anyone write about hope? For the first time, he remembered that Edward had helped Chloe make her break-through.

Feeling uncomfortable, he rubbed the back of his neck with his hand and stared out the window at the ocean. The ocean. Robbie's killer.

When Edward reentered the room, Rob said, "I don't suppose you know of anyone who's looking to buy a unit in here, do you? I'd like to sell."

His neighbor handed him a tall glass of iced lemonade. "As a matter of fact, one of my sons up in Utah is looking for a beach place. How soon would you be interested in selling?" He gestured at a vast, white leather chair, which Rob took.

"As soon as possible. I can't get away from the ocean fast enough."

"Oh, I see." Edward sipped his lemonade and cleared a place for it on the coffee table.

Maybe it was the gentleness in the old man's eyes, but Rob felt obliged to continue. "I sold my house in Newport, and Robbie and I moved down here full-time after Pamela died. Now I can't stand the sight and sound of the ocean."

"I moved down here after my wife died, too."

"When was that?" Rob asked.

"About five years ago. My son was killed that year, too. I needed a change of scene."

"You lost your wife and your son at the same time?"

"Within months of each other. But, I'd had a good many years with each of them. It can't compare with what's happened to you."

"Still, it must have been rough." Rob drank the tart lemonade. He felt vaguely guilty that he had rejected every overture that this man had made to him as his home teacher. "And you write about hope?" he asked, raising his eyebrows.

"Yes," Edward said calmly. "I write about hope."

There was a small silence in the house.

"Do you think you could talk to your son about my place? See if he wants to come down and have a look? I haven't listed it yet. We could save on broker's fees if we did the deal ourselves."

"Anthony's a lawyer, so I'm sure he'd be all right with that arrangement. He's coming to visit over the Fourth of July. He likes to wait until the fog burns off. He'll be bringing two of his boys to surf here."

"That'll be nice for you to have some family here." Rob felt his chest turn leaden.

His neighbor seemed to read his mind. "You ought to come eat dinner with me sometime, Rob. I'm a good cook, believe it or not. I make a mean lasagna, and I'm a master at desserts."

Rob felt his chest ease, and he laughed a little. "Modest, too, I see."

"Oh, I never claimed to be modest."

Indicating the mess on the coffee table, Rob said, "Just hopeful."

"Yes. Just hopeful. How about Friday night?"

"You're really serious."

"Actually, I am. I could use the company."

Rob rubbed the back of his neck again. What would be the harm? "So could I. Can I bring wine or something? Oh, I forgot. You don't drink, do you?"

"No. Sorry. But we'll have a good enough time without it."

"I've got Ginger in rehab," Rob confided suddenly. "Tossed out all the liquor when she left. It's good to have it out of the house." Speaking of Ginger reminded him of his purpose for coming. "By the way, I ran in to Chloe Greene the other day. She said she knew you."

"Yes. We've become friends."

"I'd like to get in touch with her, but I don't know where she lives or what her phone number is. I sent a thank-you for her donation and condolences to her through her publisher. Can you help me out?"

"Sure. She gave me her number the other day. Let's see if I can find where I put it." He began pawing through the papers on his coffee table.

"Maybe you could just tell me what house she's in. Do you know?"

"Yes. But here's her number. I've found it, believe it or not. Have you got something to write on?"

Rob indicated his smart phone.

"Here you go. It's 555-376-0004."

"Got it." Rob handed him his business card. "Here's my cell number in case anything comes up on the house."

"What time do you usually get home from work on Fridays?"

"Around now. Six-thirtyish. There's a lot of traffic."

"Shall we say seven on Friday, then?"

"Do you want me to pick up a loaf of French bread or something?"

"That'd be great. You're going to love my lasagna. Oh, and I'll give Anthony a call about your place."

Rob rose. "Thanks, I'd appreciate that. I'll see you on Friday."

Returning to his house, he disarmed his burglar alarm, put the key in the door, and entered. Pamela had mirrored the far wall and lined it with glass shelves so the room looked bigger than it was. It was always vaguely startling to see himself coming into the house. The fog still clung to the coastline, making it dim and cold in the room. He switched on the lamp and the gas fireplace and slumped on to the couch. He supposed he should take out a frozen dinner and stick it in the microwave, but he wasn't hungry.

He heard the roar of the surf. He couldn't go on like this—not eating, not sleeping. But what did it matter what happened to him? There was no ten-year-old waiting for him anymore. His estate would go to Ginger. That thought brought him up short, and just then his cell phone rang.

"Rob Stevens."

"Rob, this is Sandy Thompson. I am calling in response to your e-mail."

"Oh, thanks. Do you mind my asking where you live, Sandy?"

"No. I live in Cedar Rapids."

"Oh. Well, I live in California, so I guess we'll have to do this over the phone."

"What is it? What's the matter with Ginger?"

"Well, it's a little awkward. She doesn't know I'm calling you. I got your e-mail address from the guy who's the president of the alumni association."

"And?"

"Well, actually, you were good friends with Ginger, right?"

"Right. We both majored in anthro. She was supposed to go to Africa with some of us the summer after we graduated, but she opted out."

"Yes. That's part of the reason I'm calling. Do you happen to know *why* she didn't go to Africa?"

There was a pause. "I don't understand. Why don't you just ask her?"

"She's drying out," he blurted. "It all started her senior year. She became an alcoholic." He hadn't really given a thought to how intrusive he would sound. "Her therapist is convinced there was some trauma that started her drinking, but she can't get to the bottom of it."

"And you think I can help? Even if I could, I don't know that I would, *Mr. Stevens.*"

"What do you mean?"

"Surely this is Ginger's business? How would you feel if someone went around prying into your life behind your back?"

"I guess I wouldn't like it much." He sighed. "But I'm really just trying to help her here. She's in bad shape. She has been for the last fourteen years. Something must have happened."

"Well, if it did, I can safely say I didn't know anything about it. All I know is that she told us spring quarter that she'd changed her mind about going to Africa. If anyone knew why, it certainly wasn't me. I was mad at her, as a matter of fact. We were going to travel together."

Why hadn't he attached more importance to Ginger's strange decision at the time? What a self-centered kid he had been. All he had ever thought about was football. "I'm sorry. I guess you didn't keep in touch?"

"Not after that, no. I was really surprised to get your e-mail."

"Well, thanks for answering it."

"I hope someone can help Ginger. I didn't mean to seem unfeeling."

"No. It's I who should apologize. I really didn't think how it would sound."

"Well—good luck."

"Thanks. Bye."

"Bye."

Rob studied his cell phone after he hung up. Was he doing the wrong thing? Was it wrong of him to try to find out what had caused Ginger's trauma?

The therapist didn't seem to think so. But just how *would* he feel if the situation were reversed? He didn't know. If he were as bad off as Ginger and if she were sincerely trying to help—

He'd put off calling Chloe. At least until he heard what the others had to say.

In the wee hours, he still sat staring at his e-mail screen, waiting for a reply, knowing he'd be unable to sleep. The curtains were closed, though he used to love to watch the sea by moonlight. For that reason, he was totally unprepared for the searchlight brightness that shone into his little office that used to be Ginger's room.

Standing, he threw back the curtains and opened the window. There on the sand between his house and the ocean someone was shining a halogen flashlight into his house, pausing at every window. Suddenly remembering the freeway shooter, Rob ducked, barely avoiding the bullet that would have gone straight through his skull.

Crawling on his hands and knees, he moved to the other side of his home. Crouched in his bathtub, hands trembling, he dialed 911.

CHAPTER EIGHT

The day after the dinner with Edward, Chloe felt bored and out of sorts. She had been to yoga class that morning, and the galleys from her newest book had come, but she couldn't settle down to them. A little niggle inside her was trying to figure out a way to see Rob again. Just to see if he was doing any better. Her mother was on a steady diet of soap operas to keep herself away from the bottle. Chloe decided they needed to get out of the house.

"Let's go to San Diego for lunch," she proposed. "We can go to that little Mexican restaurant in Old Town."

Her mother brightened. "That's a marvelous idea, honey bun. I might even be able to manage my own mascara today."

Chloe changed out of her jeans into a pair of cream-colored capris and a terra-cotta top, and wound a royal blue pashmina scarf loosely around her neck. Tuscan colors. Suddenly, she wished mightily that she were back in Cinque Terre, sitting at the window of her little room on Madame Fiore's third story, gazing at the rocky coast with its terraced grapevines overlooking the Mediterranean Sea. She could almost smell the garlic and basil aromas that not unpleasantly wound up the stairs to her attic room.

There life had been so simple. She had written and swum and walked and eaten. She had her friends among the fishermen, the shopkeepers, and the owners of the small bistros where she spent hours writing on her laptop. And at night she had read all of Proust, French dictionary at her side. It had been idyllic. Leaving for the real world (Cinque Terre was cut off except for the sea and an infrequent little railway line) had been hard. Only her lonely mother had dragged her back to reality.

Now she French-braided her hair and was ready to go take care of said mother who was probably the only person in the universe who cared she was alive, except, perhaps, Edward. She had never allowed herself to make really close friendships since Luke. Something had closed down inside her. Even the undeniable male Italian charm could not awaken her. So she dealt with Proust's memories instead of making new ones of her own.

Her mother had managed her cosmetics fairly well. "I'm still not good enough to try lipstick, so lip gloss will have to do. And I don't look that great without eyeliner."

"Well, at least you got the mascara. That was a major job."

"You're not kidding."

The drive was nowhere near as smooth as Chloe had hoped. After Oceanside they ran into traffic. "What is this? It's Thursday morning."

"It's like this nearly all the time now, honey."

"I can't believe it. This is terrible. It's like this the rest of the way to San Diego?"

"More or less."

When they finally got to La Jolla, the traffic was still slow.

"Well, at least you'll get a good view of the Mormon temple," her mother said.

"Really? It is along here, isn't it. I'd really like to see it up close. It's an amazing place as I recall."

"Oh, Chloe, I'm starved."

"Okay, on the way back then."

As they slowly crept by the fantastical structure, Chloe remarked that it looked a little like something that belonged in Disneyland.

"It's hard to think of anything sinister going on in there," she said, studying the gleaming white façade of the castlelike building.

"They say you can be married forever in there," Martha mused.

"Hmm," Chloe replied. "I don't know if that's a bad thing or a good one, considering my disastrous taste in men."

They dropped the subject and were silent until they reached Old Town. After some difficulty finding a parking place, they finally made it to their favorite outdoor restaurant in the colorful Bazaar del Mundo. Bougainvillea covered the doorways of the little square of shops, and in the center, where their restaurant was, stood an outdoor stage. Flamenco dancers were performing. Chloe admired them as she and her mother waited in line. "They're really quite good. Remember the ones we saw in that little village in Spain?"

Her mother's eyes clouded over. "That was such a wonderful trip. It was your daddy's and my thirtieth wedding anniversary."

"Yes. They sang to you that night, I remember."

"I couldn't understand a word of it."

"No, but Daddy and I could. It was romantic and schmaltzy."

"We were so happy." Her mother turned away a bit, and Chloe heard her sniff. She wondered, not for the first time, how the Texan beauty queen with a degree in merchandising could ever have been so happily married to the complex man Daddy had been. Then she remembered that it was actually her mother who was the practical brain behind Daddy's business. Why didn't she take it up again on her own?

Finally, they were seated. Martha immediately ordered a virgin margarita.

"Mother, you've really got to get on with your life," Chloe said. "Have you ever thought about building Daddy's business up again?"

"I don't want to travel the world alone, sweetie. You know what I'd really like, Chloe? Some grandchildren."

Chloe felt herself color painfully. Her mother had never been quite so blunt before. "You know there's never been anyone who's interested me since Luke."

"And why not? What was so special about Luke?"

"He understood what makes me tick. He liked to travel, and he had a perspective on things that really broadened my mind. You might have thought he was all charm to look at him, but Luke was extremely well-read."

"He must have missed you when you were traveling."

"He came with me a lot of the time, but he had his own world, too. He's a first-class sailor, for instance."

"You seemed so happy with him. I never felt I could ask you why you split up."

"It was another woman. I lost out on the Luke stakes." She tried to sound light, but the pain in her chest was as sharp as though it were new.

"Only because you weren't there, I'll bet. If you didn't travel so much, you'd have a chance to connect with someone and stay connected. Do you know what I think?"

"What?"

"I'm addicted to alcohol, and you're addicted to running away."

Chloe was silent.

"Ever since Luke, you haven't stayed in one place long enough to form a relationship, much less keep one."

"It hurt, Mother," Chloe said. "We were together five years."

"So you're going to go through your life without love, just because of one unfortunate relationship?"

"It wasn't just an unfortunate relationship. It really went deep, Mother. I loved him. More than I've ever loved anyone except you or Daddy. He gave zest to everyday things." She was alarmed as she felt her hands begin to tremble with suppressed anguish. *Luke. Luke with the Viking blond hair and cobalt blue eyes.* The tenderness of his smile and the gentleness of his touch had seemed as though they would belong to her forever. That those things belonged to someone else now still caused her indescribable pain. Her mother was right. She hadn't wanted to risk breaking her heart again. What she didn't understand was why she had allowed herself such sentimental sloppiness. It went against her tomboy nature.

"And you broke up . . . what? Two years ago?"

"Three."

"Three years. I'd say that was a suitable mourning period. I was married more than forty years. Offhand, I'd say my addiction makes more sense than yours."

Chloe was silent again. Travel, writing, promoting, and success. They were her world, and most of the time she was satisfied. But Daddy's death coupled with Luke's defection had left a giant hole, and she would be lying if she said she couldn't hear her biological clock ticking.

But what would she do if she didn't travel and write? And how could she go about finding a relationship, assuming she even wanted one?

Gazing unseeingly at the flamenco dancers, she was startled by the interior vision of a pair of sad, brown eyes looking inside her soul and reading what was hidden there. *You don't want to love me, Chloe. I could never love you back.*

Shaking away the startling thought, she gave her attention to the waitress who finally came to take their orders. Chloe absently ordered the guacamole enchiladas.

During their coffee and flan, she began to feel the hair stand up on her scalp, as happened when someone was watching her from behind. Karma in the form of Luke Wendover visited their table, his wide smile and crinkle-edged blue eyes showing pure delight. Placing a hand on the back of Chloe's chair, he bent down and kissed her on the cheek. That was the only way she knew she hadn't conjured him up. He was real. *Luke. Here.* Well, he did live in San Diego, after all.

While Chloe remained speechless, Martha was dampening in her welcome. "Well, if it isn't Mr. Call Me Irresponsible. My stars! How long has it been? Five years?"

Chloe continued to eat her flan. It was like cold oatmeal.

"Have a seat, but please spare us pictures of the wife and family," her mother, the Steel Magnolia, continued. Though flustered, Chloe couldn't help being aware that her mother had got her mojo back. It was almost worth seeing Luke to witness the transformation.

"What have you been doing with yourself?" her mother asked, looking at him as though he were a pitiful child who was late for school.

"As a matter of fact, I just returned from a sail to the South Pacific. Sure could have used you two as crew. There were some dodgy moments."

"You *never* sailed all that way by yourself!" Martha exclaimed.

"Yes, ma'am. And broke the time record from Fiji to San Diego." He turned to Chloe. "I've been following your books. Corfu sounds like a dream come true."

"A little more civilized than Fiji, I imagine." Though she tried, she could not summon a smile. "There was some awesome rock climbing, and the sea was clear aquamarine right to the bottom."

"So you said. I did read the book, Chloe. Is it true that you swam out to 'Odysseus's boat'? Or was that an exaggeration?"

Startled, she said, "That wasn't in the book, Luke. Only the villagers knew that. You've been to Corfu?"

His eyes became solemn. "I thought maybe you'd finally found somewhere you loved enough to stay for longer than a couple of months."

"You came looking for me in Corfu?" she repeated. "Two years ago? What happened to Heather or Crystal or whatever your wife's name is?"

"We need to have a talk about that, now that I've found you again. It's karma, Chloe. I had no idea where you were."

"I've been living at the beach house for about a month now."

"If you had the brains to go to Corfu, I'm amazed you haven't paid me a visit, Luke," her mother said with obviously feigned surprise. "But then you and I never did get along real well. You're too good-looking. 'Never trust a handsome man, Chloe,' I said. And I was right, wasn't I, darlin'?" she asked her daughter in her steadily deepening Texas drawl.

As Chloe was turning beet red from the hammering of her heart, her mother continued, "So where are your kiddies? Or don't you and Jennifer have children?"

"Jennifer?" Luke asked. "Who is Jennifer?"

"Well, I'm sure her name is something like that—Jennifer or Angelica or Cameron or—"

"No children. No wife," Luke replied simply. "Here's a novel idea! Why don't you both come to dinner tonight? I can buy some steaks and a bottle of wine."

75

Her mother placed a hand on Chloe's wrist. She could feel the pressure of Martha's fingertips. "Actually, honey bun," she said to her daughter, "I didn't tell you in case I changed my mind, but I have a culinary class tonight that we have to be back for. Sorry."

Chloe thought she managed to make her sigh of relief completely internal, but Luke wasn't going to let it alone. "I'm free tomorrow. I'll drive up and make my famous jambalaya. Remember that, Chloe?"

Yes. She remembered. He made it for every reunion during the five years they'd been together. It was their celebration meal. *No wife. No children. Was this a time to celebrate?* All Chloe could feel was the hammering in her chest.

Luke took her braid in his hands as though it were a sacred object and kissed the back of her neck. "I'll be there about eight." Then he was gone.

Chloe couldn't reprimand her mother. Martha knew far too well how deep her attachment to Luke was.

"Thinks he can just walk back into our lives like Zeus playing tricks," Martha said, tossing back the rest of her nonalcoholic margarita. "You going to let him get away with it?"

"I don't know. I never imagined this happening."

Scenes of Luke and her living together in another life occupied her mind as she eyed the flamenco dancers without seeing them and gulped her coffee. She was sailing around Point Loma in the *Sunshine Girl*, the sailboat Luke had named after her, clambering up rocky cliffs in Thailand and jumping into the ocean, exchanging tender kisses in a secluded rose garden at her parents' last wedding anniversary party.

Rob's beseeching eyes disappeared from the radar of her conscious mind. So flooded with memories was she that Chloe actually asked her mother to drive home.

How in the world do I feel about this? She had absolutely no way of telling. Her emotions were in total disarray. Used to being able to squelch thoughts of Luke in their infancy, she was now flooded with images of his sapphire eyes lit with desire, his gentle hands—strong and tanned from sailing—sliding down her arms, leaving the inevitable goose bumps behind. His cocky smile the day he tried on the Frank Sinatra hat at a rummage sale for the homeless. All her anger was in danger of evaporating, leaving her completely vulnerable again.

Where Luke was concerned, she had no defense except flight. Then her mother spoke, and she came out of the memory tornado and touched earth.

"Honey, I'm afraid. Really afraid," Martha said simply.

"So am I, Mother," she said after a moment, as she realized that the force driving all these conflicting emotions was nothing akin to joy. It was straight-out fear. She couldn't still the trembling in her legs and her hands.

Then her cell phone rang, yanking her back into the present. It was Rob. How had he gotten her number? She greeted him with shades of relief in her voice. "Hi, Rob!"

"Hi, Chloe. Listen, I hope it isn't an imposition, and I know this must seem very strange, but there are a few questions I'd like to ask you. Would you like to go for coffee, ice cream, a drink?" he asked.

When she had a moment to process the question, she answered, "Coffee keeps me awake, and I'm steering clear of liquor for the time being, but ice cream would be nice." The perfect antidote to Luke?

"When can I pick you up?"

"Well, we're just on our way home from San Diego. How about after dinner? About seven-thirty?"

"Okay. Seven-thirty. Which number is your house?"

"Number twenty-three. It's got a brass pelican by the front gate."

"I'll see you then."

***

Once home, Chloe went to her room to change into a pair of frayed jeans and her Stanford sweatshirt. Conscious enough to realize that there was a cool wind blowing off the water, she anticipated fog that was even heavier than usual. Right now, she wasn't hungry for dinner and wished she hadn't given up liquor. All she wanted was oblivion.

Eventually, however, she had no choice but to face the problem of her hair. The fog made smoothing it impossible. The braid had come loose, and her hair refused to follow her hands into confinement again. Why did Luke want her back? She looked like an unruly orphan. And she was pale as a ghost. Why did someone so unbelievably handsome, who could have any woman he wanted, need her? Oddly enough, she had never asked that question in all the years they had been together. They had seemed like yin and yang, fitting together so perfectly she couldn't imagine either of them with anyone else.

Her hair was so curly, she could scarcely drag a brush through it. It looked like something wild. Pulling it back as well as she could, she anchored it with a scrunchy about halfway down her back.

As she waited for Rob, she stared at the ocean and panic seized her. Did she have no willpower? She could still feel Luke's kiss on the back of her neck.

Maybe it would be a good idea to go to New Zealand. Now.

Her phone rang again, and she saw that it was Edward.

"Chloe, did you hear about what happened at Rob's last night? I've just found out, myself."

Yanked into the present, Chloe sat down hard on her bed. "What? I've been gone all day."

"Someone shot at him right through the open window of his home office."

"Oh!" She could only breathe the one syllable. Someone had tried to kill Rob? Why on earth?

"Apparently, this incident wasn't the first time, either. Someone shot the tire of his Porsche while he was driving down the freeway. They put it down to envy or road rage. The police have absolutely nothing to go on, except the shell casing from a .22 rifle they found on the beach."

"But who would want to kill Rob? Do you know? Does he have any idea? He just invited me out for ice cream, for heaven's sake."

"He's pursuing a couple of lines of inquiry. It could be that the two incidents are entirely unrelated. The world has grown so violent. Still, I can't imagine him pursuing a romantic attachment at this juncture."

"It isn't that," Chloe told him, frowning. "He wants to ask me a question. I have no idea what."

"Well, be careful, Chloe. Someone's after him, and I'd hate for you to become collateral damage."

"We'll be downtown," she assured the man whom she realized was becoming a mentor. "No one would shoot him in the open at an ice cream parlor. This isn't a banana republic."

Leaving Luke stranded somewhere on a mountain they had just scaled together in her memory, Chloe became as practical as she was capable of being. Actually, she was immensely flattered that Rob had turned to her for help. She couldn't imagine what he needed from her, but she was ready and willing to give it.

When Rob appeared at her door, his troubled eyes grasped her full attention.

"Why on earth didn't you tell me about the shootings?" she said. "Edward just phoned."

He appeared startled. "I . . . well, I felt awkward enough calling out of the blue without dragging in something that outrageous."

She stood her ground, hands on her hips. "Did you have any intention of telling me?"

"Chloe, it's probably just two random, unrelated incidents. The world is a crazy place these days." Hands in his pockets, he cocked his head in the direction of the parking lot. "Now, are we going to go or what?"

Locking the door after herself, she walked beside him to the Audi he told her was a rental. "I don't know if they're going to be able to resurrect my Porsche. It's an old 911, and they're currently scouring junk yards for parts."

"Rob, I don't care about your car. Edward said you were working on a couple of ideas about who the shooter could be."

He helped her into the low-slung sports car, shut the door, and then climbed in on the other side.

"You remind me of an angry Yorkie," he said with a grim laugh.

But she would not be dissuaded. "So tell me."

"Well, I was up the whole night trying to reason things out," he began, backing out of the parking place and driving over the railroad tracks. "There are two possibilities, but even the more logical one is pretty wild."

"I'm not in the mood for twenty questions. Out with it!"

"I own a company that manufactures circuit boards for smart phones. My assembly plant is in Jakarta. So there's a possible terrorist connection."

Chloe took this in. Terrorists! Fanatics! They didn't count the cost of human life, were totally random in their mode of operation, and were tenacious. Worst of all, they didn't seem to mind getting caught, if that's what it took to accomplish their goal, which in this case would be Rob's death.

"How out of the blue is that?" she demanded. "Have you had threats? Have there been attacks on your plant?"

"It's tomorrow already in Indonesia. I just sent out queries a little while ago to my plant manager. But he's Muslim himself, so I don't know if he's part of whatever this is."

"Well, how are you going to find out then?"

"I have some Anglo friends there, running similar operations. I've texted them, asking them to make subtle inquiries if they can. But I don't want to put any of them in danger. I should probably go through the embassy. I think it was CIA operatives attached to it."

"There's no *should* about it!" Chloe said as they pulled into an alley off San Clemente's main street. In spite of her indignation, Rob calmly parked the car. "I don't want to raise a ruckus unless I'm pretty sure that's the problem. And there's another, even fainter possibility. That's where you come in."

With that, he got out of the car and opened her door. Part of her mind noted and appreciated the old-fashioned courtesy.

"What do you need?" she asked.

"I'll tell you once you've got your ice cream in hand. It might make you more tractable."

"Rob Stevens! How can you even think of ice cream at a time like this?"

"Actually, ice cream is essential to my thought processes and well-being. We have to be sure to take care of the inner man—or woman—during a crisis, if we're going to be effective."

Chloe stared at him. "Are you trying to turn this into some kind of joke?"

"You don't feel that way about ice cream? I was sure you would."

Stopping in the middle of the street full of tourists, she put her hands on her hips. "Of course I do, but I don't think it has any magical power over life and death!"

He gave her a half-grin, clearly amused in spite of the grimness of the situation. "You're a spitfire, aren't you? Not a yapping Yorkie. More like a mama tigress."

She stamped a foot in frustration, continuing to stare him down.

"I'm sorry. I'm standing firm," he told her, grasping her hand and pulling her along. "I assume you like Yankees?"

"If I must go along with this ridiculousness, let it be Yankees by all means," she said, not bothering to keep the sarcasm out of her voice. "Triple chocolate."

"I agree that that's what's called for."

Once she had her cone in hand and was seated at a little, round table outside, she retook the offensive. "Okay, Mr. Tough Guy, out with it."

"This is going to seem so strange that it will be hard to follow."

"I'm reasonably intelligent and well acquainted with things that are unlikely. Ritual rain dances in Central America that actually work, for instance. I even breached a secluded harem once. That opened my eyes! I doubt this could be that strange."

"Wait until you hear it." Chloe hadn't seen Rob's grin before. Even with his still somber eyes, it made him look every bit as handsome as Luke. She inhaled quickly in surprise, causing her to cough. *Heavens!*

"I doubt if it would even have occurred to me if I had been entirely rational. Staying up all night waiting for another bullet tends to color your thinking."

"Okay, already. Get on with it!" In spite of the conversation, Chloe's tastebuds paid homage to the wonderfulness of the chocolate. Rob's self-deprecating humor seemed to indicate that his ice cream was having a mellowing effect on him, as well.

"It concerns my sister," he said. "Your lovely sweatshirt confirms my intel that you went to Stanford. So did she. That's why I wanted to talk to you."

"What's her name? I saw it in the obituary, but I don't remember it."

"Ginger Stevens."

"How could I have missed making that connection?" Chloe asked herself aloud. "She was one of the people I most admired. But I was only a lowly freshman with a silly blonde afro, and she was a senior and president of the anthro club. Way above my level of existence." Once over her amazement, Chloe realized the oddity of juxtaposing Ginger with attempted murder. "How could she possibly have any connection with what's been happening to you?"

"I don't know. But clearly you need an update on Ginger." Rob had finished his cone, and he was no longer smiling. "After Robbie's death, she went into rehab. According to her therapist, she has a secret in her past that entirely changed her life when she was almost finished with college. That's when she started drinking, and until my wife's death, she lived in a little hole of a town in northern Alaska. I am now seriously wondering if she was in hiding."

Chloe was taken aback, just as he had warned her she would be. "That's truly weird, Rob. The Ginger Stevens I remember was the life of the party and as beautiful and stylish as Julia Roberts. I can't imagine her living such a solitary life." Pondering this, she tried to lure memories from where they were stored in the Stanford section of her messy brain. "I was completely in awe of her. You must know that Ginger was one of those people whom all the men loved and all the women envied. Not only that, but I seem to recall that she won some really prestigious awards because of the projects she initiated."

Chloe scrunched her forehead. "I'm afraid I didn't run in her exalted circles, so I doubt I can tell you much. But how in the world could she be involved in these murder attempts?"

"That's the part I can't figure out," Rob admitted. "All I know is that the first attempt, the one with the tire, happened when I was driving her to rehab. If she has been in hiding, the obit headed 'Stevens' would have alerted the shooter that she was living with me. He could be involved in the secret. He might be afraid that she has or will talk about it." Drawing circles with his finger on the tabletop, he continued his line of reasoning. "I know it's farfetched, bordering on delusional, but what if the secret is something criminal?"

Chloe was speechless, considering both the creativity and the complete unlikelihood of Rob's scenario. He was right. It was totally off the wall. "You definitely pulled that one out of the maze of a very tired brain, Rob." She wasn't a crime novel addict for nothing. "Whatever could possibly have happened would have been years ago, and there's such a thing as a statute of limitations."

"There's no statute of limitations on murder," he said solemnly.

She couldn't help it. Reaching over, she stilled the fingers that were still doodling on the table. "Don't you think I would remember if there had been a murder while I was at Stanford? Nothing like that ever happened. And an unsolved murder would be particularly memorable."

Rob's shoulders slumped, and she could see the tension go out of him. "I knew it was crazy, but I was hoping you'd say that."

"It sounds sort of ridiculous to say, but the terrorist plot sounds more probable," Chloe said. "I read and write suspense novels, but I never thought I'd be living in one."

Rob gave a slow grin, and she marveled at its power to stir her heart. She was glad she had been able to lift such a weight from him. "Let's take a walk," she said. "We've got to reel you back to the earth after your extravagant flight of fancy."

"Here I was picturing you as the spunky amateur sleuth, but no one except a writer would ever put together a phrase quite like that."

She grinned and, in spite of everything, her heart felt lighter.

"But I don't believe in the pathetic waif with an afro. You couldn't possibly be anything but Botticellian."

A compliment! My, things were moving along! Luke was protesting from somewhere on his mountaintop.

Rolling her eyes, she said, "Venus on the half-shell?"

"I'm not original?"

"Not when art history was a required subject at Stanford. I'm sure she was a very nice girl in her day. But I don't see her climbing cliffs or doing target practice, though I'm positive her embroidery was exquisite."

That actually drew a chuckle, warming her despite the nippy evening breeze.

They moved out on the sidewalk and started down towards the water. The fog was so thick that the laughter ringing through the air from the invisible restaurants seemed eerie. Chloe smelled some excellent Mexican food. Luckily, she'd had her fix at the Bazaar del Mundo.

"So. Have you been back to Al-Anon?" he inquired.

"Well, there's another meeting tomorrow night. I was going to go, but I'm having an unexpected guest. Are you going?"

"I guess I'll give it another try."

"I think AA is having an effect on Mother. At least temporarily.

This cooking class is the first positive thing she's done since Daddy died."

"When was that?"

"Nearly five years ago. As you probably know, anniversaries are rough."

"How did he die, if you don't mind my asking?"

"Car crash. On the Santa Ana. Just one of those random things."

He was quiet as they crossed the street, close-by dozens of others making their way to the pier. When she and Rob emerged on the other side, they heard more laughter and a low babble of voices from the diners at the pier's restaurant. The candlelight at the outdoor tables wavered in the fog. The air smelled like grilled seafood.

"I'm sorry about your father," he said finally. There was silence between them for a few minutes as their footsteps echoed off the wooden pier. "I hope I'm not intruding, but what do you think about this higher power business?

"How can you really believe in such a thing after your father's 'random' accident?"

"I'm sort of a heathen. I worship nature. That's my God, I think. And even nature can be unfeeling. Earthquakes, tornadoes, hurricanes. But, like any believer in anything, I block that out and concentrate on sea anemones and Monterey cypresses."

She was visited by the sudden memory of a road trip she had taken while at Stanford to the site of the most beautiful place in the world. "Have you ever been to Point Lobos, just south of Carmel?"

"No. I've never heard of it."

"You should take a few days off and visit. You deserve it. I've been everywhere, and it has the most beautiful trees I've ever seen. Monterey cypress. Right now, the wildflowers are even in bloom. Maybe it would soothe your soul a bit."

"When were you there last?"

"Oddly enough, on an anthro club outing." Picturing the whale-shaped sandstone mounds, the jagged cliffs, and the mist crouching over the dark green trees, a memory visited her with sudden sharpness. "Now that I think of it, your sister was acting weird. She went off by herself. I'd forgotten, but I actually think someone, Rick maybe, saved her from suicide!" She stopped and turned to face him. "Isn't memory a funny thing? Why should I think of Point Lobos just then? And I had totally forgotten about Ginger's suicide attempt. Rick caught her just as she was ready to leap off one of those craggy cliffs. It would have been a horrible death." Stopping for a moment, she said. "Rob, I'm sorry. But when you think of it, she must have really hated herself to contemplate such a thing."

He was quiet but kept walking. They had almost reached the end of the pier.

Rob stopped as they came up against the pier railing. He put his elbows on it and propped his chin on the heels of his hands. They watched as the fog-shrouded sun dipped below Dana Point and stained the fog deep orange-red.

"I never suspected," he said finally. "We used to be so close. Why didn't she tell me?"

"Maybe she was too ashamed. Self-hate is usually associated with shame."

"Who was Rick?"

"Her boyfriend. Gorgeous. Tricked himself out like the last tsar—you know, the beard and the poet shirt. He was crazy about Ginger."

"I think I got his name from the alumni association. Was his last name Niebolt?"

"Yeah, that was it."

"I haven't heard back from him yet. I'd sure like to talk to him. Poor Ginger. What could have happened? Even though it has nothing to do with whoever's after me, I still wish I knew what would cause her to do something so drastic."

"If Rick saved her then, he certainly wouldn't want her dead now. There. More nails in the coffin of that theory," she said.

"There you go again," he looked up and into her eyes. His own were searching, as though he were trying to make out her brain processes.

"What?"

"Talking like a writer."

She made a fist and gave him a light blow on his heavily muscled arm. Umm. She was a connossieur of arms, and Rob's were just plain gorgeous, as her mother would say.

They walked back down the pier in silence. Chloe began to feel uncomfortable. Who could tell what was going on in Rob's sleep-deprived brain? What an image to put in his mind! She should have bitten her tongue before introducing the idea of Ginger poised on a cliff ready to kill herself.

After they reached the restaurant, they crossed the street and emerged on the main tourist promenade. Saying little as they negotiated the crowds, they made their way to the alley that led to the back of the building where Rob had parked his car.

They had walked halfway down the alley when they were unexpectedly assaulted by high-beam headlights shining right into their eyes. A scream of tires, the revving of an engine, and there they stood, squarely in the path of an oncoming car.

Chloe stood transfixed in the headlights. Rob yanked her arm and, pulling her back, threw her to the ground between two buildings on their right. At impact, she ceased to see or know anything.

CHAPTER NINE

Rob was frantic. He stared down at Chloe's white face and wondered if he'd killed her. Taking her hand, he found a pulse in the wrist and, relieved, began chafing it. Where was the ambulance? He'd called on his cell phone what seemed like ages ago. He should never have brought her out in the open when a killer was after him! What had he been thinking?

Ah, there was the ambulance. He heard it roaring through the streets, blaring its horn, running its sirens. If only she'd wake up! Her beautiful, still face was a reproach to him. An unexpected wave of tenderness swept over Rob, and he brushed away a wisp of springy hair from her cheek. What would a higher power have to say about this? Heartless terrorists in a San Clemente alley trying to kill because it was the will of Allah?

The ambulance pulled into the alley where his car was parked, and he left Chloe's side to fetch the paramedics.

"She's back here! Still out!"

Following him with their gurney, they finally reached her side just as she was opening her eyes.

"Chloe! Are you awake? Can you hear me?"

She moaned. A short, stocky paramedic squatted down next to Rob and shined a flashlight into her eyes. "Pupils dilated. Big time. She's got a concussion. She's gonna need an MRI. Let's get her on the gurney."

Carefully, the two paramedics moved Chloe onto the stretcher and carried her to the ambulance.

"Can I ride with her?"

"Yes. There's room for the two of us. Clint's driving."

The stocky paramedic climbed in beside the stretcher and sat on a chair against the wall of the ambulance. He motioned Rob to the other one as he strapped Chloe in.

"Fasten your seat belt," he advised. "This is going to be a wild ride."

The paramedic, whose name badge said "Wolf," began running his hands over Chloe's head in an expert manner. Then he took two bags of ice from a freezer and fixed them firmly around the back of her head where she had made contact with the pavement.

"She's got one thick head of hair. It could have saved her life. There's a very large lump where she fell. How'd it happen?"

"Someone roared down that alley like it was the Indy 500. I pushed her out of the way. Unfortunately, I didn't think about her head, and it smacked the pavement pretty hard."

Wolf looked up. "Did you see the make of the car?"

"No. It was some type of van. Dark. I was more concerned about Chloe. But I suppose you need to know that this is the third attempt on my life in the past few days."

Rob halfheartedly detailed the attacks.

"And you think it's terrorists?" Wolf's eyes were large.

"For lack of a better theory."

"We need to report it." Wolf grabbed the car radio off the wall of the unit and called in to have the police meet them at the hospital. The journey seemed to take forever.

"We're going into Dana Point. She needs an MRI, and they'll give her better care there," Wolf told him.

Her eyelids fluttered finally, and the grip loosened a bit on Rob's heart. "Chloe, it's Rob. Can you hear me, honey? We're taking you to the hospital."

"Mother," she said, obviously gritting her teeth.

"Of course." Rob retrieved Chloe's cell phone and then dialed Mrs. Greene's number. He hoped she was sober.

Martha met him at the hospital as he was making his report to the police. Mascara was running down her face with her tears. Her eyes were wild with hysteria.

"What happened? Where's Chloe? Where's the doctor? I've got to see her. Now!"

He remembered she had lost her husband in a car accident, so he tried to be soothing, even though he was still rattled himself. "We got in the way of a drunk in a truck," he lied. After all, Martha Greene was in no shape to be told of a terrorist plot. "I managed to get both of us out of the way, but she hit her head on the pavement pretty hard. They're doing an MRI on her now."

Mrs. Greene repeated, "Where's the doctor? Where's someone I can talk to?"

"The ER doctor is with another patient. I know that Chloe has a concussion, but that's all they told me. They'll know more after the MRI." He didn't add that they could have both been killed. He had started trembling once they got to the hospital and the paramedics whisked Chloe away from him. It had been so close. They were incredibly lucky they'd been so near the opening between the two buildings.

The police take on the matter of the "terrorist" was serious. They had an APB out for dark vans driving in an erratic manner and said that Homeland Security needed to be briefed on the matter. They would undoubtedly take over the investigation.

Would death never stop stalking him? He continued berating himself over nearly getting Chloe killed. Could it be that she was defrosting a little piece of his heart?

When Rob was finished with the police but still awaiting Homeland Security, he found Chloe's mother in one of the plastic waiting room chairs. "How long before we know anything?"

"I'm sorry, Mrs. Greene. I have no idea. Look, I'm really sorry about this. You don't expect things like this to happen in San Clemente."

"No." Chloe's mother put her head in her hands and began to cry. "She could have been killed."

He squatted down next to her chair and handed her the clean bandanna handkerchief from his jeans pocket. "But she wasn't."

What would have become of Chloe's mother if her daughter had died? He sat down to wait beside Mrs. Greene.

It was close to eleven o'clock by the time the doctor approached them. "She has a severe concussion, but we've got her packed in ice. It's too soon to say if the bleeding will cause any damage. We'll have to keep her off pain medications for a day to make sure she stays conscious, until the danger of a coma has passed."

Rob was aware of tremendous relief tempered by a stab of disappointment. He didn't want to leave the hospital without seeing her.

A nurse directed Chloe's mother to her daughter's room. He caught up to Martha. "If it wouldn't be too much of an imposition, could you ask her if she'd mind seeing me for a moment? I'll just wait outside the door."

The woman looked him up and down in a dazed manner as though seeing him for the first time. "I'll ask her. But I don't think she's feeling too well, Mr. Stevens."

"Rob. I'm Rob. And I won't stay long, I promise. I just have to see for myself that she's okay before I leave. I don't even feel like I *should* leave until we know for sure she's going to be okay."

Her face gentled. "Let's just go see how she is, why don't we?"

He waited outside the door. It was slightly ajar, so he could hear the murmur of voices. Still, Mrs. Greene didn't come to get him. She'd probably forgotten all about him. He waited until a nurse came. She was carrying an ice bag. Before she could enter the room, he said, "Would you ask the patient if Rob can see her for a moment?"

The nurse gave a short nod and went in. About five minutes later she emerged. "She'll see you. But don't tire her. She's in a lot of pain."

Rob entered the room. It was dark, except for a small light plugged directly into the wall like a night light. He could barely make out her features, but he saw that her hair was fanned out around her pale face. Her mother was holding her hand.

"It's Rob," he said gently. "I just wanted to say how sorry I am."

"You saved my life," she said in a whisper.

"It was instinct. I threw myself on top of you. I guess I got a little too enthusiastic."

"You saved my life," she repeated. "This headache's nothing compared to being dead."

"Well, I guess that's true."

"It was a miracle. I was just telling Mother."

"I'm sorry, Rob," Mrs. Greene said. "I forgot you were standing out there."

"It's okay. You had other things on your mind."

"Why don't you go home and get some rest? I'm going to stay the night."

"I'll give you my cell number. I want you to call me if there's anything you need." He didn't add, "Or if there's any change." He knew he'd be the last thing on her mind if Chloe went into a coma. He'd just have to call the nurse's station to check on the situation himself.

"Good night, Chloe. I'll be by to see you tomorrow."

Pulling a business card out of his wallet, he handed it to Mrs. Greene. "My cell's listed on there. Be sure to call if there's anything I can do."

The woman nodded. "Thanks for saving her, Rob. I can never repay you."

"Just take good care of her."

He left the room reluctantly and went downstairs to call a cab.

By the time he got back to the house, it was after twelve-thirty, and he was reeling with exhaustion. Through the fog surrounding his home, he saw flashlights bobbing. *What in the world?* Then he realized he had parked next to a police car.

"What's going on here?" he demanded, slamming his door shut.

A broad-chested sergeant met him. "Are you Mr. Stevens?"

"Yes. What're you doing here?"

"Apparently you had an attempted break-in. Your security alarm went off, and your next-door neighbor called us. We got right down here, but the criminal had taken off."

"It's not my night," Rob said wearily. "Or maybe since you're here, it is."

"Something wrong?"

Rob recounted once again the string of near-fatal incidents. "Homeland Security was notified, but they're sure slow about getting back to me. I'm exhausted. Right now I just want to go to bed."

"You do that. We'll have someone out here keeping watch until Homeland shows up. Get what sleep you can. You're in for a grilling, I'm afraid." He shook his bald head. "Terrorists in San Clemente. Who would have thought?"

An agent from Homeland Security called him almost as soon as his head hit the pillow. Apparently, they got a lot of dubious calls and had to check out the story of his plant in Indonesia and the two previous incidents before getting in touch with him. Their resources were a bit thin due to a threat to an oil tanker in San Pedro, but the FBI had agreed to help out by sending two agents to relieve the local police. They would guard him until someone from Homeland Security could take over. Meanwhile, CIA agents based in Indonesia were checking into the situation at his plant.

He shouldn't have slept well that night. But he did. Better than he had in months. Perhaps it was the aftereffects of a double dose of adrenaline to the system, he thought the next morning while he shaved. Or maybe it was just the idea that right now a team of well-armed agents were sitting outside on his porch drinking the coffee he had given them.

Next order of business. A call to the hospital. A tired-sounding Mrs. Greene answered Chloe's phone.

"No, Rob. Still no sign of a coma. They think since she made it this far, she's going to be all right. She's still in a lot of pain, but if she stays conscious they'll give her something for that this afternoon. She'll be discharged tomorrow morning if all goes well."

"Why don't you let me take over for you? I've had some sleep, and you sound like you could use some."

"Oh, I couldn't let you do that."

"Why not? You must be exhausted."

"But you have to go to work."

"I'll bring my phone and communicate via e-mail. That's mostly what I do at the office, anyway. Our major operations are overseas."

"Are you sure you wouldn't mind? There's a hotel across the street. I could take just a short nap. I do feel like death warmed over."

"You need to get your strength back before Chloe comes home. Let me take over for the day. You go home and have a hot shower and some breakfast. Then lie down. You'll sleep better in your own bed. Besides, once they give her pain meds this afternoon, she'll probably drift off."

"Well, if you're sure."

"I'll be there within the hour."

With an agent dogging his steps, Rob was fairly sure he wouldn't be putting Chloe in further danger by visiting her, and he needed urgently to see for himself how she was.

He arrived at the hospital bearing flowers. Perhaps because of Botticelli, he associated her with Tuscany and brought a bouquet he had made up of bright blue delphiniums and golden sunflowers.

"Oh," Chloe said. "How beautiful. My favorite colors. Thank you, Rob."

"It's the least I can do."

They both said good-bye to an exhausted Mrs. Greene, who nevertheless refused Rob's offer to send her home in a cab or call a car service. She said on the way out, "Call me Martha, Rob, and take good care of my girl. I'll be back later this afternoon."

"Rob, you didn't have to do this," Chloe said after her mother had left. "I'm perfectly fine on my own. Don't you need to be talking to Homeland Security or something?"

"I want to be here," he said. "There's an agent who's been thoroughly briefed sitting outside your door, and another one at my house. The CIA is checking things out at my plant in Jakarta. It all seems absurd, but you can't really argue with three murder attempts." He decided she didn't need to know about the attempted break-in right now, though when she was feeling more herself, he intended to tell her. Two brains were better than one, and Chloe had a first-class brain.

"I'm not really good company."

"That's all right. I don't expect you to be a glittering socialite. Did you get any sleep at all last night?"

"I dozed a little. I feel like fifty million hammers are beating inside my skull."

"I'm sorry. I should have twisted so you landed on my shoulder."

"I'm amazed you had time to think at all. I was frozen in the headlights. I couldn't move. It was my 'play dead' response. It happens to me when I feel threatened."

"Well, my flight response went into overdrive. I shouldn't have flown quite so high."

"You saved my life, Rob. I don't want to hear any more apologies."

"Okay. It's a deal. I'll take out my penance by distracting you."

"It would have been terrible if we'd both died. Our alcoholics probably would have really gone into self-destruct. You saved not only us but them." A tear slid down her cheek. He was tempted to brush it away but decided that would be too intimate a gesture. She continued, "I kept thanking the Lord all night long that He hadn't left my mother alone. I know she couldn't have coped."

"The Lord?"

"No atheists in foxholes, remember? Our deliverance wasn't due to a redwood tree or any of my nature sprites. Only someone as powerful as God could have saved us, Rob. And the doctor who viewed my MRI this morning said it was a miracle the bleeding had stopped and I wasn't in a coma. Someone knew that was the one thing that my poor mother couldn't have handled."

He was amazed at her perspective. "Here you almost died, and you were thinking of your mother?"

"Of course. Don't make me sound too noble. She was weeping all over my bed."

"Well, I'm afraid I didn't spare a thought for Ginger."

"I don't suppose you've called in to the therapist about Rick Niebolt and the suicide attempt?"

"I haven't given it a thought, what with Homeland Security and a maniac in a van that almost killed you."

"Why don't you do it now? You have your phone, don't you?"

"This is hardly the time or place."

"I think it's important. Go out in the hall if you want to. I won't listen."

"It's not that."

"Then what is it?"

"It's just that you're my chief concern right now."

She managed a small, weary smile. "Then do it for me," she said.

Should he? Suddenly, Ginger didn't seem all that important. But what if he *had* died? She would have been left on her own, like Chloe said, to self-destruct. Perhaps he should just put this in train and let it play out. He still felt that someone needed to get to the bottom of Ginger's secret sorrow and try to ameliorate it so she could find forgiveness and get off the booze.

Looking down at Chloe with her reddish-gold hair fanned out on her pillow, her wan face still incredibly beautiful with its tiger eyes bigger than ever, his heart did a little trip that took him by surprise.

"I'll just go out in the hallway then, so I don't bother you."

"Okay. I'm not going anywhere."

Rob patted the hand that lay on the sheet next to where he was sitting, got up, and went out into the hallway. After dialing the number, he heard, "Renaissance House. How may I direct your call?"

"This is Rob Stevens. My sister, Ginger Stevens, is in your facility. I'd like to speak to her therapist. I can't remember her name, but she's tall with red hair."

"That would be Dr. Updike. She's in group right now. May I have her return your call?"

"Yes. Here's my cell number." Rob gave the number. "Tell her I have some information for her about my sister."

"Of course. Thank you, Mr. Stevens."

Chloe was dozing when he went back to the room, so he busied himself answering e-mails. It didn't occur to him immediately, but all his messages were domestic. There wasn't anything from the plant overseas. A nurse arrived to take Chloe's vital signs.

"I hate to wake her up," the petite brunette whispered as she fitted the blood pressure cuff over Chloe's arm.

Chloe's eyes opened blearily.

"Blood pressure's normal. You're stable there. That's a good thing. Let me take your temperature." She placed the electronic thermometer in Chloe's ear for a second. "Normal, also. Now your pulse, and I'll get out of here and leave you with your husband. Those are beautiful flowers."

Chloe blinked groggily. Rob didn't know whether to let the

misunderstanding remain or not. Would they throw him out if they knew he wasn't her husband? He decided to say nothing.

A while later, he looked up from his e-mail to find Chloe's eyes on him.

"How're you feeling? I'm sorry the nurse woke you up."

"About the same. How's your work?"

"Not a word from Indonesia. I don't exactly know what to make of it."

"It seems to support your terrorist theory."

"Yeah. I wish I'd hear from Homeland Security."

"And your phone call? How did that go?"

"I left a message. The therapist was in group therapy."

"Oh, too bad."

Rob looked at his cell. "I've been using my cell and haven't heard anything from the other line, but I'll check voicemail."

There was a message. Without thinking of moving into the hall, he called back.

"Renaissance House. How may I direct your call?"

"Yes. Is Dr. Updike available? I'm Rob Stevens, returning her call."

"She's in a private therapy session right now, Mr. Stevens. I'll tell her you called back."

"Thanks." He turned to Chloe. "I seem to be batting zero. Speaking of which, something else weird happened last night."

"What?"

"Someone tried to break into my house. Fortunately, the alarm scared off whoever it was."

"What a night!"

"That's what I say." He closed his cell phone. "I'm finished with this for a while. Why don't you tell me where you're going to set your next book?"

"Probably on a sheep ranch in New Zealand. Edward Petersen came over the other night and gave me a lot of good ideas. He lived there for three years."

Rob smacked his head. "Today's Friday, isn't it?"

Chloe appeared to consider. "I think so."

"I'm supposed to have dinner with Edward tonight. I'd better call and cancel."

"I don't see why. Mother will be back. Why go home to an empty house if you don't have to?"

"I'm not exactly in the mood for making merry after what's happened."

Chloe gave a little laugh and winced. "I can't imagine making merry with Edward. He doesn't drink, you know."

"Yes, I know. I'm supposed to bring French bread."

"Why don't you go? It'll give you a chance to talk to him."

"He'll probably try to reactivate me, and that's one thing I don't want to talk about now."

"Reactivate?"

"Yeah. I'm a Jack Mormon. Haven't been inside a church since high school. He's been assigned to keep track of me."

"You make him sound like a spy or something."

"Well, it is kind of intrusive to know he's always there, ready if I need him."

"But you do need him, Rob. You're going through an intense emotional trauma now, not to mention Robbie's death and Ginger's situation. Edward won't push you. He's the epitome of kindness."

"There you go again. Talking like a writer."

"He doesn't bite," she added.

"After last night, I'm more of a cynic than ever. Don't you realize that the agenda of these terrorists has everything to do with their version of God?"

"There have always been false gods and idols. That doesn't mean there isn't a real one. I tell you it was a miracle we weren't killed. I was praying all night in gratitude."

"You see the miracle. I see the terrorist."

"The terrorist is deluded and dangerous. His agenda is deeply flawed, I grant you that. But someone *saved* us."

Rob stared down at her. She seemed quite determined. He supposed she could be right. After all, they had been just steps away from the gap in the buildings. And he had seemed to have superhuman strength and reflexes. Plus, Chloe could have gone into a coma, and she hadn't.

"You're determined to see the glass as half-full, aren't you?"

"I was thinking about it to take my mind off the pain. Most bad things in the world seem capricious. Humans are capricious. Nature is capricious. But Edward said that comes with mortality. If there is a God, I don't believe He is capricious, like some egomaniacal Zeus. Maybe there's a good reason we don't understand why He doesn't interfere most of the time."

He felt a rush of the anger he'd been trying so hard to suppress. It tightened his jaw, and his nostrils flared. "But what about Robbie? Why didn't God save Robbie? And Pamela? Why did she have to die so young?"

Chloe didn't answer right away. Finally, she said, "There's a lot I still don't understand. But Edward is so soothing, so certain."

"I'll think about it."

"But you'll go? You'll go to dinner?"

He ran his hand over the back of his neck. "I guess. The old guy probably has the lasagna half-made by now." Irritably, he opened his smart phone and logged on once more, completely forgetting his outstanding call to Renaissance House.

He worked on and off throughout the afternoon and then started speaking to Chloe about New Zealand when she awoke at last.

"I did think I'd stay home until my mother is stable, but I think her sponsor is more help than I am. I make her feel ashamed, but her sponsor knows what she's going through and can relate a lot better."

"So you're going to go soon?" he asked, seriously jolted.

"Probably as soon as I get rid of this headache."

"You're kidding!"

"No." She looked away and started pleating her sheet with unsteady fingers.

"But why?" he couldn't help asking.

The "why" chose that instant to stride into the room in the form of Luke—big and handsome, strutting his virility. "Honey, I heard I nearly lost you for good! Your neighbor told me when I showed up for our date."

Heart sinking as though someone had just cut a hole in his new, little dinghy of well-being, Rob flashed a look at Chloe and read clear panic.

CHAPTER TEN

By the time he showed up at Edward Petersen's door, Rob was considerably disgruntled. He had finally heard from Homeland Security, and the news wasn't good. He had also missed another call from Sonia Updike. When he had called her back on the way home from the hospital, she had left for the day.

Here he was, in the foulest of moods, clutching his loaf of French bread, with the six-foot-three Agent Somers checking out the area around Edward's house.

"Come in, come in," Edward invited. "I hear there was some excitement over at your place last night."

"You don't know the half of it," Rob said. "Chloe and I barely escaped being killed earlier in the evening. She's in the hospital with a concussion."

"Oh my goodness! Is she going to be all right?"

"They thought so this afternoon. She didn't go into a coma, and she should be released tomorrow morning. It's looking better.

They're finally giving her something for the pain, but she's had a rough time."

"I'm sorry she's in pain, but I'm glad they're releasing her soon. It sounds like things could have been a lot worse. I'm amazed you showed up tonight." Looking out the window, he asked, "Is that someone I should know?"

"Sorry. I think he's trying to appear invisible. I am now under the protection of Homeland Security. The only thing we can figure out is that I am being targeted by terrorists. Homeland's take on the thing is that Muslim extremists want to eliminate Americans in Indonesia and take over my plant to use it as a source of income for terrorist activities."

"Hmm. That doesn't feel right to me. Indonesian Muslims aren't radical as a whole."

"Well, the Muslim that was working as my manager has disappeared. I got a call from HS on my way here. My plant's in chaos. The CIA agent thought it best to shut it down for the time being."

"Well, I'm sure sorry to hear that, but sit down for heaven's sake," Edward said. "Your eye sockets are like craters. How long since you've had any sleep?"

"I haven't slept much since Robbie's death."

"I know how that is. But I've never had terrorists stalking me and trying to kill me in the midst of my grief. I'm glad you came. I don't like to think about your spending the night alone after something like that. Come with me into the kitchen and tell me everything that happened."

In spite of his mood, Rob was tantalized by the delicious aromas of oregano, basil, and garlic, and the meat and tomato sauce. Dropping onto a stool beside the counter, he watched Edward slice his bread as he told his story.

"It sounds like a miracle you lived through it," Edward remarked.

"That's what Chloe says."

"And you don't think so?"

"I don't believe in miracles."

Edward was mashing minced garlic into previously softened butter. "What would you call it, then?"

Rob felt suddenly pugnacious. "Luck. I don't know. I just don't believe a God who could do miracles would let Robbie die."

"I see."

For some reason, Rob was surprised at the mildness of Edward's tone. He was silent, spreading the butter between the slices of French bread. Then he wrapped the whole thing in foil and placed it in the oven with the baking lasagna.

"Let's go in the living room where we can talk decently. The bread will take about ten minutes."

They walked into the main room of the house, which had obviously been cleaned for the evening. The clutter on the coffee table was now in one neat stack.

"I know I haven't been the righteous Mormon that I should have been, and I'm sorry for it, but it doesn't alter the fact that I'm still very angry over Robbie's death."

"I'd be angry, too."

Rob looked at the other man with something approaching shock. "You would?"

"Believing in the gospel doesn't take away the anger. I've been where you are. I lost my own ten-year-old daughter to polio. I wasn't active then, either."

"But you're writing a book on hope."

"Her death brought me back to the Church. I learned after a time that there is hope. But to feel it, you have to get past the anger."

"What can there possibly be to hope for?"

"More than we can discuss in ten—no, seven minutes. Why don't we leave this discussion for after dinner?"

Rob hid his surprise. He'd expected to have hope crammed down his throat.

Instead, they enjoyed an excellent dinner of lasagna, garlic bread, tossed green salad, and chocolate silk pie with whipped cream. Edward offered Agent Somers a plate on the porch. Looking at it with obvious longing, the agent declined.

"Can't afford to let my attention stray," the man told them.

Over dinner, Rob gave Edward details of the events in his life since Robbie's funeral, and they discussed terrorism in general.

"I don't know how much of the Book of Mormon you read, Rob, but there is this guerilla group called the Gadianton robbers that always plagued the Nephites whenever the Nephites got too wicked. The robbers were impossible to defeat and, eventually, proved the destruction of the whole civilization."

"That's a cheerful view of the situation," Rob said, feeling his irritation rise.

"What do you intend to do with your company now?"

"I'm too tired and discouraged to face that question at the moment. If I survive, I'll undoubtedly face financial ruin, losing all my assets over there, so I'm trying to keep it out of my mind. Let's talk about something else."

"I'm game," Edward said, finishing his salad.

"I met Chloe's boyfriend today," Rob told him. "Do you know him?"

"I just barely met Chloe. She's never mentioned a boyfriend."

Rob tried to hide his disappointment. He was hoping Edward could give him details. Like what the panic meant that he had seen in her eyes. "She's talking about leaving for New Zealand right after she gets out of the hospital, and something tells me that he's the reason."

"Well, I'll be sorry to see her go, but I can't shed any light on that, I'm afraid."

After dinner, they cleared the table, and Rob helped clean up the neat galley-like kitchen. Finally, they made their way back to the living room to sit in the overstuffed leather chairs.

He decided to jump in with both feet and clear the air. "You've been very patient with me over the years, Edward, so I'm going to level with you. My folks were what you would probably call 'cultural Mormons.' They died when I was in my teens. They had the big Mormon funeral and the whole nine yards."

"Where did they live?" Edward asked.

"Newport. A lot of people in their ward were the same as they were, but there were a few I thought of as fanatics. Like my Young Men's leaders. They wanted me to go to BYU and serve a mission. I was recruited by San Diego State to play football, so I went there and fell out of the habit of going to church. I didn't need it. My life was full of football, girls, and technology. I actually invented the hardware for my first cell phone when I was a senior."

"I understand. You sound a lot like me. Only I was a track enthusiast. Javelin. And there was a war on, so I enlisted in the Navy and didn't worry much about religion for years."

"But your daughter's death brought you back? Why?"

"We lived in Salt Lake City. My wife, Rachel, came from an active LDS family, but Rachel had let things slide, just like me. We had a temple marriage because that's the way things were done in our families, but we didn't really think we needed the Church. We resented it, actually. The way it intruded into everything." Edward picked up a photo from the table. "Here's Suzy's picture. My daughter."

He passed the picture to Rob, who saw a beautiful child in a smocked dress with her hair in two pigtails. Pain smote him, but this time it wasn't for himself.

"She was our only girl, so I spoiled her. And she was my shadow. Whenever I got home from the office, she was waiting for me on the front steps. In the winter, I taught her to ski. I taught the boys, too, of course, but Suzy always skied with me, before the polio. In the summer, it was sailing or waterskiing. We had two boats and went to Lake Powell most weekends."

"Then she died," Rob said, feeling Edward's sadness. "How in the world did you get from there to here?" He indicated the stack of Church magazines and books on the coffee table.

"Rachel's mother became our personal comforter long enough to teach us how to find the real Comforter—the Holy Ghost. We realized how lucky we were that we had been married for eternity and that our children would be ours forever. But we had to shape up or ship out. So, we started going to church again. One thing led to another, and here I am, telling you my story."

Edward's simple narrative rammed into Rob's brain with a thud. Pamela hadn't been LDS, and he'd married her in her hometown church in Nevada. While starting his business, he'd scarcely even been in the United States. It was easier not to make an issue of her taking Robbie to church. If Rob had been a good Mormon kid, if he'd taken life a little more seriously, Robbie would have been born into a forever family. Then maybe his death wouldn't have been nearly so wrenching. Odd that that had never occurred to him when Pamela died.

"Let's take a walk before the sun goes down," Edward suggested.

"I'm afraid it's not allowed," Rob said. "Too open. I can't make myself a target."

"Sorry. I forgot. I guess I am older than I think. Forgive me."

There was silence for a moment, and then Rob inquired, "Do you think it's possible for me to arrive at some sort of peace over my losses?"

"First, you have to want it. You have to believe peace exists. Have you ever been a believer, Rob?"

"I hung out with the Mormon kids in high school, but my parents weren't excited about getting up early to take me to seminary, and a lot of times we didn't make it to church. But I know enough to know that if I'd been married in the temple and been a worthy father to Robbie, he'd be sealed to me now."

"Do you have any desire to find that peace?"

Rob thought. "That depends."

"On what, exactly?"

"I guess I'm afraid to let go of my anger," he admitted.

"Afraid of what you might feel instead?" Edward was gentle.

Rob nodded. He looked into Edward's eyes; they seemed to mirror his own hurt. This man understood, Rob realized. He knew just how it felt. He had lost a ten-year-old to a disease that could now be prevented by an injection. He'd felt like a failure as a father, too.

"If you can let the anger go, even for a moment, just to find the desire for peace, you can work with that," Edward said.

Under the influence of Edward's calm assurance, Rob found himself wondering if it were possible for him to give up the rage inside him. Then there was the organization that was trying to kill him and take over his company. The timing was all wrong for this discussion. If there was any truth to be had in the Mormon church, he had found it too late. It was possible he could be dead tomorrow. But if that happened, what would become of him in the afterlife?

"Can it save me?" he asked, feeling a sudden wave of emotion that threatened tears.

"Yes. It has the most saving power in the universe. The only one that never fails."

The anguish he had kept at bay with his anger overwhelmed him at Edward's calm statement. Was such a thing possible? A power that never failed? His tears came to the surface, and he wept unashamedly. "I'd do anything to have peace," he said. "Anything to get rid of this pain." He reached for his handkerchief in his back pocket. "But it's too late, Edward. That terrorist isn't going to let me live."

"I know the situation is frightening and dicey at the moment. But so does the Lord, believe me. Work with HS. Do everything you can to stay alive. Then, if you really desire it, you can make things right with the Lord."

"How?"

"Give the gospel another chance, Rob. Make an experiment. Think of your desire as a seed, if you can. You can nourish that seed. It can become a tree strong enough for you to hold on to, to lean on when you need it."

Rob's tears kept coming. *What I wouldn't give for just one thing I could hold on to. One thing that wouldn't go away.* He nodded again, wiping his face. For the first time he acknowledged that the possibility of Chloe leaving had been the final straw. He had lost his family and probably his business, but somewhere inside he had just begun to think he might be able to start life all over again with Chloe.

"Jesus Christ loves you more than you can imagine. He knows your pain. He can heal it, if you let Him."

"How?"

"Through His love and understanding. I promise you this, Rob. If it happened to me, it can happen to anyone." He moved forward in his chair and fixed Rob with his mild blue gaze. "I was very angry after Rachel died. She contracted tuberculosis when we were serving our mission in Russia. I felt she should have been protected. But in time I saw that Christ hadn't been protected, even though He served the greatest mission of all. It kind of put things in perspective. Then I thought of Peter and Paul. I realized it's never been easy to be a believer."

Rob remembered that he was making an experiment. He would go along with this and see where it took him. But how could martyrdom be comforting?

Edward explained, "The mercy is that, though we suffer physical death, our spirits live on and one day will be rejoined with our bodies. It will be a glorious resurrection, just like the one Jesus Christ experienced. Robbie and Pamela will be resurrected."

Rob felt something loosen in his chest. It was as though he were somehow softening, giving in. Edward's words touched him in a place he had never been touched before.

"I never really understood Jesus Christ. All I knew was that He died and was resurrected. I didn't really see what it had to do with me."

"It has everything to do with you. Jesus Christ is your personal Savior. He's Robbie's Savior, and Pamela's. Because of Him, death is not the end. Because of how much He loved us, He suffered all things, even the worst and most despicable of sins. He did it so that we could be free of spiritual death. I don't know why Robbie died when he did, but I know that his spirit is very much alive and that someday he will be resurrected."

"Even though I never taught him about Jesus Christ? Even though he was never baptized?"

"Resurrection is a free gift given to us all by the grace of God. Rob, you must continue this experiment on your own. Did you ever pray as a boy?"

"Pray?" His mind quailed at the idea. "On my knees? Chloe didn't pray. She said her deliverance came through laughter."

"Chloe doesn't know that her meditation is actually a form of communion with the Infinite. The Lord reaches us each in different ways. But you can shorten that process by demonstrating humility. Think of what Heavenly Father and Jesus have done freely for you and your wife and son. Is that too much to ask?"

Rob pondered this. His aversion seemed foolish in light of Edward's words. "I guess not."

But to him it seemed anything but simple. It would require him to walk out on a limb, hanging over the air, possibly feeling like a fool. *But didn't I say I'd do anything to feel peace?*

Edward seemed to read his thoughts. "Remember, you're starting with a seed—a desire to believe. In time, if you proceed, you're going to grow a sturdy tree."

Rob thought about what he'd heard. He already felt a certain sense of peace. It was emanating from Edward to him—like sitting in front of a comforting fire on a cold, rainy night. He was reluctant to leave it. It was like that feeling he'd had when drinking peppermint hot chocolate in his Sunday School teacher's class sometime during his youth.

But then, memory intruded. *He wasn't safe.* There was a terrorist out there determined that Rob should die.

Rob left Edward's home in a sort of daze. It wasn't until he was halfway home, surrounded by the ever-present fog, that he registered the uneasy feeling of being followed by someone other than his agent. Immediately, his senses went on alert, and he looked around. No one. Not even Agent Somers. Of course, there were plenty of places to hide—arbors of bougainvillea, cars, patio enclosures. Even those places were hardly visible in this confounded mist. He hastened his steps but thought he heard the crunch of gravel heading away from him toward the parking lot. Whirling again, he still could see no one, but he was more convinced than ever that someone nefarious was there. At last he reached his house, disarmed the alarm, unlocked the door, went inside, and rearmed the alarm. Was he getting paranoid, or had there really been someone out there?

His heart was pounding, and the lovely, peaceful feeling he had felt at Edward's had evaporated. Now he was assailed by doubts. Had it ever been real?

He paced the small house, trying to work off his adrenaline. Shutting off the lights, he went to the side window and peered in the direction from which he had come. Nothing. In the distance, he heard a car starting up and driving away.

Turning on the lights once more, he went through his mail distractedly, finding nothing but bills and catalogues. He wasn't ready to settle down yet. Flipping on the television, he channel-surfed for half an hour, catching up on the day's news. There had been a suicide bombing in Jakarta, but it was nowhere near his plant. Still, any radical Muslim activity in Indonesia was unusual. He wished he had more information about what was going on. Slowly, his pulse returned to normal, and he began to chide himself for being fanciful.

The phone rang.

"Are you all right?" It was the voice of Agent Somers, sounding unusually harsh.

"Yes. Though I thought someone was following me earlier."

He heard a sigh of relief. "Someone was. Agent Whitlow has taken over. I'm on my way to the hospital. Your stalker shot me in the shoulder. You were lucky, Stevens."

Rob's heart began to beat like a twelve-man band. "Your shoulder! That must be really painful. Have you been passed out all this time or something?"

"Yes. For the last couple of hours, you have been unwatched.

Luckily, your friend Mr. Petersen makes a habit of taking a midnight stroll. He found me."

"Why would the guy shoot you and not me?"

"The only thing that makes any sense is that he thought I was you. The fog was obscuring the moon, and I had just set out to follow you home, so I was going in the right direction."

"Thankfully, he's not a good shot," Rob remarked.

"I don't know about that," the agent replied. "I'm being transfused and shouldn't be on the phone. You know, that bullet was just a smidge too high. He didn't miss my heart by much."

Rob collapsed into his armchair. "Thank you, Agent. You saved my life."

"You're one lucky guy, you know that?"

Rob knew. And he was starting to believe there was someone up there who wanted him alive. Why else had his life been preserved so miraculously so many times? He still didn't understand about Robbie and Pamela, but he wondered if he didn't owe that someone some gratitude instead of steadfastly denying His existence. He felt weak all over at the narrowness of his escape from death once again.

Was he ready to continue Edward's experiment? He remembered the tears he had shed. The feeling of ease in his chest. That release had been real. He had never felt anything like it.

Well, there was only one way to find out if what he'd heard was true. He got down on his knees beside his bed. Immediately feeling foolish, his doubts heightened. An experiment, Edward had said. A desire to believe. Well, he certainly had that. He'd try it, no matter how ridiculous it felt.

"Our Father who art in Heaven, hallowed be Thy name. Thank you for preserving my life, even though I haven't been the most obedient of your children." He felt his limbs tremble, still weak. Shoring himself up by his elbows on the bed, he continued, "Thank you for the resurrection, if it's real. And if it's real, please let me know that. Please let me know that Robbie is still alive in his spirit and that one day he'll be resurrected." He waited, visualizing Robbie's face in his mind. Not his dead face, but his alive, laughing face, the way it had been before Pamela died. And then, he pictured Pamela, blonde and lovely, poised and patient.

"Heavenly Father, help me to *know*," he pleaded. He waited some more, still picturing his family in his mind. Then he realized he was seeing another realm—a place he'd never seen before. It appeared to be a mountain glen. Perhaps a view of Scotland. He had always dreamed of taking Robbie to show him the land of his forefathers. The grass was a deep velvet green, and there were huge shade trees in full leaf alongside a small brook that trickled down rounded, smooth stones. The water was clear enough to see through. A perfect landscape. The peace and calm of it filled his breast, and he slowly realized that he was feeling something different. It was like the closeness he had sometimes felt on Christmas morning when his family was all there beside him, eating waffles and drinking hot citrus punch flavored with cinnamon and cloves. There was laughter. Rob was standing on his head. His parents (miraculously young) were teasing each other unmercifully, as they had done so often before dying when he was seventeen.

Rob realized that they were all, in their own way, celebrating being together. There was a feeling of joyous anticipation as though they would be doing something wonderful that day. Perhaps exploring the glen or climbing the mountains for a picnic. But they would be together. And right then, nothing else mattered.

It was delicious. There was no other word to describe it. It filled the place where the anger had been, pushing it away just like the sun chased shadows. He took a deep breath that filled him with sweetness.

Help me to hold on to this. Please. Help me to know what to do to keep this feeling forever. He waited, and Edward's countenance filled his mind. Edward had the answers. He had led him this far. He knew the rest of the way. Rob would ask him.

He knelt by the bed for a long time, reluctant to let go of this tenuous line between himself and what had felt like heaven. He replayed memories of Robbie on the beach, frolicking in the waves, at his soccer matches (where he carried him triumphant on his shoulders after he'd scored a winning goal), in the steamy jungles of Indonesia, the colorful and teeming streets of Jakarta, and the wild loveliness of Bali.

The feeling of closeness stayed, and he spent hours on his knees, weeping freely, as he pictured past happiness with renewed joy until exhaustion claimed him. He felt physically weak, only now it was from the presence of so much emotion. *Thank you, Father, thank you. Amen.*

He got up from his knees and dropped onto the bed where he felt himself falling, falling, falling into a deep sleep. When he was almost there, he realized hazily that Pamela had not been in any of the scenes he imagined. Letting go of the thought, he slept.

CHAPTER ELEVEN

When Chloe finally surfaced into awareness, she could tell by the dim night light that there was someone beside her bed, leaning forward, elbows on knees, watching her. Through her slitted eyes she could tell it was a man. Rob was big, but this man was huge. Fright overtook her. She was moving her hand as slowly as possible toward the nurse call button when the person spoke.

"Chloe! Finally, you're awake." Then she remembered. Luke.

"Where's my mother? What time is it?"

"Slow down, Chipper," he said, employing the nickname he'd always used for her. It was ridiculously inappropriate, especially now, and she realized she'd always hated it.

He reached for her hand. "I haven't seen her."

"Oh, dear," she said, feeling so weary that all she wanted to do was go back to sleep. Apparently, Luke's magic wasn't enough to combat the load of narcotics in her system.

"She didn't answer the door at your house. I was pretty puzzled when neither you nor your mom were home. Remember? It was your neighbor who told me you'd been in an accident and were in the Dana Point hospital. Your mom had him watching for me."

"Where has she gone?" Chloe knew she was subconsciously worried, but it took a few moments for her to realize why. "She's not somewhere drinking, is she?"

"I . . . I don't know."

"She was supposed to relieve Rob. She's been sober only a few days, and this accident really shook her up." Chloe sighed and looked at the ceiling, trying to remember what she had learned in Al-Anon. *It isn't my responsibility to keep my mom from drinking.*

"I know what she's going through. It's rough," Luke said. "Why do you think I was crazy enough to sail to and from Fiji all by myself?"

Startled, Chloe looked at him but could not read his eyes in the dim light. "Are you telling me you had an alcohol problem, Mr. Practically-a-Vegetarian?"

"That's what a bad marriage does to you. And regret. Tons of regret."

"I'm really sorry, Luke. Can we talk about this later? I need another pain pill."

"It's me who should be sorry." He squeezed her hand and then let go. "While you were sleeping, a nurse came in and took your vitals. She was very surprised to see me. Like she was expecting someone else." He chuckled. "She actually said, 'But you're not her husband!'"

Chloe rolled her eyes, but the action was painful. "So . . . what were you telling me about the nurse?"

"She hooked you up to a morphine pump." He handed her a little device with a push button. "I'm supposed to tell you to push that when you feel pain."

Unreasonably annoyed, Chloe said, "Well, for crying out loud, Luke, why didn't you tell me that as soon as I opened my eyes?" She knew she sounded crabby, but she didn't care. Pushing the button hard, she lay as still as possible, waiting for relief. She closed her eyes, hoping that Luke would take the hint.

Apparently, he did, for he said nothing more. When she finally fell asleep, he was gently and silently stroking her hair. How she'd missed that . . .

Sometime later, she was awakened by voices. Opening her eyes reluctantly, she saw Rob standing in the doorway, holding an adorable, purple, fuzzy monkey with long limbs and an even longer tail. Luke was giving him an amused, tolerant look—the one he usually reserved for children.

"Oh. Rob," she said. "Who's your friend?"

"King Nebuchadnezzar. I already have the sense that he's quite an eccentric."

"You would be, too, if you were purple," she giggled. Without even glancing his way, she could feel Luke looking at her curiously. She was not a giggler.

"I'm sorry we woke you up. How's the head?" Rob asked.

"Surprisingly, a lot better."

"She's on morphine," Luke said.

"Have you two met?" she asked.

"Sort of," Rob answered. "I take it that this is your significant other?"

Was he? She was confused. Probably the morphine. Then Luke reached over and stroked her hair, an action which always reduced her to a puddle of wonderful sensations, all of which she associated with a deep, nurturing love.

"Uh, he used to be. But he got married."

"Then what's he doing, stroking your hair?" Rob asked, obviously annoyed.

"Uh, I don't exactly know. He always does it. Did it."

"I am in the room, you know," Luke said. "Actually, I'm divorced."

Her eyes were glued on Rob, despite all the delicious feelings Luke was eliciting. "Are you going to give me the king?"

Wordlessly, Rob handed over the monkey. Chloe drew it close like a baby and kissed it on the forehead. "How did you know?" she asked. "This is exactly what I needed. He makes me feel safe."

"It's the morphine," Luke said.

"No, those are the special properties of purple monkeys. I checked before I bought it. Well," Rob said with a trace of regret, "I'll be on my way. Just wanted to see how you were doing this morning. Glad you're feeling better. Where's your mother?"

"I don't know. I'm worried. If it wouldn't be too much trouble, would you mind checking on her? I'm worried this has sent her back to the bottle. She hasn't been in at all, has she, Luke?"

"No," he said, his tone worried. "She hasn't even called."

"I'll do it," Rob promised.

"My key's in my purse somewhere around here. Her sponsor's number is right by the telephone, if you need to call her. If she's drunk, I know that will be a problem for you. Please don't feel obligated to deal with it yourself. I'd send Luke, but she can't stand him."

Rob gave a tiny salute, and then he was gone. Clutching her monkey, she abandoned herself to Luke's caress and drifted back to sleep.

CHAPTER TWELVE

ob pulled away from the hospital, Agent Whitlow behind him. He had given Rob a favorable report on Somers that morning. He was going to be all right. HS was taking over from the FBI sometime that day. They would brief Rob on the situation in Jakarta.

Rob had almost forgotten about his plant manager in his concern for Chloe and the incident with Somers. And he had completely forgotten about Ginger. Before he could forget again, he dialed the number he had coded into his cell phone for Renaissance House.

"Renaissance House. How may I direct your call?"

"I'd like to speak to Dr. Updike, please."

"Dr. Updike is off for the weekend. Is this an emergency?"

Rob hesitated. No, it really wasn't an emergency. There was nothing Sonia Updike could do with his information until she came back on Monday, anyway. "No. It isn't an emergency, but it's really important that I speak to her first thing Monday morning. Could you leave her a message?"

"Who is this calling, please?"

"Rob Stevens." He gave her his cell number and then turned into Capistrano Shores to check on Chloe's mother.

The first clue that something was wrong was that no one answered the door. It was locked. He tried calling from his cell phone, but there was no answer. Martha was either not home, on a bender, or had already passed out.

Checking their assigned parking place, he noted that the Lexus was there. So, unless Martha was out with a friend (slim possibility when Chloe was at the hospital), she was inside, passed out.

Reconnoitering the windows, he was able to see little slices of the interior of Chloe's home through curtains that were only haphazardly drawn. Finally, he found her. She was passed out or asleep in the recliner in the living room. He went back to the front door and opened it with Chloe's key.

"What're you up to, young man?" A neighbor with a bulbous nose confronted him from his doorway.

"Mrs. Greene is in there passed out, and she won't answer the door. Her daughter's in the hospital and needs her."

"Oh. Well, let me know if I can be of any help."

Rob felt uneasy and intrusive, entering the living room with its drawn drapes and strong smell of scotch. Ginger all over again.

Before attempting to arouse Chloe's mother, he found instant coffee in the cupboard and set the teakettle on to boil. Then, while waiting for that, he put a call in to the person he assumed was Martha's sponsor, her number taped, as Chloe had told him, on the wall above the telephone.

Trying to remain removed and rational, he explained Chloe's hospitalization and her mother's consequent drinking and present state of obliteration. Amanda promised she would be right over. Rob thanked the heavens that she was home on a Saturday.

Coffee ready, he proceeded to bring Mrs. Greene back into the real world. He stroked her face gently with a towel he had found in the kitchen drawer and then dampened at the sink. She twitched her face and turned away. He did it again. "Mrs. Greene, you've got to wake up. Chloe needs you."

Her eyes fluttered open.

"Here's some coffee. Drink it, and I'll make you some more."

"Chloe?" she said, seemingly mystified.

"She's in the hospital, remember? Concussion? They might let her go today if you can convince them to release her to your care."

Comprehension dawned, and she grasped the coffee cup, draining it quickly. Rob went into the kitchen to make another. "Your sponsor will be here soon. I'll stay with you until she arrives."

At least Chloe's mother didn't look like a drunk. Not like Ginger.

When Amanda finally arrived and took over for him, Chloe's mother was sober enough to feel embarrassed.

"Chloe was worried. She made me promise to check on you. I'm glad I did. Your daughter needs looking after, Mrs. Greene. Amanda will help you pull yourself together, okay? If you need anything, call." He handed her his business card. "I'll be at my office in Newport."

Driving down the freeway to Newport, he realized forcefully that he and Chloe had a lot in common. Those close to alcoholics must all know the drill. Maybe he should give Al-Anon another try. Especially now that he knew God was really there in His heaven.

In the office, he said hello to Mrs. Field, a plump, gray-haired widow who was a weekend staffer he'd hired to handle routine problems with the suppliers in Indonesia. He then sat down at his computer in his private office and began dealing with the e-mails that had accumulated overnight. In his walnut-paneled room, he worked with his back to the large picture window with the ocean view.

He found he was able to concentrate better than he had since Robbie's death. That was a good thing because he was in the middle of some tricky contract negotiations and a patent infringement lawsuit. Still no news from the Jakarta plant. Occasionally, he would stop and look at the framed pictures of his son that sat angled towards him on the desk. He missed Robbie horribly. That ache wasn't gone. But the despair that had accompanied it was no longer there. He held fast to the reminders of the peace he had felt the night before.

After a while, he stood up to stretch and turned to look at the view out his window. He was on the twenty-fifth floor of a high-rise building that faced the ocean. For days he had trained himself not to look at it and had even put out feelers about leasing another space without the ocean view. But now he thought he could finally live with it. He still wanted to get rid of the beach place . . . which reminded him, he needed to call Edward. He had forgotten to ask if the man had talked to his son. Calling information for the number, he sat back down and stared out at the never-ending pewter of the sea that reflected the fog and wished he were on Chloe's Corfu. Then he was connected to Edward's phone.

"Hello?"

"Edward? This is Rob Stevens."

"Oh, Rob. Good to hear your voice. Is everything okay?"

"Chloe seems to be out of the woods. And I just wanted to thank you for your advice last night. I feel more at peace than I have in years, even since before my wife's death."

He heard a chuckle down the line. "Glad to hear you took to heart what an old geezer like me had to say."

"Well, thanks for being so open with a skeptic. I promise that next time we talk, I'll be more open-minded."

"I'm going up to Dana Point to see Chloe this morning."

Rob hesitated and decided to be discreet. "It's been rough on Chloe's mom. She hasn't gotten down there yet this morning, so maybe, if you leave now, this would be a good time for a visit."

Edward answered with a "hmm," and Rob imagined that he had figured the scenario out for himself. "All right, Rob. I'll push off now."

"I'm sure Chloe will be glad to see you. By the way, before you go, I was wondering, did you get a chance to speak to your son about my place?"

"As a matter of fact, I meant to tell you last night that I had. He's very interested. He'll be down next week for the Fourth of July. How about if you and Chloe join us for a barbeque on Thursday?"

"Well, I can't speak for Chloe, but that sounds good to me. I can actually make guacamole. Should I bring that and some Doritos?"

"Sounds perfect."

As soon as Rob hung up, his land line rang. He looked at it, surprised. Who would be calling him here on Saturday afternoon?

Picking up the phone, he said, "Stevens."

"Mr. Stevens, this is Herb down in security. I've got a guy here says he's got a delivery for you. I know you sometimes work Saturdays. Wanted to make sure you'd be there to accept it."

"Delivery? On Saturday?"

"The guy says he works for a private firm. Does Saturday deliveries. He's in a brown van."

Rob asked, "How did he know I was here?"

"He was just going to leave it with me if you weren't."

"Odd. I don't know who'd be sending me anything on Saturday. I guess you'd better send him up."

Rob waited until he heard the brisk knock in the outer office foyer and then went to the door. Outside stood a man chewing a huge wad of gum and wearing sunglasses and a baseball cap over shaggy hair.

"You Mr. Stevens?"

"Yes. I am. What do you have for me there?" Rob looked at the medium-sized, brown cardboard box.

"Special delivery."

"Okay. I guess you'd better put it down over there." He pointed to his secretary's desk.

The man wordlessly walked to the indicated desk, left the package, and walked away, closing the door after himself. Rob was left feeling there was something off-key about the whole thing. He was ready to open the box when he heard his cell phone ring in his office. He walked in there quickly and grabbed the phone before the caller could give up.

"Rob Stevens."

"Mr. Stevens, this is Sonia Updike calling . . ."

KABOOM!

The explosion threw Rob on the floor behind his desk and blew out the window, covering him in shards of glass. *That was no ordinary window.* Next he heard the crackle of flames. Standing, he viewed his outer office on fire. For several moments he couldn't think but just stared as his office took on the look of a disaster film. There had been a bomb in that box! Now flames were licking the desk, the carpet, catching onto the paper all over the desk.

"What was that?" the doctor's voice came through his panic.

"An explosion." Without telling her good-bye, he hung up and dialed 911.

The overhead sprinklers came on, emitting only a dribble.

"This is Rob Stevens at Stevens Communications, 1215 Costa de la Mar, Suite 2500. A bomb just went off in my office. Get someone here as quickly as you can. I'm going down the fire escape."

Rob disconnected and, hearing the hungry crackling of the fire in the outer office, took the time to grab his laptop. He ran out into the outer office, now cut off from the front door by a wall of flame. Dodging to his right, he coughed at the smoke and tried to hold his breath. The doorknob to the supply room was burning hot. Grabbing the handkerchief out of his back pocket, he used it to open the door and, entering the small room, shut the door behind him. Then he opened the back door into the CFO's office and darted inside. Never had he been so glad that Tom had had that door cut through so he could keep his files away from the outer office. Blessing Tom's paranoia as he unlocked the doorknob to his office, he ran into the clear air. Smoke was starting to seep through Tom's office door, but Rob headed for the door to the outside hallway that Tom had also insisted upon. He didn't like people monitoring his comings and goings.

The smoke alarms finally started blaring. Switching his laptop to the other arm, Rob unlocked the door to the hallway with his key and ran towards the fire escape at the end of the hall. He didn't have any desire to walk down all twenty-five flights. Maybe just a couple of floors to be on the safe side, then he'd go out onto another floor and risk calling the elevator.

Then, suddenly he remembered. *Mrs. Field! Was she trapped in the fire? How could he have forgotten her?*

Putting his laptop on the landing of the fire escape, he ran back to Tom's office door and threw it open. The smoke was thicker now. Pulling the handkerchief out of his pocket, he covered his nose and mouth before venturing into the supply closet. Taking a deep breath, he flung that door open and then the door to the main office. The flames were raging out of control, burning along the carpet. The smoke was so thick he could hardly see. He swiftly closed the door behind him, so as not to feed the fire with fresh air. Staying close to the back wall that was farthest from the flames, he choked his way along until he reached the door to Mrs. Field's office. It was closed. He tried the knob with his hand wrapped in his handkerchief. It opened, and he heard the roar of the blaze behind him as fresh air raced past him.

"Mrs. Field!"

The widow was cowering in the corner, receiver in hand as she talked furiously to someone.

"They're on their way!" Rob shouted impatiently. "Come on! If we hurry, we can still make it out through Tom's office."

He took another deep breath and choked on the incoming smoke. "Here," he said. "Put this over your nose and mouth." He handed her his handkerchief and then pulled his polo knit shirt over his head and used it to cover his own face.

They plunged back into the inferno. The flames were closer to the back wall now. He motioned to Mrs. Field to do as he was doing and flattened himself against the wall, inching sideways. He heard her begin to cough. She had stopped moving. He pulled her by the arm and, coughing himself, kept stepping slowly sideways until at last they were at the supply room door. Mrs. Field dropped to the floor.

In desperation, he threw open the door, bent to pick up Mrs. Field, and attempted to throw her over his shoulder. He was not successful. She was a dead weight. With no hand free to hold his shirt over face, he was choking on the smoke.

We just have to make it to Tom's office. Dragging Mrs. Field with his arms around her, he had to let go for a moment to open Tom's office door. His head reeled as though he were going to faint too.

The air in Tom's office was smoky but not as bad as where they'd come from. Rob's vision cleared somewhat, but he still hacked at the smoke in his lungs as he dragged Mrs. Field towards the door to the hallway.

Stopping, he finally managed to get the widow over his shoulder in a fireman's carry. He flung open the door to the hall and staggered out into the fresh air. Taking deep breaths, he felt the world right itself as he stood bent nearly double under the weight of Mrs. Field's body. He made his way to the elevator. He would have to risk it. He couldn't get his employee down the fire escape by himself, and she needed help as quickly as possible.

Summoning the elevator, he watched as the smoke stole from under his office door, and he prayed that the door would hold until the elevator arrived. The hallway was getting smokier by the minute. He leaned against the wall with his shoulder to ease his burden. Finally, the elevator came, and he stepped on board and pushed the button for the lobby. He felt as though he were going to break in two, and his lungs were heaving and hurting. Would Mrs. Field make it? She must have asthma or some kind of other breathing problem that made the smoke especially dangerous for her.

When they reached the lobby, he saw Herb on his telephone.

Rob stumbled out the door and cried hoarsely, "Herb! There's a fire in my office. Help me with Mrs. Field."

The stocky security man was on his way to where Rob had nearly collapsed at the stairway.

"I heard the explosion clear down here," he said. "When that 'delivery man' came running out of the elevator, it took me a few seconds to process things, but I called the police to give them a description of the van before it could get too far. Then I called 911 for the fire department and an ambulance. All that time, I was praying you'd make it." He helped Rob lower Mrs. Field gently to the floor. "Was it a bomb? Did that creep bring a bomb to your office? How did you get away?"

"It was difficult. Mrs. Field is out from the smoke."

"I'll get started on her. I know CPR," Herb said.

Herb began mouth-to-mouth resuscitation, but Mrs. Field remained limp. Rob stood by helplessly, remembering his own efforts on Robbie. He hoped Herb would be more successful. Finally, the woman began to cough. Herb propped her up. "Breathe," he instructed her. "This is clean air."

The woman kept coughing but managed to breathe a little in between. "You're going to be okay, Mrs. Field," he told her. "An ambulance should be here any minute with some oxygen."

She nodded, unable to speak.

Rob patted Herb on the shoulder. "Good work. Stay with her. I've got to go back up for my laptop. It's got all my business files on it."

"But, Mr. Stevens, you can't go back into that fire!"

"It should be all right. I left it inside the fire door of the fire escape."

Rushing back to the elevator, he pushed the button for the twenty-fourth floor, still heaving from his exertions. For the first time it occurred to him that not only were the sprinklers almost nonfunctional but the elevators should be stuck on the first floor for the firemen. Clearly, this building was not up to code. Once the elevator stopped, he rushed out and ran to the fire escape. Climbing up the stairs one floor, he gratefully retrieved his laptop and made his way downstairs one floor and back to the elevator.

Was the fire out into the hall by now? He didn't know. The elevator, fortunately, had not left the twenty-fourth floor. He was able to get to the garage level with no further problems. There he made his way to his rented Audi, pushed his remote to unlock the trunk, and put his computer inside. Slamming the trunk closed, he unlocked his car and realized he was trembling so much he couldn't get his key in the ignition.

He forced himself to take calm breaths as he listened to the sirens. His lungs still hurt. They were almost here, surely. At last his hands were calm enough to start his car. He roared through the garage and up to the street level, where he parked in a handicapped spot, climbed out, locked his car, and was making for the lobby when he saw Agent Whitlow lying on the pavement behind a parked car.

Approaching, Rob saw a bullet hole in his head. *Another death.* He could hardly register it. Torn between leaving the body where it was and his memories of TV shows screaming at him not to disturb the crime scene, he just stood there.

In a moment, a black-and-white vehicle pulled up beside him.

"This the bomber?" a tall, rangy policeman with black hair asked him.

"No." Rob closed his eyes, took a deep breath, and began coughing. There was still smoke in his lungs. "This is the FBI agent who was watching me. Whitlow. Probably got out of his car to check the package the bomber was bringing up to me and got shot. Bomber must have pulled his body over here. I'm sure he used a silencer. The one that got Whitlow's partner last night used a silencer. That's why Herb didn't hear him."

At that moment, a fire engine and an ambulance roared into the parking lot, pulling up to the building's entrance. Rob and the policeman watched as the firemen, hauling huge extinguishers, ran into the building.

"You got everyone out?" the policeman asked.

"Yeah. Mrs. Field got too much smoke, though. She needs the ambulance." Breaking off his conversation with the policeman, Rob ran back to the ambulance to brief the EMTs on his employee's condition.

"You okay?" the EMTs asked.

"Just shook up and coughing a little, but other than that I'm much better than I have any right to be."

"Why is the FBI watching you?" asked the lieutenant.

"Guarding me until Homeland Security takes over. Whitlow told me that was supposed to happen sometime today." Rob mopped his brow. He was still shaking but tried to concentrate. "Terrorists have apparently targeted me because I own a business in Jakarta. This is the—" Rob counted in his head: the tire, the shot from the beach, the van that tried to run over him and Chloe, the attack that shot Somers, and now the bomb—"fifth attempt. My manager in Indonesia is missing."

"Five attempts! And you're still standing? Terrorists generally get their target. Man, you've got some guardian angel."

An image of Chloe darted through his mind. It steadied him, and he began to think more rationally. "I'm beginning to think so. But we only hear about the terrorists' successes most of the time." *He must think!*

"And this last attempt makes me wonder if there's more than one terrorist after me and that they're not communicating very well. The guy that shot Somers last night took him for me. He would think I was dead. On the other hand, this deal with the bomb would take time to set up. Probably a couple of days to purchase the ingredients in a way that wouldn't arouse suspicion. And how would he know I was going to the office today?"

"Those are good questions," the lieutenant acknowledged.

"Herb, the security guard, already called in a make on the van."

"Good. I'm going to call Homeland Security and have them get a guy here now. I know the threat in San Pedro harbor has spread them thin, but I don't want a sixth incident that leaves you dead."

Walking away from Rob to sit in his patrol car with the door open, the lieutenant began talking on the phone. The conversation became quite heated from what Rob could see as he stood rooted to the spot.

What is going to happen next?

The lieutenant came back to him after shutting his phone. "I'm supposed to tell you that they're getting a team here immediately. The bomb seemed to convince them that this is truly an HS matter. They also have news for you about your plant."

CHAPTER THIRTEEN

It seemed like hours before Rob was sitting in the Paradise Bakery near his gutted office, talking to two hard-bitten men who looked all business. The one called Christensen reminded him of a seasoned Ben Affleck. The grooves between his nose and mouth and between his brows were deep. His eyes were sharp and probing. "I'm afraid the news out of Jakarta is bad."

The other agent, Northridge, had little eyes that darted continually around in suspicion. He also had a small, drawn mouth, pinched in an expression of permanent disapproval. Rob had never liked people with small mouths.

"How bad?" he asked.

"The CIA found your manager this morning in the jungle with his throat slashed. He'd been there several days. A warning note was pinned to his body."

Rob shook his head. "I hired the man myself. What a disaster. What was the message?"

"They want money through the embassy to spare your life. They gave specifics about delivery. As you know, we don't negotiate with or pay ransom to terrorists," Northridge said. "So that means we've got to wipe out this cell. We think it's part of the same thing that's going on down in San Pedro. They're sending assassins up here, perhaps different guys from one day to the next."

Rob explained his theory about the terrorists' haphazard communication, as indicated by last night's "success" and this afternoon's bombing.

"You've got to understand that life is so cheap to them, they'll go after you as many times as it takes. If one assassin dies in the attempt, they send another one. They've probably got a dossier on you, in Afganistan or somewhere, and as long as they were threatening to blow up our harbor, they decided they'd take care of you on the side. The bomb for your office may have been a scenario they planned just to ruin your headquarters. They wouldn't have cared if the security guard got killed instead of you, either."

"What's happening in Jakarta?" Rob asked. "Now that my manager is dead?"

"They don't have any market for the stuff you make. They're not businessmen. You might as well say good-bye to your operation there. They've threatened the workers, telling them they shouldn't be working with 'Jew-loving Anglo scum.' There's an armed guard at the plant now, and it's shut down—the workers were afraid to come in, anyway," Christensen told him. "Our idea is that the terrorists are going to try to find someplace to sell your inventory of circuit boards on the black market and then blow up the facility or use it for some purpose of their own. But, like I said, they're not businessmen."

"So what am I supposed to do?"

Northridge tapped his fingers on the table. "Well, the big picture is that our sources under deep cover are trying to get the bombs removed from as many freighters as they can. The whole thing started with only one ship whose captain was lucky enough to uncover the bomb by accident when he had a diver go down to repair the screws on his engine. They don't know we're following them as fast as we can, checking every boat in the harbor. The oil tanker is the biggest problem. We still haven't found the bomb. We're sending dogs on board now, thinking that they may have rigged this one topside."

"Back to your situation," Christensen said softly. "We think the whole thing is set up to go off on the Fourth of July. But we're only running down one of their agents at a time. They're not talking, of course, but we think we're near the hive." Christensen looked at Rob intently and leaned forward across the table. They were in the banquet room of the restaurant and the doors were locked, but the agent clearly felt the walls had ears. "They work underwater at night, so they must sleep during the day. If we breach that hive today, we'll take as many alive as we can. Then we'll question them and try to find which ones are working on you by offering them some kind of a fake deal."

"Some fireworks," Rob said. "So I'm just a side issue."

"Sorry, sir, but that's what we think is going on. If it weren't for your operative in Jakarta being killed, we wouldn't even have gotten involved in your case. One-on-one isn't their style; they want to take out big targets and lots of people. They're more likely to have bombed your whole development. It was only the bomb today that really clinched it for us. Sorry, but as you can see, we're on a tight deadline here.

"I expect they'll leave one guy behind to detonate any bomb we don't manage to find, but the rest of them will be dug back into their base of operations somewhere in the country. We'd sure like to find it. And we'd sure like to catch them before they get out of Dodge."

"I understand," Rob said, running his hand over the back of his neck. "You must feel pretty silly watching me when the whole harbor is in danger, not to mention what damage a blown-up tanker can do."

The agents did not hesitate. "We do hope we can catch the guy or the team that's after you. Send 'em for some real interrogation. Now, who knew you'd be here today?"

"My son was killed two weeks ago. I've been working Saturdays since then."

They questioned him further about when the attacks began and about the nature of each one.

"I swear, this doesn't sound like terrorist activity. Until today, they've been playing 'too nice.'"

"Remember my plant in Jakarta," Rob reminded them. "That has got to tie in."

"That's another thing that's odd. Jakarta is not exactly friendly to Islamic extremists."

"I think the reason I thought about it was that an Anglo friend of mine received threats about his plant there."

"What happened in his case?"

"He moved his operation to India immediately. It was more portable than mine."

"Did he report the threat?"

"I have no idea."

After taking down the details of Rob's friend's business and the threat he had received, the two men rose. "Where are you going now?"

"I suppose I've got to go home and tell my employees not to come to work until I've got new offices and the danger has passed—let's hope you guys round up the cell or the hive or whatever it is. Besides that, I guess all I can do is continue to dodge bullets."

"It would be better if you let us put you in protection some-where. Then we could rotate watch. You'd be safe, and it would take only one of our men."

Rob shook his head. "Sorry. I'm not staying holed up somewhere until after the Fourth. It seems to me that as long as I'm on the loose, you have a better chance of drawing them out. Just try to do a better job than the FBI did."

"You're willing to act as bait?"

"Look. My family's dead. My business is wiped out. Can you think of anything better for me to be doing? I want these guys caught more than I care about being safe. Particularly if they're part of the harbor plot."

The two agents looked at each other. They gave a synchronized nod and turned back to Rob. Christensen asked, "So you got a look at this delivery man?"

"I'm sure he was in disguise," Rob said. "The sunglasses should have tipped me off that something wasn't right. I already thought the Saturday delivery was strange. But who expects to be bombed?"

"So what did he look like, aside from the sunglasses?"

"Long, straggly, mouse-colored hair. Probably a wig. He had on a plain navy blue baseball cap. Jeans and a maroon sweatshirt with-out a logo. Clean-shaven. Nothing distinctive about his face that I can remember, except he had a dimple in his chin."

The agent called in a description of the bomber. Rob realized his hands were still trembling, but he felt as though he'd been given a stimulant that had heightened his awareness of everything. "Thursday night. I was almost run down in an alley. That was a dark-colored van," he said. "Those two attempts are probably linked."

"Think," Agent Northridge said. "Is there anyone else who could possibly want you dead?"

The crazy idea about Ginger's "crime" was a nonstarter now that his manager had been killed. It was too fantastic to share with the agents. Still, he wanted to track down the origins of her alcoholism. It would give him something to do other than worry about having his brains blown out.

"No. Nothing even remotely fits with the facts we have," Rob told him.

"No one who wants to cash in on your insurance policy?"

"My sister is my only living relative, and she's in rehab. Lockdown. Besides, she's not my beneficiary. My son was, and I haven't updated the policy."

"Anyone who wants you dead for business reasons?" Northridge asked.

"No. No one that I can think of. The company is privately held. My CFO and I are the only shareholders. But he wouldn't want me dead because control of the company would go to my sister, since she's my next of kin."

"He could buy her out."

"He doesn't have the money. What would be the point, anyway? He's not some power-hungry twenty-something. Tom's over seventy. He was a friend of my father's."

"What's his name?"

"Tom Treherne." Rob flipped his cell phone and punched up his CFO's number. "Here's his number. He's likely to die of shock, so tread carefully. His heart's not good, and it's because of his precautions that I was able to escape."

"How's that?" Northridge was copying numbers from the screen of Rob's cell phone.

Rob described how he'd managed to flee the office.

"Tom's older, like I said. He doesn't trust computers, and he doesn't trust secretaries. He likes to do things his own way. I've got the company's financial records on my laptop at my insistence, but Tom kept his own paper backups of everything," Rob said. "They're probably nothing but ashes now."

CHAPTER FOURTEEN

L uke had insisted on accompanying Chloe home and seeing that she was settled in the recliner with unnecessary blankets heaped on her, the TV remote to hand, and even a glass of hot milk with honey next to her pain medicine.

She would have been spared these ministrations had her mother not turned up at the hospital still suffering a hangover. Chloe knew her mother was sufficiently ashamed and didn't want to add to her guilt in front of Luke. Chloe had refrained from scolding her, telling her simply that she was glad to see her, kissing her cheek and telling her Luke was going to drive her home later, after the hospital released her. When they arrived at the beach house, she assumed her mother was lying down in her room because the door was shut.

The morphine had dulled her reactions to Luke, which was undoubtedly a good thing. He had stayed with her all night. She didn't even know if he'd eaten dinner the night before or breakfast or lunch earlier that day, as she had been asleep almost all the time.

Now, to his annoyance, she was clutching the purple monkey

Rob had given her and was trying to figure out how she felt about Luke. It was certainly odd, but when Rob had appeared in the doorway that morning, a curtain had risen on the day. Pain and the remnants of terror had fled. It had been as though her knight in shining armor had arrived.

Looking out at the sea, she watched the waves breaking. *Rob is emotionally unavailable to me. Luke is miraculously free and more than anxious to make amends. Once I loved him with a passion that made colors brighter, emotions deeper, and the slightest touch a caress. Could we ever get that back?*

First, she had to find a way to forgive him and reassemble the pieces of her heart. She hadn't trusted *anyone* in three years. How was she supposed to trust Luke, of all people? And another question had begun troubling her: *If I loved him so much, why did I leave him every year in order to write my books?* Was there a part of her that was "just Chloe," that needed to be alone in order to sort through her own impressions, free of Luke's overpowering presence?

"If you're planning to stay," Chloe told him, "you'll have to stop pacing and do something useful. As I recall, you're a great cook. I'm not hungry, but Mother must be. Can you still do that great stir-fry? I make it occasionally, so I keep all the stuff on hand. I even have frozen shrimp."

"It'd be a relief to have something to do, Chloe love. Stir-fry it is. Do you have cashews, too?"

She nodded and realized she was due for another pain pill. But the pain was easing on its own. She'd just take a half. Partly due to her mother's proclivities, Chloe had a horror of addiction.

At the smell of shrimp frying with coconut, vegetables, and cashews, her appetite woke up. Without thinking, she said, "Too bad you can't move in and be our chef."

"Just say the word," Luke said, his voice as cheerful as it had been in the past.

"I was joking."

"You'll just have to move back to San Diego."

As her thoughts spun around this statement, the phone rang beside her hand. It was Edward. With enormous relief, she answered it.

"Chloe, did you watch the local news?"

"No. Why? What's wrong?"

"Rob's office was bombed this afternoon. It's a miracle he's alive."

Rob! Panic accelerated her heart, and the pounding in her head resumed at this response. Her overall weakness caused tears to spring to her eyes. "No. No, I can't believe it! Is he hurt? Where is he?" *Someone had tried to kill Rob again?*

"It's true. I just talked to him, and he's not hurt at all. Another miracle saved him. Fortunately, he'd left the scene with Homeland Security before the reporters arrived, so they didn't talk to anyone but the cops who were there. No one mentioned terrorists, so they didn't get any publicity out of it."

"That may make the terrorists angry," Chloe said. "Next time they may not be so particular and blow up the whole development!"

"Chloe, this is no time to foretell disaster. As soon as I talk to you, I'm going to talk to Hiro—you know, the Capistrano Shores Homeowner's Association President—about hiring a rent-a-thug for the gate." The wooden arm that supposedly kept people out unless they knew the password was broken. "No one will be able to get in unless they are on the photo ID list Hiro has or a resident goes down to the gate to let someone in."

"Sorry, Edward. Of course you would think of a plan. But why don't they just have Rob in protective custody? He would be safer."

"He wouldn't have it. He thinks his life is of so little value now that he is willing to act as bait."

Chloe closed her eyes and sighed at the thought that Rob would value his life so cheaply. "Edward, would you consider staying with him? I can't bear to think of him so alone and thinking that crazy way! He needs a talking-to."

Luke had taken the stir-fry off the stove and was standing by her side, frowning.

"If I tell him you suggested it, he may go along."

"Why?"

"He's got a soft spot for you, Chloe. Knowing that you care that much may make him care a little more about what happens to him. He's been asking about your boyfriend."

Chloe looked up at Luke. Should she be giving Rob false hope? That would be worse than nothing, wouldn't it?

"Then just give him a message for me, okay?"

"What is it?"

"Tell him I'm putting off my departure for a bit."

"Departure? Oh, New Zealand. Were you serious about that?"

"It seemed the best way. But it's cowardly, and no one is going to say Jonah Greene's daughter is a coward."

"Okay, sweetheart, I'll give him the message. After I call Hiro. And I'll try to get Rob to invite me to stay."

"Thank you." Chloe put her hand to her head, taking a deep breath of relief. *Rob's okay. Rob's okay. Rob's okay.*

"How are *you* feeling?" Edward asked.

"Much, much better," she said. "It's good to be home. Mother had a terrible time, but Luke's making dinner. Oh, I forgot, you don't know about Luke."

"The boyfriend?" Edward guessed.

"Yeah."

"Is he staying with you?"

"I hope not, but he has a mind of his own. I'm not exactly in fighting trim. Isn't that what they say about ships?"

"You strike me as a young lady who's always in fighting trim—remember, you're the captain of the ship in your own home. I'll keep you informed, Chloe, if Rob doesn't. You take care of yourself and try not to worry about all this—just get well."

"I'm fine. I just wish there were something I could do to help Rob."

"There is. Pray. He's had a lot of miracles so far. I don't think it's his time to go, Chloe. Pray that he'll continue to be protected."

"Okay. I will."

As she hung up, a picture flashed into her head of that morning when Rob stood in the doorway of her hospital room, holding King Nebuchadnezzar and looking confusedly between her and Luke.

Was his confusion caused by the fact that he hadn't known she had a boyfriend, or was it something more? Well, she had five years of history with Luke. Five years that had been marred only by her disconsolate periods over Daddy's death. And she really knew nothing about what Rob was like. She was falling into the maiden-in-distress syndrome by making a hero of the man who had saved her from death by van.

She slumped further into the recliner, suddenly depressed.

"What was all that about?" Luke asked.

"Someone tried to kill Rob this afternoon. A bomb. At his office." Chloe covered her face with her hands. "Can I have my stir-fry, please?"

"In a minute. Who's Rob's enemy? Any idea?"

"A terrorist. Rob has a plant in Indonesia," she replied. "Please don't tell Mother."

"I wasn't going to, but I think you'd better steer clear of that guy and come down to San Diego with me. You're not safe around him."

She couldn't help it. It just popped out: "Probably safer than I am with you."

When Luke narrowed his eyes, she knew he was getting ready for a jealous blowup.

"Look, Luke, I'm not romantically involved with Rob. But I can't possibly stay away from him. He needs people who care about him now. He has no one."

"And New Zealand? Do you mind telling me what that was about?"

Chloe decided that she needed to tell him straight out. "I was going to run away to my next project so that I wouldn't be tempted to fall in love with you again. You hurt me more than you will ever know, Luke."

Leaning down, he stroked her cheek. "Chipper, if I had things to do over, I would never ever have left you. You're solid gold, through and through. I have lived in horrible anguish and regret these past two years. That was where the drink came in. And it was because of you and the hope that someday there might be another chance that I took that sail to Fiji to dry out—for good."

Looking into his troubled face, Chloe's heart ached. "I want to believe you wouldn't hurt me like that—that such a thing couldn't happen again, Luke. But I don't know if I can. However, I promise you, I'll think about it and pray about it."

"Pray?"

At that point, her mother emerged tentatively from her room.

"What's that I smell? I'm starved! How are you feeling, Chloe?"

"Much better, thanks. Luke just made dinner. Come and join us."

"I'm so sorry, honey bun," her mother said. Chloe was glad there

147

was no plaintive whine in her voice. She probably had Luke's presence to thank for that. "I really let you down when you needed me. It won't happen again. Luke, thanks for coming through."

Chloe could hardly believe her ears. Her mother was *thanking* Luke?

"I'm trying to talk Chloe into going down to San Diego to finish recuperating," he said in elaborately casual tones.

Her mother said firmly, "That's up to Chloe, but I'm certain she's really not ready to make any life-altering decisions at the moment, are you, darlin'?"

"Hardly!" Chloe said, thankful for the respite. She knew that in her emotionally and physically weakened condition, she could easily slide back into life with Luke. Her mother's sudden show of spunk made her realize that Luke had absolutely no right to ask such a thing at this point. "We have lots and lots of unfinished business, *Monsieur Luc*, before anything like that is likely to happen."

He compressed his lips, threw her a determined look, and then said with counterfeit sweetness, "Will *Mademoiselle* dine at the table?"

"But of course."

Their use of French brought Proust to mind, fortunately, and grabbing at the topic, she told him about her reading. Luke was of the opinion that Proust was dull and overrated, and a lively but friendly discussion ensued.

As soon as he and her mother had cleaned the kitchen, Chloe pleaded exhaustion. "Thank you so much for everything, Luke. I think I'd prefer if you left now and we saved the heavy emotional stuff for another time. Good night."

He looked as though he might object, but then his face relaxed into the loving one she was familiar with. "Take it easy, Chipper," he said, kissing her cheek. "I'll be in touch."

When he was gone and her mother was settled in the recliner, remote in hand, Chloe kissed her and said, "Thanks for rescuing me from myself. Good night, Mother. Feel better."

"I really meant what I said," Martha told her. "It was unforgivable of me to take to alcohol when you needed me. Sometimes we need to hit bottom before we realize which way is up."

"Then maybe, all in all, it was a good thing," Chloe said.

As soon as she reached her room, she went straight to her bed and, for the first time in her life, knelt beside it in prayer.

"God, why is this happening to Rob? How could you allow this to happen to him now when he's so grief-stricken about Robbie? Please help me understand! Oh, and thank you, thank you, for whatever miracle it was that saved him. Please help me to know if there's anything I can do. I want this to stop! I don't want Rob to die! Please, if you care for me at all—if you care for him—please spare his life!"

For a while she simply stayed on her knees, receiving the complicated impression that somehow this all had meaning. Finally she said amen and crawled into bed.

Ginger was nearly hysterical by the time Rob remembered to call her—after Edward had informed him that the explosion had made the news.

"Rob! I couldn't bear it if anything happened to you. You're all I have left!"

Trust Ginger to put a personal spin on things. "Well, I don't much want anything to happen to me, either."

"Some horrible men were here, asking questions. They acted like I'd hired a killer or something!"

"I'm sorry if the police upset you. I told them you had nothing to do with it."

"But who would want you dead? I just can't believe this!"

"I know. It's hard to wrap your mind around it. The only thing we can think of is terrorists. Because of the plant. My manager has been murdered, and they, whoever they are, have threatened me and demanded ransom. Meanwhile, they're trying their best to kill me."

After he hung up from talking to his sister, Rob made another call to the Renaissance House main number.

"Can you get a message to Dr. Updike?"

"Yes. If it's important."

"She called me. In the middle of our conversation there was an explosion. I just wanted her to know that her phone call saved my life."

"Oh, my goodness. Are you all right? Is this Mr. Stevens?"

"Yes. I suppose everyone in the place knows all about it."

"Of course. The police were here."

"Well, I'm all right. If you could just let Dr. Updike know?"

"I will, for sure."

Sonia Updike called while Rob and Edward were eating Stouffer's fettucine and unwinding to a New Age composition by David Lanz that Edward had brought for a calm ambience.

"I just talked to Margaret at the center," she said. "What happened?"

Rob gave her a condensed version of the afternoon's events. "So, anyway, I appreciate your calling me back this afternoon."

"You know, I just had this feeling that I should. I'm glad I followed through. It sounds as if it really did save your life."

"It did. I can't thank you enough."

"It makes me a little shaky, actually. Phew. By the way, what was the information you had that was so important?"

Rob switched gears mentally. "It might not be important at all, but it may give you somewhere to start. I've tried contacting some of Ginger's friends from college. I found out that she had a boyfriend, Rick Niebolt. I've tried to get in touch with him by e-mail, but he hasn't replied yet."

"It could be an old e-mail account or something. Did anyone give details?"

"Well, I found out that Ginger was actually on the point of suicide when Rick saved her from jumping off a cliff. According to the woman who told me, Rick really loved Ginger, so he's not the cause of her drinking. I wondered if it might have been a relationship gone bad, but if it was, it wasn't with him."

"Hmm. I appreciate your help. I'll have to approach this carefully. Have you tried finding him on the Internet?"

"No. Not yet. I've been a little preoccupied, as you can imagine. That will give me something to do instead of waiting for the next attack. I'll let you know if I find out anything."

"Did you get in touch with any other friends?"

"One basically told me to mind my own business. Rick Niebolt and a woman called Brooke Sampson didn't reply. I got the information on Rick by chance from an acquaintance of mine who didn't know either of them very well."

"It's interesting that those two never answered your e-mail."

"They probably just didn't want to be bothered. I remembered something else, too—Ginger introduced my late wife to me. They were actually roommates. Pamela kept a journal. I'll dig it out and see if I can find anything. "

"That's probably a good idea. I hope it won't wreak more havoc on you emotionally. How long has Pamela been gone?"

"Eighteen months. There are other things I need answers to. You know, for closure and all of that."

The therapist's voice turned unprofessionally soft and warm, "I hope you find your answers then, Rob. Good luck."

"Uhh—thanks." *Good grief! Is the woman coming on to me?* He hung up abruptly and then stared at his phone as though it were a snake.

Moments later, Edward had finished the dishes, such as they were.

"Thanks for your help, neighbor. I'm sure you know how depressing eating alone can be."

"Anytime, Rob. I'm glad you're letting me stay with you. It was Chloe's idea, you know. She didn't want you to be alone."

Rob was warmed by her concern. Then he remembered the blond Adonis that was probably staying with her and sighed. He had no rights where Chloe was concerned, and he had enough on his plate right now without a romance. But when he thought of Luke's hands caressing Chloe's reddish-gold hair with such tenderness he felt slightly ill. Mentally chastising himself, he knew he had less than nothing to offer her. A home he was trying to sell. A business that no longer existed. A heart bruised and battered by grief. He didn't even know if he'd be alive tomorrow, despite Edward's efforts at the gate and Agent Christensen concealed outside his home. Trying to put Chloe out of his head, he said, "I need to do a little research on the Internet and go through Pamela's old journals. I'm trying to find out some things for Ginger's therapist. I'm a rude host. Can you keep yourself occupied?"

Edward tapped a book that looked like a biography. "Just picked this up today and I'm eager to read it. I'll close the blinds and settle here on the couch, if that's okay."

"You'll be sleeping in Robbie's room. The one with the sports pictures all over the walls."

"Are you certain you want me in there, Rob? This couch is very comfortable."

"There's no one I'd rather have in there than you. I'm sorry I've been so rotten to you all these years when you were trying to 'rescue' me."

"I'm just glad I'm here now."

"I did that experiment, you know. Planting the seed. Last night. It yielded surprising results. Robbie is okay. The Lord sent me a wonderful reassurance. That bomb blew it right out of my mind, but I meant to tell you: I'm going to change my ways."

Edward walked over to where he stood and gave him a hearty embrace. "Welcome home, brother."

Chapter Fifteen

Martha came in after Chloe's prayer, bringing a glass of water, fluffing the pillows, and offering to brush her hair. Sensing that her mother needed to do those things for her, Chloe made room beside herself on the queen-sized bed and let her mother go to work on her wiry mane. Closing her eyes, she tried to pretend she was young again—a princess with the world at her feet. Why had she been born in the days of terrorists?

Would she have preferred the Second World War? The Depression? The First World War? She reluctantly realized that every generation had its challenges. At least she had been born into a wonderful family.

"Mother, what do you honestly think I should do about Luke?"

Her mother said nothing for a while. Finally she spoke. "Until he told you about this other woman, did you ever have any reason to doubt him? Why didn't the two of you get married?"

"He wanted to marry me, but he had a condition: I had to stop running away to other places to write books. He wanted a normal life with a family. I just wasn't ready. A lot of that had to do with Daddy. I saw your grief and thought I could never, ever, go through something like that. It was bad enough as a child to lose a parent. But I didn't want any part of losing a husband."

"But, Chloe! I wouldn't give up those years with your father for anything. Even if I had known the precise hour of his death, I wouldn't have given up those years. He had scooped me up and carried me off like a real-life Rhett Butler. I *had* to marry him, or I would have regretted it all my life."

Chloe considered that. "Well, then, I guess I didn't love Luke enough. I always needed my freedom to roam as a fall-back position. I couldn't surrender completely."

"Oh, darlin', that's such a shame. Do you think you'll ever be able to?"

"That's what I'm wondering." A fragment of memory teased her. "What did you mean when you said people could get married forever in the Mormon temple?"

"That's what they tell you. But maybe they just say that to get you baptized. I mean, I suppose anyone could *tell* you they were marrying you forever. But that doesn't make it true."

Chloe thought of Edward and wondered if that was the source of his hope. His peace. She probably *could* marry someone under those conditions. But it would have to be someone she trusted. She wouldn't want to be married forever to an adulterer.

"It would be very hard to be married to Luke," she said.

"Why is that, honey bunch?"

"He is too good-looking. I am really attracted to him, and I suppose that's good, but so is every other woman in the world who looks at him. He would be constantly tempted to stray. I don't know if I could live with that. I want to be enough for my husband, so he won't think the grass is greener elsewhere every time we disagree."

A thought hit her with great force. "That is probably the reason I wouldn't let go of my traveling. I think I was really testing Luke. To see if he would stray. And he did. And now I wonder how many times he did."

"He knew himself, at least," her mother said unexpectedly. "That's probably why he wanted you to stay home with him and start a family."

"But what about when I'm fat and pregnant and unappealing? Will he be tempted to go elsewhere?"

"Your father thought I was cute when I was expecting. He used to talk to you in my tummy. And he rubbed you down with lotion every night so you wouldn't give me stretch marks. Glory! I was terrified he wouldn't love me if I got stretch marks. And then I found out I couldn't have another baby, and I was sure it was because I was such a drama queen when I was pregnant!"

"I know Daddy never would have left you. He totally adored you, Mother."

Looking at her mother's face, Chloe thought that tonight she looked as warm and beautiful as she ever had. But her mother had something more than beauty. She had grace and a loveliness that went clear through her—when she wasn't drinking. Martha was the classic Steel Magnolia. As tough as Daddy had been, Martha was really the tougher of the two. She had seen through people who might have deceived Daddy. Letting him dream about the big picture, she had always taken care of the details. They were the ultimate yin and yang. Perhaps that was why she had been so sure that she and Luke together were the same. And yet, had she really? Had her mistrust of him come only because he was too good-looking?

Oh, I'm so tired of thinking about this! As her mother continued to brush her hair, there crept into Chloe's mind the ultimate test for Luke.

Rob Googled Rick Niebolt on his laptop, set up in Ginger's old room. He realized that he missed her. When she wasn't drunk, she was the best of companions—funny, smart, interesting. What had robbed her of those characteristics that made her so lovable? What had turned her into a sloppy, peevish drunk? And why hadn't he cared sooner? She was his sister! All the family he had. And he was all she had. Here he had gone on, living his prosperous, happy life, not giving a thought to why Ginger was in a town where her next-door neighbor was probably a moose, where it was dark half the year, subsisting on Scotch. What did that say about him? Nothing good, that was for sure. He hadn't even called her until he needed a nanny for Robbie. And if he had known what an addict she was, he wouldn't have called her at all, would he?

Determined to reform, Rob pledged that in the midst of all the madness around him, he would try to unravel the mystery of what had driven Ginger to give up on life. Rick Niebolt had several Google entries. He was Rotary Club president in Irvine, and there were excerpts from the Irvine community newspaper, telling of community awards he had won, giving brief biographies. From them Rob determined that Rick was a tenured professor of anthropology at University of California–Irvine, married to Dr. Ruth Phillips, a professor of sociology, and was the father of three daughters, all of whom were active in soccer, and though they were only junior high age, had traveled abroad playing together as a piano trio.

He seemed to be a solid citizen. Rob would try to connect with him through the university. If anyone knew why Ginger had tried to take her life, it would certainly be her boyfriend at the time.

Even after his prayer, however, Rob found he couldn't sleep.

He'd left something undone. Then Rob remembered the journals he'd taken out of his storage unit in Costa Mesa that morning before he went into the office. He was going to find out if Pamela knew anything about Ginger's transformation. And possibly why Pamela and Ginger had acted like strangers every Christmas. He was certain Pamela must have known something.

The journals started when Pamela was fourteen. Skipping forward to her senior year at Stanford, when she had roomed with Ginger, he began to read. After only a few pages, his hands went rigid while holding the journal written in Pamela's neat and precise hand. *What in the world?*

Scrambling back through her old journals, he found the one from her junior year and then went back to her sophomore year. There he stopped and rubbed his jaw and the back of his neck. He had been clenching his teeth. *Why had Ginger never told him about this?* Because she had her own problems and couldn't see past them? Obviously, if she had almost committed suicide. He wondered now whether that was before or after his own first date with Pamela.

Afraid of what he would find, he skipped forward to Pamela's graduation. He had been right to worry. The more he read, the more shocked and disoriented he became. But he was like a man hooked on a melodrama. He read the journals, unable to connect them at all with the Pamela he knew, until it started to get light outside. To himself, he kept murmuring, "Oh, Pammie, Pammie. Why didn't you tell me? I would have listened to you. Things would have been better. You would have been happier."

As he climbed into bed wearily, he pulled his pillow over his head to block out the light and the sounds of the gulls feeding outside his windows. He had not known his wife at all. He now understood their lack of intimacy, the feeling that she was like quicksilver, sliding out of his emotional grasp every time he tried to get closer to her. The eleven years of their marriage had been nothing short of a complete sham. *Is Robbie even my son?*

Of course he is. He was the spitting image of me when I was his age.

But Rob's discoveries had rocked the foundations of his life. Everything he remembered had to be recast and revised to include what he now knew was the truth. As he lay there, scenes from his family life passed before him like an old-fashioned slide show, and he mentally edited Pamela out of the pictures. It was not as painful as he might have supposed. She had, he realized, always kept herself on the sidelines, except with Robbie, whom she had loved with all her heart and soul. Her passivity and lukewarm nature had not made their own attachment a passionate one. It had actually been quite convenient, he realized now, while he struggled to get his business going and afterwards, when he had spent so much time in Indonesia. Once or twice, he had wondered if there shouldn't be more, but he had always been grateful that he had been spared moods and chastisements for his absences.

Remembering back to his vision of life in the hereafter, the one that the Lord had shown him a few nights before, he realized again that Pamela hadn't been there. Why hadn't he questioned that?

It was going to take a while to adjust his thinking, but looking back, he realized that Pamela had actually orchestrated their marriage. He, a busy entrepreneur who nevertheless knew he wanted a family to replace the one he had lost when his parents died, had simply gone along for the ride.

Even his memory of their getting engaged was hazy. He tried to summon it up.

Rob, do you love me enough to marry me?

Shocked at the question, he realized that Pamela was not as much of a women's libber as he had thought. She had initiated all the physical intimacies between them, but he had never thought they had meant that much to her. For him, they had been only casual, but now, thinking they must have meant more to her, he felt guilty.

Of course, Pamela.

Finally, his confusion exhausted him, and he fell asleep.

CHAPTER SIXTEEN

On the following day in the early afternoon, Chloe made her way, behind a huge pair of sunglasses, over to Edward's house. He had called to see how she was feeling, and, needing to escape her dark bedroom and the conundrum about Luke, she asked if she might visit him for a while. Edward had said Rob was going to be spending the afternoon with him as a break from his own company. It seemed Rob was feeling pent up as well.

She had left a distinctly peevish mother preparing homemade spaghetti sauce. But Chloe's head was much improved, she had some questions for Edward, and, she had to admit, she felt an overpowering need to see for herself that Rob was all right.

"Chloe! I'm so glad you're well enough to come over. Rob isn't here yet. Come in."

Entering, she made her way to the deep leather chair she favored. "Any more news about the bomb?"

"I haven't talked to Rob today. He was going to be tied up this morning with e-mail and the phone company."

Edward looked tired. Chloe doubted he had slept well. "You're really worried about this, too, aren't you?"

"I spent a long time on my knees last night, Chloe."

"I said a prayer, too. I pleaded for his life. I hope it helps."

"So do I."

Just then, they heard the knocker on the door. Edward went to answer it. There stood an exhausted Rob. Chloe noticed immediately that there was something different about him. He averted his eyes from hers and shook hands with Edward. Seating himself, he looked down at his hands, throwing out an apology. "Sorry I'm so out of it. I only slept an hour, late this morning."

"Any news?" Chloe asked. "I've been so worried about you."

He looked up, and she was surprised to see a different Rob Stevens. His face was defined by lines of stark cynicism.

"How's Luke?" he asked.

"What does he have to do with anything?"

"He looks like the kind of guy who gets pretty much everything he wants out of life."

"Whoa!" Chloe said. *Is Rob jealous or just angry at the world?* She decided to take the most tolerant view. "I wouldn't say that. He just emerged from a hellish marriage."

"Then he has my full sympathy," Rob said, flummoxing Chloe completely. Was he referring to his own marriage? He'd always appeared to genuinely mourn Pamela, to the point where Chloe realized she'd wondered if he could ever love anyone else.

"I didn't come here to talk about Luke," she said. "I want to know about you. You must be really strung out if you got only an hour's sleep. What can Edward and I do to help?"

Rob's hands were balled up in fists, and he clamped his jaw.

Anger. And anger implied vulnerability. He had nearly died how many times? Her hurt dropped away, and all she wanted to do was hold him in her arms. To feel him warm and alive, heart beating through his shirt.

Even Edward's presence couldn't dissuade her. Walking over to where he sat, she said, "Rob, stand up for a moment."

Looking up sharply, he asked, "Why?"

"You just need to."

He stood, putting his fingers in his belt loops, looking at her with clear defiance. But compassion impelled her, and she put her arms around him all at once and held his rigid body to hers. There. She could feel his heart. And it was beating fast enough to belie his reluctance. *What is wrong with him?*

"I'm so glad to see for myself that you're okay. You have no idea how hard I've been praying."

At these words, she felt whatever emotion was raging in him dissolve. He raised his arms and returned her embrace. "You forgot your monkey."

"Nope," she said, pulling off her sun hat. "Nebbie is right here, waiting to surprise you." She pulled the monkey from her hat and wound its arms around Rob's neck, fastening the Velcro strips on its hands.

"Nebbie?" he gave a one-sided smile, and she was glad to get that much.

"Make no mistake. He's a personage to be reckoned with. He will set you absolutely straight on any issue in or out of his expertise. Now, for the last time, any news?"

Rob stroked the monkey's silky purple fur, relaxing more with each moment. "They found the van."

"I assume you're talking about the van the bomber was driving," she said. "Where was it? Any fingerprints?"

163

"In a parking lot at Fashion Island. Apparently abandoned. Now they're looking for the person who sold it to him. It was a new purchase. There weren't any fingerprints or anything." Tickling the end of her nose with Nebbie's tail, he peered into her eyes, "It really is good to see you, Chloe. I'm sorry I was such a bear. How are you feeling?"

"Improving hourly," she answered.

She was glad for the physical contact, however minimal. "My head is getting better. But I'm worried about you, to say the least. When is Homeland Security going to step up to the plate?"

"They're with me now." He explained about the situation in San Pedro. "I told them to use me as bait. Maybe they can isolate the terrorist who's after me and follow him home to the hive."

"But, Rob, that's so dangerous!"

"It is, a bit. Normally they would drive me where I want to go and stay with me in my house, but they're having to be a bit more 'hands off' since they want to attract the guy. We've got beefed-up security at the gate of the development, however, and a 24/7 watch on Edward's and my houses, so there won't be any bombs detonated here, at any rate."

Edward spoke up. "All the articles I've been reading lately have remarked on the incompetence of the present-day frontline terrorist. Terrorist groups are having trouble with recruitment, apparently."

"Well, I'm not going to bet my life on an incompetent terrorist," Rob replied. "There was nothing wrong with that bomb I was given. It even blew out the window of my office."

"Why don't we all sit down?" Edward suggested. "How are things going with putting the pieces of your business back together?"

"I haven't figured it out yet. It depends completely on what happens in Indonesia. All my assets are there. That's where everything is assembled. The employees here do the developing, and I'll try to hang onto them, but sales and marketing won't have a product to peddle until we're up and running again. Everyone is really shaken up, and I can't offer them much reassurance." Rob stood and began to pace the small living room, his back to the ocean. "My employees here don't have an office anymore. I'm reluctant to tell them to look for other jobs until I find out if we can salvage anything, but at the moment the warehouse in Indonesia is being guarded by a Muslim insurgent with an AK-47. No one is allowed in or out. The terrorists could decide to bomb it to smithereens if they want to. I don't know if there's anyone in that cell or its leadership who knows what to do with circuit boards for smart phones."

"Pardon the personal question," Edward said, "but how much of your net worth is tied up in this operation? Are you going to be all right financially if the business fails?"

"The beach house is worth a million dollars, at least. So I'll have capital to start a small operation somewhere more stable, if I can live in a tent for a while."

"For heaven's sake, Rob. You know I'd love to have you here. You just say the word."

"I don't think you're prepared to house a start-up out of your back bedroom," Rob said, grinning, "but I appreciate it. I'll have to find a hole-in-the-wall somewhere for my developers. Cash flow is going to be a problem. Fortunately our receivables are healthy at this point because we just got ahead of the game with a new product. Enough of them have been sent out to our accounts this past month to pay a couple month's worth of salaries to my guys."

"Well, if Anthony buys your place, I'll insist that you bunk here with me, at least."

"Thanks."

"I'm just so glad you're still alive," Chloe interposed. "I think you should stay in your house with the security alarm set and not go anywhere."

"Not a bad idea, actually. Except that I need to see about finding said hole-in-the-wall for my developers ASAP."

She had an idea. "Why don't you let me take care of that? I can find something. I've lived here on and off my whole life. Do you want something closer, like Dana Point or maybe even Capistrano? Neither of them would be as expensive as Newport."

"You would really do that for me?"

"Of course. Even though you have your own protection, it sounds like he's going to keep his distance so the terrorist won't spot him."

Rob stared at her, his brown eyes studying hers intently. "But it's my business to draw him out."

"Rob," she said gently, "you've had an average of at least one attack per day for the past few days. I've lost count. You need to rest and see what you can do long distance to salvage your business. You must have options. Don't Indonesians welcome American business? Start with the embassy. Just take some time to slow down and *think!*"

"But Homeland Security says this San Pedro thing is most likely scheduled for the Fourth of July!"

"That's next Thursday. Don't worry, that gives them plenty of time to find you. All I'm asking is that you stay put tomorrow."

"Okay. I think the developers would like to be near a beach or a park so they can jog or play Frisbee during lunch."

"Dana Point sounds about right. How many guys do you have?"

"About ten. It would be nice if there were possibilities for expansion, if you're right and I can get my business up and running again. Then we wouldn't have to move again."

"Okay. I'll look for a hole-in-the-wall for ten people, near a beach or park, with possibilities for expansion of said hole."

"You talk like a real estate agent now. Where's my writer?"

"She has vanished, as though behind a discreet veil." Chloe took Nebbie back and slung him around so he was hanging down her back. "I am, at the moment, believe it or not, my mother's daughter. She's the expert businesswoman, if you need someone to help you pull things together. She ran my father's retail import business. He'd have been lost without her."

"Okay, then. But I'll have to go and inspect . . ."

"I won't sign anything. I won't even make a deposit. Rentals are so low right now with the economy the way it is that, except for beachfront property, it's a buyer's market."

Chloe felt a glow of satisfaction inside.

At that moment, Rob's cell phone rang. He answered. It was obviously another employee with questions. Rob excused himself and moved into the kitchen.

"I'm sorry. I kind of took over there," she said to Edward.

"I should have thought of it myself."

"I just wish these terrorists would all blow themselves up."

"Don't say that," Edward said earnestly. "They'd probably take all of downtown LA along with them."

When Rob returned to the living room, he firmly turned his cell phone to vibrate. After he had seated himself, Chloe said, "Now that that's decided, let's get on to some more uplifting topics. Is that okay, Rob? I think you need something else to think about that's positive."

"Go for it, boss," he said.

Chloe hoped she could sound sufficiently casual. "When my mom and I were driving by the San Diego temple the other day, she said, 'People get married for eternity in there.' What did she mean?"

Rob perked up. "My parents were married in the temple."

A genial smile crept over Edward's face. "It's the crowning ordinance of the gospel and the source of all my hope. Faithful members of the Church can be sealed for eternity. Not just 'until death do us part.' And all your children will be sealed to you for eternity as well. It is a beautiful ceremony."

Chloe's face lit up, and she clasped her hands in front of her chest. Taking an intentionally deep, cleansing breath, she said, "That is the most wonderful thing I've ever heard. What security it must give you, Edward! I'm sure it's the secret behind your serenity."

Rob's cell phone vibrated, and Chloe could see his attention was torn, but the caller ID convinced him to answer. "I've got to get this call, and I should go, anyway. I'll be in touch, but it was wonderful to see you for a minute, Chloe. Thanks for helping out. Edward, I'll see you later."

He walked to the door and let himself out, talking earnestly into his cell phone. Chloe watched out the window as a man in Bermuda shorts with very white legs and brown socks followed him at a distance. It was so absurd, she almost wanted to laugh. "Don't they teach them how to dress for undercover assignments in Homeland Security? That man needs a visit to a tanning salon and some flip-flops."

Edward joined her at the window. "I agree. But then I never did look particularly good in shorts, either."

With regret Chloe watched Rob round the corner. She and Edward resumed their seats.

He wore what she thought of as his "earnest" face, which he wore to discuss anything about God. "Chloe, the promise of eternal marriage is a great one, but there are a lot of things you need to know about the gospel first. There are young men who are uniquely prepared to teach you the gospel in a way that will answer all your questions. They're missionaries, like I was. Do you think you're ready to talk to them?"

"Why can't you teach me?"

"Because I'm first and foremost your friend. You are your mother's daughter in a lot of ways, and I want you to feel free to go at this with the gloves off. The missionaries receive special blessings that come with their callings that will enable them to help you find the answers to all the hard questions that might come up."

"Why are you backing out? Do you think I won't believe what you tell me?"

"Let's just say it's going to require faith. I'm a man like any other. I can fail you. But the Lord won't. The sooner we get you depending on Him instead of me, the better."

Chloe squirmed. "That makes me more than a little uncomfortable."

"Well, I haven't done a very good job then." Edward looked regretful. "I should have left this up to the missionaries."

"I'll have to think about this, Edward."

"Good. And don't forget to continue your prayers. They're your own personal line of communication, and they don't depend on me or anyone else."

Chapter Seventeen

Chloe was almost home when her cell phone rang. It was
Luke. "Hello?"

"Chloe, I thought I'd let you know I'm on my way up.
Traffic's bad, but I'm about a half hour away."

"How did you get this number?"

"From your mother. I think I woke her up, or she'd never have
been so cooperative."

"You're probably right."

"It's great to hear your voice again."

"Thanks." She knew she was sounding short and unresponsive,
but she was suddenly feeling drained after her show of strength for
Rob's sake. "You realize Mother will be there to protect my honor?"
Chloe's palms began to sweat. Luke must emit strong pheromones
even over the phone. In spite of everything against it, she suddenly
longed for the familiar comfort of his arms and a world where there
were no terrorists. She slammed on her mental brakes. It had felt

wonderful in Rob's arms, too. Wonderfuller. She was obviously needy right now.

How in the world could she see Luke when she was in the middle of this? Her emotions were on overload as it was. Well, maybe it was best to get it over with. Otherwise she'd just be left wondering. *Do I still love him, or is it just a physical thing because I'm so love-deprived?*

Chloe pleaded a headache to her scolding mother and went to her room to lie down. She fell asleep immediately.

She was in a small, dark place. It was stuffy, and she had something over her head. Her hands were tied, but someone hadn't done a very good job. Yanking at the string that bound her, she kept screaming, "Rob! Rob! Stay away! Don't come here. Don't ever come here! They're going to kill you!" And she knew deep down that they were going to kill her, too. As soon as Rob got there.

Someone was shaking her more and more vigorously. "Chloe, it's Luke. You're all right. Wake up. You don't have to scream. I'm sure Rob's all right. Just wake up, and you can call him."

Little by little, she rose out of the terror and focused on Luke's concerned face. She concentrated on the cleft in his chin. *Was that dream left over from the morphine? Or was it a warning? Why would I be locked in a closet screaming for Rob to stay away?*

The knowledge, or the interpretation, or whatever it was, came to her with certainty. She was going to be used as bait for a trap to catch Rob.

Scrabbling for the phone at her bedside, she pushed in Rob's number.

"Chloe?"

"Are you all right?" she asked, knowing she sounded as though she'd just downed a fifth of her mother's Scotch.

"Are *you* all right? You sound awful."

"I just woke up. From an awful dream. I don't know how you

feel about dreams, but sometimes they can be warnings. I've had that happen before." She had. Twice. The last time was the dream that had warned her that all was not well with Luke. She had had it on the airplane and afterwards was grateful for at least a little preparation.

"Okaayyy. I'll take your word for it."

"If I call you and tell you to come to get me for any reason, *do not do it*. It will be a trap."

"Do you think we should have a code word?" His voice was playful.

"You think I'm bonkers."

"I think you've had a very bad dream."

"Well, just in case, even if you don't believe me now, the code word is . . ." She wracked her abused brain. "Naomi. Naomi—there was an awful girl by that name in my algebra class. If I say something like, 'Don't bring Naomi,' you'll know it's a trap."

"My dear Chloe, you have lost your mind. Do you think I would leave you in a trap?"

"This isn't a movie, Rob. You know better than I do how serious it is."

Luke was hovering over her, his brow creased forbiddingly.

"I should go. Remember what I said."

Hanging up, she fell back on the bed and put the back of her hand over her eyes. Her head hurt.

As though he had read her mind, Luke asked, "Do you need to take a pain pill, Chipper? Well, Not-So-Chipper at present."

"No. That would just put me to sleep again, and you drove all this way. Maybe some extra-strength Tylenol. I'll get it." Luke had been making for the bathroom, and that suddenly seemed too personal. "Wait for me in the living room, okay? I promise I'm not demented. I just had this awful dream."

"I heard. Is there any real likelihood of you getting kidnapped?"

"Not if I have anything to say about it. Good grief, Rob must have thought I was Looney Tunes."

When Luke left her, she grabbed a turquoise East Indian caftan and slipped into the shower to wash away the damp terror of her dream. The fog always made everything so muggy. She would be glad when the Fourth of July came and they had their usual miracle of a suddenly blue sky. Then she remembered San Pedro Harbor and knew it wasn't safe even to pretend everything was all right. It wasn't.

To fortify herself against Luke, who had been looking too incredibly handsome, she whistled the oldies' song her father always used to sing about Luke: "You're So Vain." The funny thing was, it wasn't true. Luke managed to act as though he were just accidentally handsome. He never made an entrance, so the song didn't work. Instead, she remembered the day they had ended their five-year relationship. She had just returned from ten months in Avignon, where she had been researching a historical novel about one of her ancestors. Those notes still lay buried under her heavy sweaters in the bottom of a sea chest from somewhere in the Far East. Luke had been with her part of the time.

When she got home to her mother's house, he left her bags in the car and said they had to have a stroll on the beach to revive her after her long flight. That's when he broke the news. Despite their long separation, he wasn't even holding her hand, and his welcome kiss at LAX had been a mere peck.

Luke looked down at his feet as he told her. She'd been gone so long. He'd gotten so lonely. There had been this woman at work. One thing had led to another. Now they were getting married. He'd looked at her then, his deep blue eyes pleading for forgiveness.

A fog of disbelief had shrouded her. He was joking with her. He had to be. Joking with a painfully straight face. In all his e-mails, he'd never mentioned anything of the sort. She'd never suspected.

She remembered now that when he wouldn't respond to her teasing, she still hadn't been able to take it in. She had just put her hands up to her mouth to stop her lips from trembling and turned blindly away, running as fast as she could back to the beach house. She'd not seen him again until the other afternoon in San Diego.

Was this a mistake? How could she keep seeing him after that catastrophe? She looked at herself in the mirror. She looked frightened. What had her mother said? That she was addicted to running away. Maybe if she finally faced up to Luke and saw that he was just an ordinary man, it would cure her. She clenched her fists at her sides.

She came out of her bedroom and went into the living area, where her mother and Luke seemed to be enduring a strained silence. Martha was busy heating up the leftover spaghetti sauce and making fresh pasta.

"Don't you look nice!" she exclaimed.

"Do you think so?"

"I'm going to kill him," her mother said in a whisper so vicious it could have killed a horse. "You're feeling insecure. You. Chloe the Fearless."

She gave her mother a hug. "I'm glad you're here."

Now that she really saw him in the full light of the day, Luke looked great in his white knee-length shorts and the sapphire blue polo shirt that made his eyes compelling. She could scarcely look away.

"Hi, Chipper." His eyes lingered on hers a moment before he

grinned his wide, Viking grin and looked towards her mother. *Funny. That grin had never before struck her as predatory.* "Martha, have you put away all the knives?"

"This is not a joke, Luke. You're here on sufferance. If I had my way, you wouldn't be here at all."

"Let's sit," Chloe said, heartened by her mother's solid partisanship. "I know I look as strong as an ox, but I'm actually a bit droopy still."

Luke gave Martha his trademark sheepish grin that said, "At least I know where I stand."

Martha plopped down in the middle of the chintz couch, forcing Luke to take one of the mauve chairs. Chloe took the other.

"You're looking beautiful, Chloe," he said. "That caftan makes your eyes look turquoise. Like the bay at Corfu."

She felt herself blush and hated it.

"Well, what happened, young man? Chloe's strong enough to discuss it now. How do you come to be divorced?" Martha asked.

Chloe felt that she should protest her mother's manners but stopped herself. She wanted to hear the answer.

"Same old story. She left me for someone else."

Who would leave Luke?

"Why?" she heard herself ask.

"Never let it be said that the Greenes beat around the bush." He frowned. "He had more money. At least, I tell myself that. It's easier than thinking she fell out of love with me and fell in love with him. Or that she never loved me at all."

"I lost you to someone like *that?*" Chloe asked, incredulous.

"Yeah."

"Serves you right," Martha said grimly.

"Yes, I guess it does."

"What I don't understand," Chloe said, "is why you never told me anything until I got home. You even visited me in Avignon. I thought everything was just the same between us."

"I was leading a double life. I kept telling myself that when you came home, I'd break it off with Valerie. But then I saw you, so fresh and honest and trusting, and I knew I couldn't go to you. I'd been unfaithful. You'd trusted me. I decided Valerie was what I deserved."

His words were like a physical assault as Luke's deceit hit her anew. As fresh as yesterday. She couldn't say anything.

"In a way, I suppose I left you because I respected you and loved you too much to give you what I had become," Luke continued.

"Thank you," she said and meant it.

"Well, that's honest, at least," Chloe's mother said. "I'm glad you lived to regret it."

"Oh, I regretted it immediately. But the damage was done, you see."

"Do you think it would have happened if I hadn't been gone?" Chloe asked.

"There's no way I would have looked at another woman if you'd been here. But that doesn't excuse it."

"You're right there," Martha said. "Don't you go blaming yourself for this, Chloe."

"But it never would have worked, then. My work made it impossible for you to be faithful," Chloe said, sitting up straighter. "It was a test. You failed."

"I've changed, Chloe. Nothing was worth losing you. Nothing."

Chloe was silent. How could she ever trust this man? If she wanted to be with him, she'd never feel secure, even supposing she gave up her career.

"Let's change the subject," she said finally.

"Yes," Martha agreed. "What's your business these days, Luke?"

"I have an online printing company. Brochures, ads, invitations, stationery. I make it easy for my customers. I have templates for them to use to design their own, or for a higher fee, I do custom work." He paused and looked at Chloe, a sparkle in his eye. "The great thing is, I can do it anywhere and just forward the JPEGs to my print shop. My employees can do the actual printing and send out the orders."

Chloe's guard went up. *Is he trying to tell me that now he can follow me anywhere?*

"Any leads on the bombing and the near-accident that put you in the hospital, Chloe?" Luke asked.

"Terrorists want Rob dead. Radical Muslims have taken over the factory in Indonesia. One FBI agent is dead. Another is in the hospital. The rest I can't talk about."

"And you're still hanging out with him?"

"Some. But he doesn't want to put me in danger. There's no one nicer than Rob. And he doesn't deserve this. He just lost his son and, eighteen months ago, his wife. Drowning and cancer."

Luke must have heard something in her voice, for he looked at her closely. "Are you sure you're okay?"

"Just the occasional headache." Like now.

"And this Rob," he said. "Is he someone special?"

"You've got nerve all right, Luke," Chloe's mother said. "Waltzing in here three years later, expecting Chloe to be just the same. She's lived in three countries since you ended things so badly. Do you think that she didn't meet and date other men during that time?"

"Martha, I was just trying to make a point. A point you should appreciate. It must have been really bad to have come so close to losing Chloe after Jonah's death. You can't tell me you're comfortable with her hanging out with a man who's almost gotten her killed."

"I told you, he doesn't have anyone else," Chloe said. "All of his family are gone. Except his sister, and she's in rehab."

"So, you're trying to tell me he's a charity case?"

"Of course not!" Chloe exclaimed. "Just that I'm not going to leave him to fight this all by himself."

"And what does he have to say about that?"

"Oh, he doesn't want me to endanger myself, of course."

"And so you shouldn't, Chloe," her mother said.

"At last, something we agree on," Luke said with a sigh.

Chloe looked from one of them to the other. "You two would have me abandon someone in need?"

"But what can you do, Chloe?" her mother asked.

"Be there for him!"

"So he *is* someone special," Luke said.

"Not in the way you mean. He's still in love with his wife."

"So there's hope for me?"

His appealing eyes! How many times in the last three years had she fantasized that something like this would happen? She hadn't ever been able to adjust to life without Luke. Now she could have it all for the taking. But fear she couldn't have predicted held her back.

"I'm only considering friendship at the moment, Luke. Especially after hearing about your marriage."

"I'll continue to hope, if there's no one else. We had something wonderful, Chloe."

"*Had* is the operative word."

"For me, the spark is still there. I can't believe that it's gone out entirely for you. I have to hope."

She shrugged. "I'd be lying if I said the spark was completely gone. I just wonder if it's wise to blow on it."

"Just give me time to prove to you how wise it is."

Chapter Eighteen

Chloe was up by eight A.M., showering and singing a lusty version of "Cry Me a River" in her most sultry voice, her headache gone.

> *Now you say you love me.*
> *Well, just to prove that you do,*
> *Come on and cry me a river,*
> *Cry me a river!*
> *I cried a river over you.*

Why, after all the happiness she'd had with Luke, was she now so attracted to Rob, so concerned for his happiness and well-being when she hardly knew him?

As she shampooed her hair, it struck her that Rob had absolutely no sense of entitlement. Unlike Luke. Luke truly believed that she belonged to him and wasn't even the least bit jealous of Rob. It had never occurred to him that she might not eventually come back to him.

"Honey bunch," her mother said through the bathroom door, "I sure like your attitude this morning."

"Comb my hair out?" she asked.

"If you make the coffee," her mother answered.

So, while her mother struggled with her tangles, Chloe watched the waves roll in and foam over the little section of beach by their patio. *One terrorist cell to take care of. No problem.*

"By what you were singin', I guess you're going to send Luke on his way, darlin'?"

"Umm, haven't actually decided yet, Mother. That's what you'd do, isn't it?"

"Who knows how many times he cheated on you? Your daddy was an exception, but normally I don't take to handsome men."

"Do you think Rob is handsome?"

"Hmm. I wondered if he might be in the picture. He's more what you'd call 'all-American.' But those shoulders and arms, umm hmm. Gotta love 'em. If only he didn't have this habit of getting shot at."

"Now that he's got professional bodyguards, I think things are going to get resolved pretty soon."

Her dream had ceased to trouble her, and she laughed as she remembered Naomi, who had called her names and spread vicious rumors about her. Her junior high days had been a version of hell because of one girl with a huge chip on her shoulder. Compared to Naomi, Islamic extremists would be no challenge. Especially ones that had missed their target as many times as these had. She just had to lure one out and follow him back to the hive. Then she'd treat them all to a grown-up version of Naomi's fate: raspberry Kool-Aid from a squirt-gun all over her prom dress. That had been brilliant!

That idea had burst into her head before she offered to find Rob's so-called hole-in-the-wall. Whoever had driven that van had observed her with Rob and no doubt had watched his visits to the hospital, thus deducing that she meant more to him than she actually did. She was willing to bet that when she emerged from the shut-down Capistrano Shores, there would be at least one terrorist watching. Hopefully, he would figure that she would be the perfect bait to lure Rob out. In fact, she was counting on it.

Her hands trembled a little as she stuck her Taser gun in the outside pocket of her huge black leather bag with the rhinestone straps that her mother coveted. She vowed for the hundredth time to buy her one the next time she visited the Florence Central Market. Dressed as a professional in the midnight-blue stretchy pantsuit she wore on airplanes, she assessed her footwear. Something comfortable but made for action. Her black Hush Puppy loafers with the waffle soles would be just the ticket.

Feeling like the heroine in one of her beloved "strong female" crime novels, she sang out to her mother as she left. "I'll see you when I get back. Have some business to take care of."

"Can you pick up some more coffee, sweet girl?"

"Italian roast?"

"Whatever strikes your fancy, darlin'."

⌒〜

She was about a mile up Pico Avenue when she saw the dirty white pickup behind her. The man behind the wheel could be either Latino or Middle Eastern—she couldn't tell. Pulling up at Rosemary's Real Estate and parking her mother's Lexus, she watched the truck pass her and then park up the street. She got out, but the truck's occupant didn't. So far, so good. A random Latino would have no reason to follow her.

Rosemary was tickled to see Chloe so unexpectedly. She explained her errand to find an office for Rob's business.

"Oh, sweetie, I was wondering what I was going to do with my day. Business has been the pits." Picking up what she called her Gucci power bag, she continued, "I've got some ideas. We'll have fun looking and then eat at the Fisherman's Cave. I haven't had sea bass in an age."

"I should also tell you that there might be a little side action," Chloe said. "Nothing you can't handle, but something you should know about. I know you think it's wimpy, but bring your Taser, okay?"

"Girl, what have you gotten yourself into?"

"I'm being followed by a member of a terrorist cell that is trying to blow up San Pedro Harbor."

Rosemary only clucked like a mother hen, asking, "What in the world does he want with a slip of a thing like you?"

"I'm bait for a bigger fish." As they walked out to Rosemary's black Escalade and started driving towards Dana Point, Chloe outlined Rob's situation.

"So you finally got over that cad Luke. Good. I hope Rob realizes what a treasure you are," Rosemary commented.

Chloe wasn't surprised. Rosemary would take even a shoot-out with terrorists with aplomb. Though Chloe managed to forget it most of the time, her friend had once been a deputy sheriff in Texas. Worries about how the heat of west Texas was aging her fair skin had driven her northwest to the damp, skin-friendly climate of San Clemente.

"Why in the world are we only armed with these wimpy Tasers?" her friend asked. "They'll have real guns, you know."

Chloe shrugged. "We'll just have to surprise them and be quick on the draw. I don't want to kill anyone, even a terrorist."

"Well, I'm taking a real automatic too, just in case."

Rob realized suddenly that he no longer wanted to die. Things had changed. Staring ruefully at the stack of Pamela's journals as he ate the breakfast of bacon, eggs, and fried tomatoes that Edward had served him, he wondered what was different. In the midst of a living hell, with a whole cell of terrorists who wanted him dead, he had found out that his quiet wife was an impostor, a betrayer, a sneak, and a liar. Less important than either of these things, but still a concern, his business was in serious jeopardy. But it had all combined to bring out the scrappy fighter that had been the best quarterback in San Diego State's history. Even though he didn't know what was around the next corner, he wanted to survive. In the fog that surrounded him, a barely discernible image of heavenly benevolence and a pair of golden eyes spurred him on.

Chloe, bless her beautiful heart, had just called with a possible address for his developers. Knowing the building and deciding the rent was more than reasonable, he talked to her friend Rosemary, the realtor, and instructed her to draw up a contract. Then he called his employees to give them their new office address. Then he telephoned his sales and marketing crew heads and told them about the situation in Indonesia and the efforts he was making to salvage his business.

"I won't blame you if you go after other employment. I don't know how long this is going to take, or if it will even work out, but I am going to try everything to put us back together, and I would love to have you back when the time comes. I'll get Mrs. Field working on the receivables, so we can get some cash. If we have enough after paying rent and salaries to the developers, I'll see that you get as much severance as I can afford."

Edward was vacuuming the bedrooms when Rob sat down to compose an e-mail to the American Embassy in Jakarta, initiating his attempt to enlist the help of the Indonesian government in ousting the insurgent group from control of his factory. It felt good to be acting instead of reacting, and he blessed Chloe's positive influence. She might look like a Botticelli sprite, but she had brains and *chutzpah*, and for the first time since Robbie's death he felt energized and positive.

Pamela's actions lingered like a wound, but surprisingly, the hurt didn't go as deep as he would have imagined. He had already begun to wonder if he knew the true nature of passionate love. Pamela had surely never offered him such. And now his guilt over his many absences was completely erased. Still, he was wary. What if he had loved her as much as he should have? This new knowledge would have cut clear through nerve and bone, amputating a vital part of him.

Once he had completed his e-mail and sent it on its way, he went in search of his home teacher. He found him scrubbing toilets.

"For heaven's sake, Edward! What do you think you're doing?"

"My Monday bachelor duties. What do you want for lunch?"

"Actually," Rob said, taking a fortifying breath, "I need to talk."

"Oh? Well, just let me finish here."

Minutes later, they were seated on the porch, watching the tide go out and the gulls swooping onto the water in search of prey. A handful of surfers were trying to ride today's puny waves, and somewhere about was Agent Christensen, watching the house while Agent Northridge watched the whole development from a higher perch with his binoculars.

"What would you do, Edward, if you found out after Rachel's death that she had been in love with another man since before she married you? And that she had an affair with that man up until the day she died?"

Edward's forehead drew into a frown, and his green eyes looked into Rob's face with concern. "The journals?" he asked.

"Yes."

"You must be in shock. I would be. I think I'd have trouble distinguishing what reality was. I mean, your ideas about your marriage must be . . . oh, it's useless. I can't even put it into words." After a moment, Edward said, "Betrayal. The worst betrayal."

Rob was very glad Edward was there to understand his confusion. "Yeah, big time. But I've realized that I didn't love her as a man should love his wife, so, surprisingly, it didn't hurt as much as it could have. Still, I should have guessed. It's left me wondering about a lot of things, like if I'll ever be able to read a woman's true feelings—or my own, for that matter."

"Was it anyone you knew?" Edward asked.

"Rick Niebolt. The guy that was in love with Ginger. Chloe told me he saved her from suicide. Turns out Pamela hated Ginger. She only married me on the rebound from Rick." He rubbed the back of his neck, his agitation increasing. "Then, after Robbie was born, she and Niebolt picked it up again. It's hard to get my mind around the fact that I never knew the woman I was married to for eleven years. I thought she was sweet, passive, patient. But she was playing a part the whole time."

"All women aren't deceitful, Rob."

Rob's mind flew again to Chloe. Then he saw the Viking/Adonis in the hospital, announcing his possession of her by intimately stroking her red-gold hair. Pain darted through all his other emotions, and his drive faltered. A man like that wouldn't disappear from her past or present very easily. He sighed heavily.

As though reading his mind, Edward said, "Chloe isn't like that.

She would never be like that. She's too wholehearted. I don't think she has it in her to be deceitful."

"What do you know about the boyfriend?"

"She hasn't discussed any boyfriend with me. You mean the guy at the hospital with her?"

"Yeah."

"I'll sound her out on him if you like. But I've seen her look at you, Rob. She doesn't look at him that way."

Rob dug his knuckles into his sleepy eyes. Was he going to let the fog overtake him? Betrayal. Confusion. Danger. Grief. How many more emotions could he hold inside his mind and body? Was there even any room for love? Was he just so starved for light and love in his present state that he was imagining feelings that weren't really there? Was the blond hunk the reason that the beautiful, intelligent, talented Chloe had never been married?

To keep from calling the woman who was so much on his mind, he decided to check on Ginger. If it weren't for her, he would never have read the journals, would never have discovered Pamela's secret. Did Ginger know of it? He doubted it. She had practically dropped off the face of the earth by the time he married Pamela. And, in all fairness, at this moment she was probably worried about him.

He phoned the facility, waited the requisite twenty minutes while Ginger was paged and made to wait by the pay phone, and then called back.

"Rob, how *are* you? I've been worried to death! No more close calls?"

"I've lost count. But I've got some real pros on the case now, so don't worry."

"Good. I'm getting kind of antsy in here, Rob. I don't know if I'm going to be able to stick it out."

"Anything in particular?"

"That therapist. She's messing with my head."

"What do you mean, Ginger?"

"Well, I think she's got this idea that if she can figure out my past, she can figure out my drinking."

"Well, is that right? Is there anything in your past that caused it?"

"I don't want to go there, Rob," she said firmly. "I don't want to get anywhere close to my past. That's why I don't want her messing with me anymore."

"But what about your drinking? How can you overcome your drinking if you don't square yourself with your past?"

"It's not something I'm willing to trade off. You have no idea what's involved, nor do I ever want you to."

"Tell me, Ginger, does it have anything to do with Pamela?"

There was silence on the other end of the line. "No, Rob." She sounded completely puzzled. "Why should it?"

He bought it. She wasn't on the defensive. He knew Ginger on the defensive.

"So where does this leave us?" he asked.

"I want to get out of here. I think I'll go out of my mind if I have to stay here any longer."

Rob was stunned by the panic in her tone. "Ginger, this is the worst possible time," he said. "People are trying to kill me. You'd be putting your life in danger."

"Do you really think so?"

"Yes. Until we get this settled, I think you'd better stay right where you are. I can change your therapist if you think that'll help."

"No. I really like Sonia. That's just it. She so sympathetic. And I'm not worth it. I'm not fit to live, Rob. I'm really not. If you knew everything . . ."

"Knew what?"

"Nothing. I'm getting all shook up."

"Well, I'll have a talk with Dr. Updike. I'll tell her to go easy on you, Ginger. But you've got to get your life cleared up sometime. And if you think you're not fit to live, I can get a restraining order to keep you in there. I won't let you be a danger to yourself."

"Rob!"

"I mean it, Ginger. Alcohol has taken your last fourteen years. Don't let it take your life. Look at it from my point of view. You're the only family I have left."

"And you'd be better off without me."

"That's not true," he said. "I'll speak to Dr. Updike. Just one more thing. Whatever happened to you and that boyfriend you had your senior year at Stanford? The one you were dating when you set me up with Pamela?"

"You mean Rick?"

"Yeah, that's the one. What happened between the two of you, anyway?"

"I guess our relationship was just another casualty. He hung around for a long time after I told him to leave. The whole thing was pretty one-sided. I never would have had a future with him."

"Oh? Why?"

"He was too controlling. I wouldn't be surprised if he turned out to be an abuser. Forget about me, Rob. You have your own stuff to worry about."

Do I ever! "No. This is important."

He called Sonia Updike next and managed to reach her between sessions. "I've just spoken to my sister," he said. "She seems most upset."

"Yes. She is. I don't know precisely why. I told her I wanted a social history on her and tried to get her to take me through her college years. It was like we hit a brick wall."

"So you were right. Something traumatic happened."

"At a guess, I'd say so."

"She wants to leave Renaissance. She's in a panic."

"I know. I've been trying to think of another way we could get at this. I don't think it's just a love affair gone wrong. I think something really bad must have happened."

"You mean—like some kind of crime?"

"I don't think it's that. It's something she's really afraid we'll find out about."

"What does she have to say about Rick Niebolt?"

"Now, Rob," she cautioned. "You know I've already stretched the rules. What she told me has to remain completely confidential. Do you think you could get any more from those two friends you talked to? Maybe something bizarre that happened at the time?"

"Like what, for instance?"

"Oh, she could have been caught cheating. Stanford makes a big thing over its honor code."

"Not big enough to cause a fourteen-year drinking bout. I'm going to try to find out more about this Rick Niebolt."

"Why?"

"I have my reasons for not trusting him. They're confidential. If I find anything that connects to my sister in any way, I'll let you know."

"All right. I look forward to hearing from you."

Again, that come-on warmth in her voice. Rob shuddered and hung up the phone. More for something to do than anything else, he began to go over the things he had harvested on Rick Niebolt from the Internet.

But then Chloe called, and he forgot all about Rick Niebolt.

CHAPTER NINETEEN

When Chloe and Rosemary finished their meal at the Fisherman's Cave, they walked out of the restaurant to find their terrorist tail sitting cross-legged on the ground with a sign that said, "Will work for food."

Though Chloe realized the sign was no more than camouflage, she decided that the best way to accomplish her goal was to take the man up on his offer. Seen close up, he was definitely Middle Eastern with a short beard, dressed in gray workpants and a dirty white T-shirt. He fit perfectly the part of a poor indigent.

She approached him. "Hi! I'm Chloe. I'll help you out. I need the roof of my house fixed. There's a leak."

She knew he understood only that she was taking him up on his offer. His nearly black eyes turned startled and confused, but he unfolded himself and followed them to Rosemary's Escalade. As he got into the backseat, she could see the gun tucked into his waistband under his oversized T-shirt. From her quick nod, Chloe knew that Rosemary had observed the weapon, as well.

Rosemary started the car. No sooner were they out of stop-and-go traffic than the terrorist pulled out his gun and held it to Chloe's head. "You go there," he said to Rosemary, pointing to the north-bound entrance to the freeway, his voice tight.

Chloe felt a thrill of fear shoot through her. Had her impetuosity led her into a fatal situation? How many terrorists were there anyway? Gulping, she wondered at herself. Was she so empowered by her freedom from Luke's spell and her desire to save Rob that she had completely lost her mind?

Her mother's voice sailed into her head. "Now, honey bunch, you know no self-respectin' Texas lady would let a bunch of hooligans get the best of her, especially when she's got her sidearm on her. You're gonna do just fine."

The gun held next to her skull didn't waver.

They kept going on the San Diego freeway until it merged into the Santa Ana. Their captor urged them off at an exit in Anaheim that Chloe knew was the heart of Little UN, where Latinos mixed with Vietnamese, Laotians, Cambodians, and Middle Easterners. Drive-by shootings were an everyday occurrence amid warring ethnic gangs. Perhaps their own show would go unnoticed.

She knew that at any moment they would reach the house where the hive of terrorists hoped to lure Rob with her as bait. The small bungalows were sprayed with graffiti, and almost all the lawns were dead. An occasional yucca plant held onto its spring blooms. Anaheim was usually desert-hot in the summer, but today the fog had rolled into this inland slum, veiling everything with just enough eeriness to make the whole scene unreal.

This is how it would look on TV. Pretend you're Ziva David, trained assassin for the Mossad. This Jihadist would soon be writhing on the floor.

She and Rosemary had mapped out a rough scenario over lunch. The killer with his sign had made it just that much easier. As they pulled to a stop in front of a tired, pale green house with a cracked concrete driveway, she felt her confidence flag. Could she really do this?

God, please help me! Throwing her prayer out into the universe, she pulled her Taser from the outside pocket of her purse when her captor began wrestling with his door. Rosemary had locked it automatically from the driver's seat. Turning, Chloe fired straight into the terrorist's chest. He collapsed.

Chloe put the terrorist's gun in her back waistband. She certainly hoped she wouldn't need it. She and Rosemary counted to three in unison, as Chloe's friend yanked her keys from the dash. They threw their doors open and locked the car. Their captor-turned-captive wouldn't be in any shape to go anywhere.

Darting quickly to the far side of the driveway, they crept up its perimeter, their Tasers held out in front of them with both hands. Chloe hoped the police would not choose this moment for a cruise through the crime-ridden neighborhood and that the neighbors would know enough to keep their heads down.

Rosemary gave Chloe a quick nod, and they began a simultaneous mental count to thirty. Chloe climbed the chain-link fence to the backyard in ten seconds. Then, while Rosemary began sidling towards the front door, she crouched and ran under the windows in the weed-choked backyard. *Twenty.* With her back to the house and her arms outstretched in front of her, Taser clasped tightly, she moved slowly to the back door. There she stood, head cocked for any sound, as she completed her count. All was ominously still. Putting her hand on the knob, she turned it cautiously. Unlocked!

At the count of thirty, she quietly opened the door. Rosemary had brought her Glock as well as her Taser, for Chloe heard her shoot the lock off the front door. Instantly, bedroom doors flew open and three men in their underwear, wiry black hair wild from sleep, came out firing. Rosemary stayed outside. Chloe fired first into the back of the man closest to the front door. As he fell, the other two whirled and let off a barrage of gunfire that she heard from behind the freezer where she had ducked. Rosemary entered the house, firing her Taser, and one villain fell at Chloe's feet. The other approached Rosemary, tossing aside his empty gun. As he kicked out, Rosemary grabbed his leg and flipped him onto his back, where she tasered him.

Chloe wanted to cheer. A nice job and a wonderful gift to Rob and to Homeland Security! She and Rosemary took out of their pockets the cord they had bought during their office hunt that morning. Using a knife from the kitchen drawer they cut it in lengths sufficient to bind the terrorists' hands and feet before they could regain consciousness.

When all were bound, they stood and grinned at one another.

A car. Chloe heard a car pull into the driveway. Through the ragged sheer curtains, she saw another man, this one in full Islamic garb, climb out of the car and go to investigate the Escalade. In a split second, he whirled, drawing an AK-47 out of his voluminous robe.

Chloe yelled, *"Down!"* as a spray of bullets came through the front door, smashed through the front window, and struck the wall opposite it. Then the automatic fire swerved back the way it had come. Chloe thought the shooting would never stop and put her hands to her ears.

Rosemary, however, was Texas tough. Crawling to the shattered window, she poked her head up while the assassin was shooting the other side of the house. Bringing her Taser to the window, she aimed with a miraculously steady hand and brought the extremist down with two shots to the chest.

Doors started opening up and down the street. In the distance,

Chloe could hear a siren. She and her friend ran out the bullet-splintered front door as Rosemary used her remote to unlock the Escalade. Chloe climbed in the back with their hostage, who was mercifully still incapacitated, tied his hands, and then dumped him in the street. Rosemary gunned the engine of her powerful SUV and squealed out of the neighborhood. Within minutes she was on the freeway, and Chloe had pulled out her cell phone. Pausing for a deep breath, she dialed Rob's number.

"Chloe?" he answered.

"Reporting, sir!" she said, assuming the voice of a seasoned veteran. "Five terrorists lying tasered by person or persons unknown at 316 Magnolia Street in Anaheim, awaiting a visit from Homeland Security. Don't know how long they'll be out, so I recommend urgent action. I hope someone understands their language."

CHAPTER TWENTY

As Rob listened to Chloe, he thought she must be joking. "Aren't you going to tell me not to bother to bring Naomi?"

"Rob," her voice was weary. "Rosemary, my friend, and I just took out the cell. We really did. You need to send your agent over there. Tell them it was an anonymous tip from a neighbor. You're the only one who needs an alibi, and you have Edward and the agents. So we're not going to run into any red tape or need a lawyer or anything. I can ID one of them as the guy that was tailing us this morning, so there's your connection. He wanted to hold me hostage, I imagine, but I turned the tables. Of course HS doesn't need to know that part."

"Chloe!" he demanded, sprinting for the door, his heart accelerating to a drummer's cadence. "Are either of you hurt? Who in the world is Rosemary?"

"You talked to her. She's your realtor and my best friend and self-defense instructor. Now find Agent Whatsit or the other one! We're on the Santa Ana, speeding home."

Rob exited the house, still unable to believe that the petite Chloe, his pocket-sized Venus, had brought down five terrorists. "Just a minute, I've got to yell. I have no idea where they're hiding."

Lowering his phone, Rob shouted, "Agents, agents: All clear, all clear. I just got a tip from a neighbor at 316 Magnolia Street in Anaheim that five men have been found tasered and unconscious. They could be our terrorists."

Agent Christensen poked his head out of the bougainvillea. "Is this a joke, Rob?"

"Absolutely not, sir."

"Did you at least get caller ID?"

"Called it back. It was a payphone. But my girlfriend was followed by one of the terrorists who have been stalking me when she left this morning. She managed to lose him, but I'll bet that she can ID him if you pick up these guys and take them wherever you take them."

"Rob, what have you done? Hired vigilantes?"

"No, sir. I had nothing to do with this. Could be they had a patriotic neighbor who figured out they were up to something. I'd move quickly on this if I were you."

"Where's your girlfriend?"

"Out shopping. Where should she meet you?"

"Federal building in Santa Ana."

Going back inside the house, Rob finished his conversation with Chloe. "Meet the agents sometime soon at the federal building in Santa Ana. Do you know where it is?"

"Rosemary's SUV has a GPS. Thanks, Rob."

She hung up before he could begin to thank her.

"I don't believe it." Collapsing on his couch, he relayed the information to Edward.

A slow smile crept over his friend's face.

"I hope she didn't have to kill anyone," Rob said from his daze. Then apropos of nothing, he gazed out to the sea. "It's so foggy I doubt you could see your hand in front of your face."

In a moment, they heard the screaming tires of the Homeland Security Ford Expedition as it peeled out of the subdivision.

"You're free, Rob," Edward said with a chuckle. "Rescued by your maiden."

Rob batted his hand as though he were shooing a fly. "She's not my maiden, remember? Her Viking is probably the one who taught her what she knows. Then there's Rosemary. They sound like Thelma and Louise. I just hope they don't drive off a cliff!"

He began pacing. Was it really over? For him, maybe. But could they make the terrorists talk and give up the location of the bomb on the oil tanker? Chloe had almost been killed, he was sure. She'd risked her life for him! Did she make a habit of this kind of thing? Going up against a cell of terrorists with nothing but a Taser?

Suddenly, he couldn't stand the waiting. "C'mon, Edward. Show me where the federal building is in Santa Ana."

His friend chuckled. "I don't think she needs rescuing anymore."

"No, but I need to see her. Right now."

When they arrived at the nondescript building in seedy downtown Santa Ana, they found that Chloe was already looking at a lineup. Rosemary would go in separately.

He couldn't see either of them yet, so he paced the floor.

"It's all right, son. Calm down. No one's going to hurt Chloe. She's not going to get arrested. No one would ever believe her story."

After three cups of nasty coffee and what seemed like hours, he finally saw Chloe coming down the hall. She was frowning.

"What's up?" he asked.

"Well, they can hold them for questioning indefinitely under the Patriot Act, but the only one they actually have anything on is the one Rosemary and I identified. I could tell they were suspicious about the whole thing, but they just kept shaking their heads. And they still don't know where the charge is hidden on the tanker. They are all pretending they can't understand English. Everyone's waiting for an interpreter to be helicoptered in from LA."

Her hair had escaped its braid and was blooming all around her classical face. She looked as fragile as the Renaissance painting he had seen hanging in the Uffizi in Florence. But her golden eyes had seen violence that day.

"Have you done this kind of thing before?"

"Not exactly. Once I went undercover in a burka for a month in a suspected terrorist cell. I had a friend with the CIA, back before Daddy was killed. The friend convinced me to do it, but Daddy was livid and got me out. Nearly got shot himself. It was wild!"

Without another thought, Rob gathered her into his arms and held her tight. "You've freed me, Chloe. I'm no longer a walking target!"

The unlikely gunslinger curled herself into his chest. "Yeah," she said. "But what about the tanker?"

"We have until the Fourth, honey bun. They can always fly them to Gitmo for interrogation. The interrogators down there will get it out of them."

"Only my mother can call me honey bun. And you *think* we have until the Fourth. It's not for sure that the Fourth is really part of their timetable." Raising her face a few inches off his chest, she looked up into his face. "I'm so glad you're not in danger anymore."

"I'm in awe of you, Chloe. How in the world did you learn to do something like that?"

"Well, mostly from TV. I love NCIS. But Rosemary taught me to shoot. She said that with my lifestyle it might come in handy."

"Where *is* Rosemary?"

"She left half an hour ago. They questioned her first, and she had a client to meet at the office."

"She sounds like quite a woman. Business in the morning, wiping out a terrorist cell after lunch, then business as usual in the afternoon."

Chloe grinned. "What do you expect? She's one tough Texas lady. And she didn't even break a fingernail." She eased herself from his embrace. "I just hope we got them all. They're going to take prints and make sure there aren't any others in the house where they were staying."

Edward rose from where he sat and came over. "My turn," he told Rob.

Chloe threw herself into his arms. "Edward! I didn't see you!"

"I'll bet you're pretty tuckered out. Does your mother know where you are?"

"Good grief! I'm not four years old!" she protested. "I told her to expect me when she saw me."

"Is she bound to take to drink when she hears of this little to-do?"

"Mother? Heavens, no! She packs a Beretta like a proper Texas lady. She has a concealed carry permit and carries her gun at all times."

Edward shook his head in apparent bewilderment. "A little lady like that?"

"Well, I'm not so big," she said. "Size has absolutely nothing to do with it. Especially if you're a Texan."

"Well," Rob interrupted, feeling his impatience percolating into the danger zone, "Edward and I need to hear this story. And I can't wait until we've driven all the way home."

"There's a doughnut shop next door," Edward informed them.

Over a box of doughnuts, Chloe told them a story that did

sound just like a TV episode. Rob would bet his beachfront property that Chloe had been impersonating Ziva David, the Mossad assassin on NCIS. It hardly fit his image of her though. He found that he was having to adjust to it. She had risked her life for him. She could shoot better than he could. Would he have been able to pull off such a gutsy thing? Maybe being a woman had actually been to her advantage. Still, he could no longer think of her as a sprite. He was uncomfortable with his sudden eruption of male chauvinism. Yet, she had curled herself against his chest like a kitten.

When she got home, Chloe found that her mother was out, and the light was blinking on the answering machine. Could it be that it was only 4:00 P.M.? The fog had socked in the entire shoreline, and it seemed as dim as twilight outside.

Now that the ordeal was over, she felt something of a letdown. Rob had been appropriately grateful, but now that he was no longer in danger, she felt a bit brazen. Why had she allowed him to embrace her like that? It had seemed so natural. And she had needed his steadiness and acceptance after the grueling interrogation. That had been worse than the shoot-out, which had actually stimulated her. She could see why people were drawn to a career in law enforcement. Catching the bad guys was a terrific high.

Setting her Taser on the kitchen counter to be cleaned later, she punched the button on the answering machine. "Chloe, this is Luke. Give me a call when you get in. I want to take you sailing."

She had no idea where Rob fit into her life now that she didn't have to worry about his safety anymore. And she had made her peace with Luke. Her hurt would make her wary of him, but she no longer turned into a puddle of disgusting goo when he walked into the room. She felt perfectly certain that she was no longer in danger from her treacherous hormones. All in all, she would love a sail. But then she saw the fat package of galleys for her latest book sitting under the circulars. *Work before play, Chloe.*

Upon the heels of this stricture, she suddenly realized what she had actually done that day. *Rosemary and I wiped out a nest of terrorists. I don't even remember how many I shot. I've never shot anyone before.*

Sitting down, she went through the whole sequence in her mind again, starting from when the Escalade pulled up in front of that horrible house. She remembered the hasty prayer she had sent up for safety. A little gratitude was in order, to say the least. There was no other way to account for the fact that she, a novice, had contributed to bringing five dangerous men to justice and had not so much as a scratch on her.

Falling immediately to her knees, she expressed her gratitude to the Lord for her safety and for Rosemary and Rob's safety. She confessed that while the determination had been hers, she knew the skill had been lent by a power higher than her own. Something had been added to her usual moxie that enabled her to perform beyond her natural ability. That was a humbling realization for Chloe.

Standing, she decided to call Luke before opening her galleys.

He answered immediately.

"Chloe?"

"Hi, Luke. You called?"

"Yeah, hours ago."

"Sorry. I just got in. Was it urgent?" She was finding it difficult to focus on her former lover's voice. The shots from the gun battle still echoed in her head, and the exhilaration and adrenaline had not yet worn off.

"Well, I managed to free up tomorrow, and I wondered if you'd like to go sailing."

"There's actually nothing I'd like better, but I've got a set of galleys to go through for my new book. Can we go Wednesday instead?"

"You're sure you don't need a break?" He was clearly disappointed.

"I just got them today and haven't started yet. I need to get a good solid day of work in."

"I guess Wednesday would work. I could shift my meetings from then to tomorrow. I'm the boss, so no one can complain."

"Do you still have the same boat?" *The one you named after me?*

"Yeah. So you'd have to drive down here. Would you mind?"

She knew she had a lot to process emotionally. The galleys were nothing more than an excuse, really. But by the day after tomorrow she'd probably be ready for a good sail. And she'd have had time to see Rob and get the latest news on the interrogation of the terrorists. She realized, now that she was coming down from her high, that there could be others they had missed.

She wasn't feeling as vulnerable to Luke as she had at first, but it would be easy to slip back into the easy camaraderie they had always enjoyed. Luke was the only man she'd ever loved until now. She'd known him for years. Rob's face flashed into her mind. Whatever intimacy they had had been forged in crisis. He still loved his dead wife. He was selling his house and had his hands full reconstructing his business. It was unlikely that things would continue with the same urgency and frequency that she had known over the past week.

I want to marry someone I know I'm number one with. But how long would I stay number one with Luke?

"No, I don't mind. Wednesday would probably work fine. Should we meet somewhere?"

"How about Diego's? We can have lunch, and then I'll take you out on the boat."

Diego's had been their favorite Mexican restaurant. She hadn't been back there since Luke, either. This was going to be a trip down memory lane. Chloe began to rethink her decision. Before she could progress very far, Luke broke in. "It's coming up on the Fourth of July, so the tourists are pouring in down here. I'll make reservations for around 11:30. It shouldn't be too bad."

Chloe breathed deeply and said, "Fine. I'll see you then."

Knowing she couldn't possibly concentrate on her galleys, Chloe took a long, hot shower, dressed in her jeans and sweatshirt, and turned on the news. Laden with shopping bags, her mother walked into the house during the story of the terrorist roundup. Fortunately, the HS agents had kept her and Rosemary's name out of the news.

"Five alleged terrorists were captured today in a shoot-out in Anaheim. The suspects, all practicing members of the Fundamentalist Islam sect, were found shot with Tasers and bound. Their target in the United States is still uncertain, and Homeland Security is asking for assistance from any persons who have noticed unusual activity that might be linked to a terrorist act. Neighbors of the alleged terrorists who rented a house on Magnolia Street in Anaheim as well as workers at the docks in San Pedro Harbor are particularly asked to consider this plea. A reward will be given for any information which leads to the prevention of any planned attack."

"Thank you, God," Martha said, as she unloaded her groceries. "What have you been up to today, honey bun?"

"Oh, finding new office space for Rob. Rosemary and I had a long lunch at the Fisherman's Cave in Dana Point."

"Fun! Now that those awful men have been caught, why don't we celebrate? I can whip up that chicken and green chili casserole, so why don't you call Rob and invite him to dinner?"

"Great idea!" Chloe agreed.

Rob, however, had made plans with Edward for a night on the town. He asked Chloe and her mother to join them.

Chloe carried the cordless phone back to her bedroom. "Normally, my mother would be proud of my antics today, but now that she's in recovery, I don't want anything to rock her boat. So don't mention them, okay?"

Her mother was excited at the prospect of eating at A Tavola Ferrantelli, the exclusive and enormously expensive Italian restaurant in Dana Point.

"We'd love it! I miss Italian food so much," Chloe told him.

They arranged to meet at seven in Dana Point, and Chloe, revitalized, went off to consider her wardrobe of classy Italian skirts and tops. She wouldn't have time to wash her hair. Maybe she could get her mother to weave it into a French-braided coronet.

CHAPTER TWENTY-ONE

To say that Rob was deeply stirred by Chloe's life-threatening actions that day was inadequate. What he really wanted to do was to fly her to Paris on his business jet and treat her to dinner at a fabulously expensive restaurant on the Champs-Élysées. In his present circumstances, he couldn't afford the fuel. Dana Point would have to do for now. But he did have a little talk planned for later. There were several things he needed to have set straight.

Rob inhaled sharply as Chloe walked into the restaurant behind her mother. She had dressed for the occasion in creamy gauze with tiny sequins and a gold thread running through it. Her glorious hair was pulled into a woven crown around her head. Never had she looked more like Botticelli's version of Venus. There was something magical about her. Thinking of her taking out a bunch of filthy terrorists that afternoon was impossible to picture.

He couldn't get words out, so he whistled. Playing it up, she twirled around. "A seamstress in Cinque Terre made it by hand. I've been dying for an opportunity to wear it."

es sparkling.

They raised their water glasses and drank a toast to safety and another one to Rosemary, who had a hot date she hadn't been willing to break.

"Do they have any evidence tying them to the bombs they found in the harbor? Do they know where the one is on the tanker?" Chloe asked in a rush.

"After the newscast tonight, several longshoremen called in, saying they'd seen the men in the televised mugshots studying the harbor through binoculars. The captain of a freighter that docked late one night last week actually saw one of them putting on his wetsuit at two A.M., right at the water's edge," Edward said. "You know, I've heard they're having trouble finding quality men for the front lines of al-Qaida. This sure bears that out. All the terrorists with brains are hiding in caves somewhere."

"Well, our Homeland Security isn't particularly impressive," Chloe said. "It's taken them long enough to bring the terrorists in."

"Makes you wonder, doesn't it?" Rob asked, with a smile for Chloe. "I wonder who the anonymous vigilantes were who took them down."

"You never answered my question about the tanker," she said.

206

"They can't get anything out of those men. Edwards Air Force base has a jet flying them to Guantanamo overnight. They know how to get answers down there."

Martha said, "I could probably show them a trick or two. Too bad I sold my daddy's branding iron in a garage sale before we moved down here. They would have looked real cute with a Bar Z brand on their foreheads, not to mention their backsides."

"Now, Martha, I don't think they're allowed to leave any marks," Edward said. He chuckled. "I sure don't want to get on your bad side."

"Then don't try to convert my daughter," she said, robbing the words of offense by whispering them in her coy manner and batting her eyelashes.

The dinner was a great success. Rob was able to indulge his appetite for bruschetta, pears and honey with lamb cheese and walnuts, slices of Tuscan melon wrapped in prosciutto, mushroom ravioli in a divine cream sauce, and a chocolate tiramisu to finish. He hadn't eaten this much in what seemed like a lifetime.

As he was drinking the last of his coffee, he whispered in Chloe's ear, "I don't suppose you're much good at chess."

She grinned, and the corners of her eyes went up, enhancing her resemblance to a sprite. "Oh, you don't, huh? What if I told you that my Texas mama taught me chess when I was still in diapers?"

"I'd quake in my boots, knowing your mama. What else did she teach you to do that I should know about?"

"Well, I can lasso a calf and make it into a steer."

"Ooof. I didn't need to know that."

"Do I understand you'd like to test my prowess at chess?"

"Are you too tired?" he asked in a low voice. "I mean taking down bad guys must have knocked some of the stuffing out of you."

"I can do chess."

"Good. We have some private matters to discuss."

Later, as he and Chloe sat in front of the gas fire in his living room, the chessboard between them, he let her win the first game. Rob figured he owed it to her, but he had to admit she was an adroit player.

During the second game, he said, "I want you to tell me about the guy in the hospital."

Puzzled, she looked up. "I don't know anyone in the hospital."

"When I brought you Nebbie," he clarified.

For a moment, she looked puzzled, and then understanding appeared to dawn. "Oh, you mean Luke! Luke is . . . well, I'm not sure what Luke is right now. Maybe I'll know more after Wednesday."

"What's happening on Wednesday?"

"We're going sailing. It's something we used to do every weekend when I was home. Before . . ."

"Before what? C'mon. Level with me, Chloe. The guy was stroking your hair, for crying out loud. Is he an ex-husband? Ex-boyfriend? Current boyfriend?"

She chewed her bottom lip, considering a move while she drove him crazy.

"Well, I guess you'd say he's a bit of all three," she said finally. He felt his heart dive. "We were together for five years when I wasn't abroad, but we never married. Then, three years ago, he got engaged to someone else." She gave a heavy sigh. "It was hard. I thought I would never get over it, would never love anyone else. But last week he found me again, and it seems he's divorced. Now he's the one who wants the relationship, but I . . . well, I can't seem to make up my mind. He was unfaithful once. I don't know if I can trust him again."

Rob's heart rebounded.

"You'd think after loving someone that much and being that

brokenhearted, I'd fall right back into his arms. But I guess I've got a chicken heart. I'm afraid, and I don't know if there's anything he can do to make me feel secure again."

Watching her move her knight, he asked the next question, "Okay. I get that. And believe me, I understand what you're saying. Maybe someday I'll tell you why. But how, if you were so much in love with him, could you leave him every year and go off someplace for however long it took you to write those books?"

"You know," Chloe said, putting her head to one side, "I've been wondering that myself. I came up with a very strange answer."

"Which was . . . ?"

"You probably noticed how attractive he is. The man's a magnet."

"I could hardly avoid noticing, could I?"

"Well, I think some part of me instinctively distrusted him. I mean, you've got a man that handsome, and you know every woman who sees him has got to fall in love—or at least lust—with him." She looked up from under her eyelashes in the same provocative way Lauren Bacall had perfected. "I think I was subconsciously testing his love for me. Three years ago, I came home to learn he was engaged. He hadn't even bothered to let me know but had just gone on e-mailing me as though he were as devoted as ever."

"Well, that kind of takes the shine off things," he said.

"You could say that. Add to that the fact that my daddy, whom I adored, had died two years before, and I was still grieving. You know what I think?"

"What is that?"

"I think that when I had that experience with Daddy when I was meditating, it freed me from the worst of the grief over his death. I was sitting on the floor laughing! Until then, I think I'd been locked into an endless loop of PTSD. God rescued me by giving me just enough of my daddy that day to know he still existed, somewhere, somehow."

"And what about your mourning over Luke? Is that still going on?"

She looked straight into his eyes. "Until you rescued me from being run over by that van on the same day that Luke found me again, I was still a sorry mess. But the trauma of almost dying and being preserved by such a miracle knocked that Luke trauma right out of my head."

Rob grinned at her, more relieved than he wanted to express. "So now you are sort of militantly ambivalent."

"That describes it perfectly," she said. The twinkle was back in her eye. "It's anyone's guess whether the magic will come back, but at least I don't feel like I need to run away to New Zealand tomorrow to get away from my feelings."

Rob wondered briefly whether a kiss would help change her mind. But part of him held back. He wanted Luke well and truly decided upon before he risked his heart. Pamela's infidelity had sorely messed with his confidence, giving him trust issues as big as Chloe's.

They played in silence until the quiet became uncomfortable. It was a foggy night, and, even though he knew intellectually that he was safe, he still felt like a target sitting there with the lights on and the fog masking whatever evils lay within it.

"Would you mind talking about Ginger?" he asked.

"Not if you think it will help. You still haven't figured out what caused her drinking?"

"No. And she's stonewalling her therapist."

"It must be something she's deathly afraid to let out," Chloe guessed. "I still can't imagine what it would be."

"I thought maybe a rape had traumatized her, but it's not that.

It's something she thinks she's done wrong. She thinks she's a horrible person."

"She was wonderful," Chloe said. "She treated me so kindly, even though I was so wet behind the ears."

"I'm going to try to catch up with that old boyfriend. He hasn't answered my e-mail, but it may be an old account he doesn't use anymore. I found a lot about him on the Internet. He's still in the area. But it would really help if you could think of a big scandal that happened that long ago."

Putting her hands to her temples, she murmured, "This is all a plot of yours to rob me of my concentration."

"Then the scales are even. Just sitting across from you all decked out like that is robbing me of mine."

Spritely grin.

Then she closed her eyes as though divining spirits. She spoke. "There was nothing that involved Ginger. There was a football scandal. Our quarterback was found guilty of cheating and was kicked out of Stanford right before the Big Game, and a girl I knew pretty well committed suicide. She was a Mormon, in fact. Sad. Her parents were really broken up over it."

Rob's brows came down. "Nothing else? No dirt in the anthro department?"

"I was as low on the totem pole as you could get. It would have had to be a pretty big pile of dirt for me to see."

Opening her eyes, she scowled at the chessboard. "I wonder why that Mormon girl killed herself. I've always wondered. She was such a wonderful person."

"Depression can hit anyone."

"Yes, that's what they say." She was silent for a moment as though she were picking through her thoughts. "As I recall, Rick was awfully strung out at the time of Ginger's suicide attempt. I mean, he was white as a sheet and wouldn't let her go."

"Devoted, huh? It's nice to know that someone in her life felt that way about her at one time."

"I don't think she appreciated his saving her. She was crying and hysterical and trying to make him let her go."

"Wow. The more I hear about this situation, the weirder it gets. Are you sure you don't remember anything else?"

"I just have the vague sense that Ginger sort of drifted away after that. Like a ghost of herself."

"And Rick?"

"I don't think he ever stopped trying to get her back. It's possible that he sank into depression, as well. But I don't know that. The anthro club was not a cheery place the rest of that year."

Rob rolled these facts around in his mind. "Hmm." It was all starting to make an awful kind of sense. Thinking of his sister in so much pain harrowed him up inside, as though his vitals had been raked through with a tractor. He looked up at Chloe. Her golden eyes were studying him as though trying to read his mind. If things continued like this, she was going to enter that wounded soul of his, and he'd have a triple heartache going when she went off with Luke. The problem was that today she had virtually saved his life, and her smile was his balm of Gilead.

"Check," she said, glowing with satisfaction.

In a few short moves, she had defeated him. Again, he could have avoided it, but he knew that if he kept her there much longer he was going to kiss her, and then it would be all over but the crying, as his grandmother used to say.

Disarming the house alarm, he walked her out into the damp fog, quietly, so as not to wake the neighbors. Chloe followed. As they walked out onto the driveway, Rob thought he noticed a spark of something by his rental car. Though the fog was still thick, he aimed his flashlight toward the Audi. A bullet whizzed by his head.

"Down!" He clutched Chloe by the back of the neck and forced her flat onto the small bit of lawn beside him. There was another shot, this one whizzing just over their heads.

Lights went on in the house next door. Old Mr. Havers stuck his head out. "What's the noise?" Then he saw Rob and Chloe flat on the ground. "Gunfire? Are they after you again, boy? Well, don't you worry."

Mr. Havers was back seconds later with a semiautomatic shotgun, spraying shot in the direction of the parking lot. "You there! Come out with your hands where I can see them!"

They heard the kick start of a motorbike. Followed by another burst of shot, the intruder made off down the roadway in the foggy mist that shut in the night.

CHAPTER TWENTY-TWO

Rob quickly dialed Agent Christensen. By the light of his flashlight, he'd seen a brief glimpse of a man in a black ski mask. His clothing was dark, too, except for the light-colored running shoes with reflectors on the heels. Those reflectors were what had caught his attention through the fog.

"Christensen here."

"I don't care what forensics says, there's another terrorist loose. He just shot at me. Black ski mask and a motorcycle. Probably left behind to detonate the bomb on the oil tanker."

"Oh, no," the agent moaned. "One of us will be over shortly. Stay low and locked up in that tin can you live in."

Chloe popped up during his conversation. She had apparently landed partially on the gravel, and her knees were bleeding through her gorgeous dress.

"Tell him about the car!" she said.

"Oh, Agent, I almost forgot to tell you. Bring a mechanical forensic specialist. He was monkeying around under my car."

After hearing a couple of swear words, Rob hung up, cutting off the stream.

"I'm sorry about the dress, Chloe, and your knees. Do they sting?"

"Not nearly as much as my head would if that bullet had gone through it. And no worries about my dress. My mother can get blood out of anything."

"I'm starting to believe your mother is supernatural."

"Well, she's starting to come around again. But even though she doesn't turn squeamish at the sight of blood, I'm going to tell her I fell down your stairs."

What a day she'd had! "I think you'll sleep well tonight. One day you're going to have to teach me to shoot."

She grinned. "Better get Rosemary to do that. She's the expert."

"I'm surprised you didn't say your mother taught you. But I'm longing to meet the legendary Rosemary."

Heedless of the agent's advice, he was walking Chloe home.

"Actually, my mother's aim isn't that good. She won't wear her glasses, even at the shooting range. Vanity is the only flaw in her armor. And Rosemary will probably have your lease ready for you tomorrow. A real overachiever type."

"You should talk! Is there anything you can't do?"

"I can't seem to write a straight novel anymore." She sighed. "My first one, the one you're reading, was my best. But my natural bent seems to be crime and adventure. I can be sitting in the most placid of surroundings—and take it from me, it doesn't get much more placid than Cinque Terre in the winter—and I can still come up with a plot that will curl your hair."

"You're a best-selling author," he said.

"Yeah, but the Stanford grad in me feels like I ought to be going for the Pulitzer or the Booker Prize. Don't we always want to be who we're not?"

"I guess."

"You know, that was really a close shot. But these terrorists don't seem to be very good at what they do, thank goodness," she said.

"I thought you were going to tell me it was another miracle."

"Well, it must be. I mean, they have to have been trained somewhere."

"I'll bet it was in some desert, and the fog throws them off."

Chloe actually giggled. "Let me know about your car."

"I'm not going near it until forensics have finished with it. Here we are. The Brass Pelican. You are home, princess, bloodied but unbowed."

"Thanks to your neighbor. When he gets back from his chase, be sure to give him my regards. He probably saved our lives."

"Our aged angel in pajama bottoms."

"You know we have to face it, Rob," she said, suddenly serious. "That guy wants revenge. Big time. He must think you are the one who caught his team." She wrapped her arms around herself for warmth, shivering.

"I'll take care. I'm getting good at it." He shook his head. "I guess our celebratory dinner was a little premature."

"Yeah," Chloe agreed, hanging her head. They stood before her door.

He needed to pull himself together. "Something about this attack felt different. He must be the leader of the pack or something."

"Because he was on a motorcycle?"

"Did you see any sign of a motorcycle at the house?"

"No. The guy might be staying somewhere else, just in case something like this happened. Maybe he's the only one with brains. I sure hope they find that bomb before he detonates it."

"I think they're going to move the ship out of the harbor to-night, actually. Agent Christensen wanted to make sure it was out at sea on the Fourth of July. All hands will abandon ship once she's out far enough."

"Then it may be out of range of the detonator."

"Unless they have access to a helicopter. Or maybe this guy with the motorcycle is a suicide bomber and is planning on detonating it on board. That's the reason these guys are so dangerous. They're crazy. You can't predict what they're going to do."

He put his hands on her shoulders and squeezed them reassuringly. "But our luck's going to hold." What he really wanted to do was to put his arms around her and hold her close to make certain she was safe.

"Maybe Daddy is our guardian angel. He was always fiercely protective." She gave him a lopsided grin.

It was that little grin that did it, Rob thought afterwards. Suddenly, she was in his arms, and he was kissing the top of her head, her forehead, her nose, and finally her lips. Chloe responded by giving him a bear hug and then extracting herself. "I'd better go in," she said as she unlocked the door. "Let me know what Agent Christensen has to say."

Rob felt as if she had just drawn a line in the sand. This far and no farther. His stomach twisted with anxiety. *Why did I do that?* "I think it would be safest if you stayed away from me until this is all through, one way or the other," he said.

Chloe stopped with her hand on the doorknob, hesitated, and then quickly, as though she were afraid that someone would see, stood on her toes and kissed him firmly on the mouth.

"Don't fuss. Everything's going to work out." He couldn't help what he was certain was a goofy grin of relief. She looked as if she were going to some hip cocktail party, except for the bloody scrapes on her skirt. Her Botticelli grace had never failed to cheer him, especially now, when he added to it the picture of her with a probably oversized Taser. She made such a definite statement: *Here I am: Chloe Greene. Fresh from the imaginations of gods. Venus. Womanly perfection.* Completely under her spell, he grinned at her. The thing that made her so undeniably charming was that she seemed entirely unaware of her beauty. And from what he was coming to know about her, from her frantic attempts to save Robbie down through their joint journey towards some kind of faith and her beyond-gutsy surprise raid on the terrorist cell that was trying to kill him, her inner strength was even greater than her outer beauty. Pamela had been stunning, but he had never been able to get past those silver eyes of hers.

Before he could even attempt to put these things into words, Chloe had opened the door and gone through it.

The next morning, Chloe attempted to put the events of the previous day out of her mind. They quite easily assumed fictional status as she lost herself in the imaginary crimes contained in her printer's galleys. She had put in three hours of working on those galleys when she decided it was late enough to call Rob and see what he knew about the car. She realized she also needed to tell Edward what had happened.

Knowing that her mother was busy in the kitchen making homemade rolls, she proceeded to give Edward an unexpurgated account of the night before. Summing it up, she said, "So, there's a rogue terrorist somewhere, but our guardian angel is still operative."

As she expected, he said, "I'd better get over there and see how Rob is. How's your mother taking this latest development?"

"I haven't told her, so don't you tell her, either. I don't want her to worry any more about terrorists. As far as she's concerned, they were wiped out single-handedly yesterday. Period."

After she hung up, she dialed Rob's number, peeking her head out of her room to make certain her mother was nowhere in the vicinity. She heard sounds coming from the kitchen.

"Hi, Chloe. I hoped you were still asleep."

Chloe closed her door and took the cordless phone into the adjoining bathroom for extra measure. "How are you doing today?"

"Well, considering I met your friend, the six-foot femme fatale, not bad. I can't believe she fired a gun with those fingernails. They're like daggers."

"So you signed the lease then. Good. How was your sleep?"

"It's really funny, but after these things happen, I seem to sleep like a log. Post-adrenaline overload, I think."

"Well, I'm glad of that. What did they find out about your car?"

"The guy was in the process of dismantling the alarm. So we don't know what he was up to, but the police suspect a bomb wired to the ignition."

Chloe shuddered. "That's what I figured. Straight out of one of my books. You were really lucky you stopped him."

"Yeah. I'm just glad you didn't get hurt."

"Me, too. What did Agent Christensen say?"

"Just that the oil tanker was clear of the harbor. They've got the Coast Guard on alert in case the guy moves up his plan and tries to take us by surprise in a helicopter or some kind of boat. Where are you going sailing tomorrow?"

"No worries. I'll be in San Diego. Unless you need me here for some reason."

"Well, think of me, confined to this tin can, as Christensen calls it, eating pretzels, with my bodyguard somewhere out there."

"Do you need groceries? I can pick some up. I'm just working on galleys."

"No. I've got a freezer full of frozen Stouffer's and plenty of ice cream, which is the main thing. Pretzels are good stress food too."

"I've been meaning to ask you. Did you ever contact the embassy in Jakarta?"

"I heard from them this morning. They're leaning on the authorities to arrest the guy with the AK-47, but it's really politically sensitive. They want American business, but they don't want to seem as though they're against their own people."

"So the terrorists holding the plant are Indonesian? That's bad news."

"You're not kidding. Everything's always been so friendly and peaceful. My employees felt lucky to have their jobs."

"Please keep me posted."

"How are you doing today?"

"I'm just fine. I'm getting some good editing done. Mother doesn't know anything about the shots last night, but she's still being protective. She's actually making homemade rolls this morning."

Rob chuckled. "We keep this up, and she'll become a regular Martha Stewart."

"You promise you'll stay in today?"

"It'd be a lot more fun if you'd come play chess with me, but I don't want you in any more danger. A gasoline bomb through the window would burn this thing to a cinder in no time."

"Don't even think it. Hopefully, there's only the one guy left, and he's distracted by his target sailing out of reach. Edward's on his way over to keep you company."

Some promises can't be kept. Rob received a call from Ginger. Now that she supposed the terrorists had been caught, she wanted to get out of rehab. He decided he'd better go visit her and try to calm her down. Knowing he was being tailed by Christensen in case their lone suspect made an appearance, he drove to Renaissance House, preparing to be firm.

Gaining admission to the facility was as bad as trying to visit a prison. They didn't normally accept visitors. Rob had to explain that he was the one who had committed his sister, that now she wanted to leave, and that he was trying to convince her otherwise. He had to wait in the plush, mint green lobby while they telephoned Dr. Updike for permission.

Finally, having been cleared, he was led into a small room furnished in blond wood with sky blue walls. He waited there for Ginger.

"Rob! It's so good to see you!"

Ginger looked terrible. Her eyes were hollow with exhaustion and her hands were shaking. What was happening to his sister?

"Ginger, you look like a ghost," he couldn't keep himself from saying.

"No. Just someone who's drying out and needs a drink."

"You look like you're not sleeping or eating."

"I haven't been doing much of either."

"Why not?"

"No booze."

"You need booze to sleep and eat?"

"You don't understand, Rob. It's like medicating myself when I drink. When I'm sober, all I want to do is die."

Rob stared at his sister. She wasn't exaggerating. Perhaps he'd bitten off more than he could chew in trying to get her to conquer her addiction. "Do they have AA in this place?"

"Of course they do. But I can't go along with it, Rob. God doesn't want trash like me."

He was speechless for a few moments. Finally he managed to say, "Whoever put the idea in your head that you're trash?"

"I did. It's true. If you knew what I was really like, you'd never claim me as your sister. I've already cost you your son."

"So this is about Robbie?"

"Among other things."

"Well, expecting you to stay with Robbie was my error in judgment."

"Oh, come off it. You didn't know I was drunk. I'd started earlier than usual that day. I didn't expect you to go out again."

"Okay. So none of us exercised good judgment. You, me, or Robbie. He's dead. That doesn't mean I want you dead, too."

"You don't know the half of it, and you're never going to find out. So you might as well let me out of here. I'm never going to stop drinking until I die."

"You want to drink yourself to death?"

"There's nothing to live for now that Robbie's gone."

"Yes, there is, Ginger. There's a whole world out there. You have a brilliant mind. How can you pickle it in alcohol?"

"For the last time, Rob, it's the only way I can stand to live with myself. Look, I won't come back to the beach. I'll go live somewhere else."

Rob felt defeated. She had absolutely no intention of staying sober. And she could check herself out at any time. He was surprised she hadn't already. Maybe she didn't know she could. He'd bank on that.

"Well, I've got a terrorist on my tail right now, and Homeland Security is still taking care of me. You'll have to come back to the beach for a while at least. We should have this guy in a day or two. Either that, or I'll be dead."

"The news said they were all caught."

"One wasn't."

Rob recounted the attack of the night before.

"But that's terrible! And here I come whining to you with my troubles. I guess a few days more in here won't hurt me."

"That's the spirit," Rob said, attempting to be cheerful. He recognized now that drying her out was probably a lost cause. Unless Sonia Updike could get through to her. He was still counting on Ginger telling a stranger whatever it was she wouldn't tell him. Maybe without the alcohol, the strain would get to be too much, and she'd spill her secret. He could only hope. Summoning a smile for his sister, he said, "I'll keep you posted, and you hang in there."

Rob left Renaissance House in an even worse frame of mind than when he'd entered. What could Ginger be hiding? What could be so terrible that she'd rather drink herself to death than face it? He couldn't imagine. Then his mind took a horrible leap. In spite of what Chloe had said, *was* it something criminal she could still be prosecuted for? *Was it murder?* He had been thinking only in terms of Stanford. It could have taken place in San Francisco, and Chloe never would have connected it or even remembered it. His heart jolted with sudden anxiety. What if it was some unsolved crime, like a hit-and-run when she was returning a little drunk from a party or a rock concert?

For the first time in his life, he felt real anger towards his parents for not raising them with the Word of Wisdom. What a different life Ginger would have had if she'd never tasted a drop of liquor. And he would have married in the temple. Robbie would be sealed to him, and his anguish would be tempered by that knowledge.

Pulling out his cell phone, he requested a page be put out for

Dr. Updike. She called back just as he was pulling into his parking place. He explained his new theory to her.

"That would account for a lot of things—her sense of extreme guilt, her refusal to talk about it, her desire to punish herself by drinking. What I don't know is how to get her to tell me."

"She might crack under the pressure of not having any liquor. By the way, she seems to be under the impression that only I can get her out of there. Didn't someone read her her rights when she committed herself?"

"Of course. But she wasn't thinking very logically at the time. She feels like she's doing time for Robbie's death. Only you can release her from that."

"She's promised to stay in a few more days."

"Then we'll make the most of them."

Rob searched for signs of the terrorist watching his house but didn't see any. He disarmed Edward's alarm and let himself in. Edward greeted him and listened as he railed against his parents. "They were so caught up in the faux social whirl of Salt Lake City's east side that they took for granted our values would be the same as theirs. They didn't prepare us for life in the world outside Salt Lake."

Chapter Twenty-Three

All the way to San Diego, Chloe found herself thinking not of Luke but of Rob. She remembered the look on his face just before he'd kissed her. It had seemed a natural, intimate gesture, like the kiss she'd given him. He had looked so tender, so dear with his troubled brown eyes and serious mouth. The lamp glancing off his light brown hair had made him look young and very appealing. Almost like the surfer boys she used to hang out with. Luke was a surfer. *Why am I such a sucker?*

She told herself that at least the woman in Luke's past was someone he no longer cared about. Reminding herself once again that the woman in Rob's past was still very much alive in his mind, she came up against the hard rock of truth. Pamela was Robbie's mother. He loved Robbie heart and soul. Chloe would never be first with Rob.

As she passed the Mormon temple in La Jolla, she knew she wanted to be sealed there. That's what she wanted—that kind of security.

So. Rob was out of the question. She was a forever kind of woman.

That line of thinking brought her mind around to the Mormon church. Did she want to listen to the missionaries and learn more? If it meant she could eventually be sealed to her future husband, she did. But not until this mess was cleared up. Hopefully, today would be the day. They would catch their renegade terrorist making a break for the tanker, and Rob would no longer be in danger. She was coming to care a great deal about Edward and didn't believe that he was delusional about something as basic to him as "the gospel."

Remembering the evening she had enjoyed Daddy's presence and the good laugh they had had, she was surprised by the peace that stole upon her while she was driving in the car. It enveloped her heart with warmth. It seemed stronger than thought. Yes. That's how she would describe it—a peace that was stronger than thought. It pervaded every dimension of her. Her doubts faded into the background as she envisioned the temple spires.

When she drew up in front of Diego's, she was still feeling that remarkable calm. Realizing it was time to face Luke, she knew she was unprepared.

He was looking his best, dressed in white shorts for sailing with one of his trademark blue shirts. "Chloe. You look positively radiant," he said, taking her hand and holding it in both of his own.

She came down from her cloud and felt the protective shield go over her heart at the look in Luke's eyes. "Thank you. Is our table ready?"

Peering into the dimness of the little adobe restaurant with the terra-cotta tiled floors, she noted the same Mexican flag adorned the vestibule. It was all coming back to her.

"Yes. They're just waiting for us."

A slim Latino waiter dressed like a bullfighter led them to their table. It was tucked in the corner away from the small windows that provided the only outside light to the interior. Theirs was the last table available. Diego's was already packed with diners.

The waiter handed them their menus and retreated. Chloe opened hers and tried to concentrate while she felt Luke's eyes on her. They made her nervous. How many women had Luke looked at like that? She wanted to trust Luke, but as memories of his deceit flooded her mind, she floundered. Rob had advised her to take her time. She would. Luke wasn't going to like it, but if she couldn't have Rob, she at least wanted someone that was faithful.

"I'll have the huevos rancheros," she said finally.

"I knew it," Luke said. "They were always your favorite, day or night."

"What're you going to have?" Luke hadn't opened his menu.

"Guess."

"The combination plate."

"You remembered." His eyes were soft as he smiled at her. They brought memories that were instinctive.

"Did you come here much with Valerie or Sonia or whoever she was?" she asked.

The soft look turned reproachful. "Never, as a matter of fact. I never wanted to bring her here."

"Even when I was in Corfu?"

"Especially when you were in Corfu. This place will always mean 'Chloe' to me."

She didn't know what to say.

The waiter approached then, bringing a basket of chips and salsa. He took their order. Luke asked for a margarita and raised his eyebrows at her in question.

"I'll have a virgin margarita," she said.

"Why?" Luke asked as the waiter left.

"I'm off liquor for the time being. My mother's an alcoholic, if you remember."

"Yeah. When did that start?"

"It's been getting worse since Daddy died. I'm hoping she'll find a reason to stay on the wagon before I go on my next trip. I'm afraid to leave her right now."

"I'm so sorry to hear that. She doesn't seem the type somehow."

"You never know how you're going to react when you lose someone you love," she said flatly.

"How did you react?" he asked, his eyes probing hers.

"By throwing myself into my work. I've written five books since my father died. But I've found some peace with it now. I was just thinking about him, as a matter of fact."

"What were you thinking?"

"About how much I love him and how close I feel to him sometimes."

"That's wonderful that you're able to feel that kind of peace."

"Yes. It is. I think it's a special gift."

Their drinks arrived. Luke took a sip of his margarita. "Ah, just as good as I remembered."

Chloe sipped hers. She found she didn't miss the tequila. Edward would be proud of her.

"Have there been any more incidents with your friend?" Luke asked.

"As a matter of fact, yes. The night before last. We caught the guy trying to do something to Rob's car."

"We?"

"I was over there playing chess."

Luke raised an eyebrow. "What did he do when you caught him?"

"Rode away on his motorcycle."

"What did he do to the car?"

"He didn't have the chance to do much except start to disable the car alarm."

"Do you often play chess with Rob?" Chloe had the impression that Luke was trying hard to restrain unaccustomed jealousy.

"That was the first time, actually."

"Chloe, are you sure he isn't someone special to you?" Again the eyes probed. She was uncomfortable under his brooding look.

"He's special to me. But not as husband material. He's a widower who is still in love with his wife."

"I really don't think you should hang around with him, then. You could have been hurt last night if that man had been armed."

Chloe looked down into her drink. She had never been very good at hiding things from Luke. She took a sip, glancing over his shoulder at the serape hanging on the wall.

"Chloe?"

"Umm?"

"Was he armed?"

"The bullets didn't hit us." She casually reached for a chip and dunked it in the salsa. Avoiding Luke's eyes, she studied the serape again.

"You could have been killed! Chloe, you can't keep taking these risks!" He reached across the table and grasped her hand. "I couldn't bear to lose you again."

"You don't have me, Luke," she said.

"Not yet."

Chloe simmered at his presumption. "Why don't we talk about something else?" she asked. "Tell me about this new online printing company of yours."

Luke let go of her hand and settled back in his seat as their food was placed before them. They spent the rest of the meal talking about his company.

Chloe became nostalgic once she was on the three-masted teak boat that Luke had found and restored himself. She couldn't believe three years had passed. The trim little sailboat, *Sunshine Girl*, was just the same. Every surface shone with Luke's loving attention. She sat in the bow as Luke turned on the outboard motor and steered them clear of the slip and the marina. Once they were out on the water, she followed the captain's orders, and soon they were sailing against a cerulean blue sky across Mission Bay. It was glorious. All other thoughts floated away on the wind. Sailing had always been this way for her. A complete escape. She'd missed it, she realized. And down here in San Diego she had finally escaped the fog.

Filling her lungs with the sea air, she said, "How could I ever have forgotten how wonderful this is?"

"You haven't been sailing in a while?" he asked, busy securing the mast.

"No."

"When was the last time?"

She turned her face away from him into the wind. Her hair flew out wildly behind her. "When I was with you."

"Oh." He paused. "Well, I didn't do much sailing myself the year I was married. My wife didn't like it." His Viking features were hard as she turned to look at him.

She was shocked. "How could you even think of marrying someone who didn't like to sail? It was practically your life!"

"I don't know. Pretty dumb, wasn't it?"

"Just what was it about her that you did like?"

He grimaced. "The usual. It was a physical thing."

Chloe felt ill. His answer stabbed her heart. He had given her up for a mere physical relationship? That didn't say much for her.

The old wound inside her began to ache. How could she ever marry a man who would compare her to another woman in those most cherished moments? Valerie or whatever her name was must have been sensational for him to have married her.

She suddenly wished she weren't on a boat with this man so she could get away. *Whatever made me think this could be a good idea?*

"If I wasn't enough for you then, I certainly wouldn't be now," she said.

Luke had his hands full, so he couldn't go to her, couldn't touch her. But he said, "You're all I want, Chloe."

"Until your glands strike again, Luke. How could I trust you?"

He was silent. They sailed for ten minutes without speaking. Finally, he said, "I'm willing to go wherever you are, Chloe. I can run my business long distance if I have to. It's Internet-based."

She stared at the water and then looked up at the swelling sail. "So you don't trust yourself, either?"

He cursed. "I just want to be with you. It's not right for people in love to be separated for such long periods of time."

She looked down at the white, canvas deck shoes she had bought that morning. How could she answer that? He was right, and she knew it. The wind blew her hair back into her face, as Luke tacked in the opposite direction. She didn't dare look at him.

"We could try it and see how it works," Luke said.

Chloe should have expected this. "You mean live together?"

"That's the general idea."

Edward's face flashed into her mind, followed closely by Rob's. "No. No, I couldn't do that. I don't want that kind of relationship."

"What do you mean?"

"I've changed, that's all." Her toes curled inside her shoes. "There hasn't been anyone since you, and there won't be until I'm married."

He stared at her. "You're kidding."

"No. I'm perfectly serious."

"But how will we know if it's going to work for us if we don't try it out first?"

"I'm not going to risk that kind of heartbreak again. I've had enough."

"Chloe, what can I do to make you believe in us again?"

Memories continued to cut deeply through her soul, sawing like a dull knife. Those horrible moments on the beach. What he'd said about being unfaithful to her.

"I don't know that there's anything you can do. I don't know if I'll ever get over it."

She looked at Luke then. His eyes were stormy, his jaw set. "There must be something I can do."

They were silent a long time as she thought about what her life was like now, compared to what it had been when she was with Luke. Then it became obvious. She thought of something that might go a long way towards salving her wounds. If he went along with it, there might be hope for them after all. "What do you think of religion, Luke? We never discussed it."

He appeared puzzled. "I didn't think you had a religion."

"But what's your religion?"

"I don't really have one." He adjusted the sails again.

"Do you believe in God?"

"I suppose so. I've never really thought about it much."

"Would you consider thinking about it?"

"What exactly are you asking, Chloe?"

"I've discovered that I believe in God and Jesus Christ." She felt suddenly exposed, telling Luke her innermost thoughts. This really hadn't been a good idea. Squirming mentally, she asked, "Why don't we start back?"

"We can, if you like. Here, help me." They brought the boat about, heading back towards the marina.

"So when did you make this discovery?" he asked.

His casual tone made her cautious. "It was a process."

"And you'd like it if I'd go through this process? It would make you feel more secure?"

"It would help," she admitted. "It's a big part of who I am now."

Luke looked at her curiously. "What brought this about?"

"Oh, a lot of things. I needed hope in my life, and I found out how to get it."

"I can see this means a lot to you."

"More than just about anything."

"And you're sure about it? It's not just wishful thinking?"

Chloe thought about her own doubts. Then she weighed them against what she had felt in the car that day. A peace stronger than thought.

"No. It's not just wishful thinking. It's something very real."

"What do you want me to do?" Luke asked. There was resignation in his voice.

"I'd like you to talk to my friend Edward Petersen. He's a wonderful man. He's the one who helped me find hope."

"Okay. If you think it'll help, I'll give it a try. When do you want me to talk to him?"

"I'll have to check with Edward. I don't know what he's doing this weekend."

"You're really anxious about this aren't you?"

"I just want to see if it's going to work. You might not want the person I've become."

"I can't imagine that. The more I'm with you, the more I remember, and the sorrier I am for what happened. I can see that it's been harder on you than I ever imagined."

"I don't take things lightly."

"Yes, I know. In the end that's why I chose to deprive myself of you. I couldn't deceive you any longer."

"Let's not talk about that. It hurts too much." Chloe wondered if it would always hurt too much.

"Yes, it does."

Another silence overtook them. Then he said, "You said your next book would be set in New Zealand. What did you have in mind?"

Though she was far from sure about her feelings or her future now, they talked about New Zealand the rest of the way back to the marina.

CHAPTER TWENTY-FOUR

Wednesday morning Rob woke feeling surprisingly refreshed. After he had updated Edward on the situation with the terrorists and the oil tanker the previous evening, he and Edward had begun reading the Book of Mormon together. Its distant familiarity had warmed Rob's heart. He placed a call to Agent Christensen immediately after his shower.

"This is Rob Stevens. Was there any activity overnight?"

"Nothing reported."

"No one followed me to Renaissance House?"

"No. I really think he's trying to figure out how to get to that tanker."

"Any luck finding the bomb?"

"No, but the tanker is far enough out now that we've dropped anchor and what little crew they needed to sail her is being evacuated."

"An oil spill of that magnitude would be awful but more preferable than blowing up the ship in port with a full crew."

"Fire would burn off a lot of the oil."

"So your main concern is catching this guy."

"Yeah."

As Rob was checking his morning e-mail, he was surprised to finally hear back from Brooke Sampson, the only friend he knew had still been in touch with Pamela when she died.

> Rob:
>
> Sorry, I've been away from my computer on a cruise. Just got your e-mail. Am so sorry to hear Ginger is ill. Can you tell me where she is so I can go visit her? I haven't seen her in years.
>
> Best regards,
> Brooke

The thought that had been niggling in his mind suddenly assailed him. What if Rick knew that what Ginger had done was criminal? What if Brooke had known as well? What if he and Brooke were trying to protect her by their silence? Rob was in a quandary as to how to answer the e-mail. Brooke couldn't visit Ginger. But he needed her help. How much of Ginger's condition should he reveal?

Brooke had been a friend of Pamela's. Perhaps she already knew Ginger was an alcoholic. He finally composed an e-mail:

> Brooke:
> I'd like to talk to you about some things in person. I have plans for the Fourth tomorrow, but how about Friday? Let me know what you think. I'm sure you'll agree that we need to help Ginger by helping her to make peace with her past.
>
> Rob

During the rest of the day he worked, contacting all of his

developers and proposing that they open for business again on Monday. They were in the middle of developing the hardware for a new Nokia phone, and he didn't want to postpone it any longer.

He wanted to talk to someone. He knew Chloe was sailing with Luke, and his hands balled into fists of tension whenever he thought of it. Edward had had something to do in the temple that day, but he had said he would be home by four. May he should give him a call and find out about the details for the barbeque tomorrow. Day zero for the terrorist, as far as they knew. Would they be able to see any explosion from the shore? And after that, would the remaining terrorist come after him as vengeance for his captured coconspirators?

"Come on over about two tomorrow," Edward told him. "Anthony's arriving late tonight, and he and the boys will be sleeping in. That'll give him a chance to have a swim in the late morning. The boys will be surfing. We can talk, and you two can get to know one another. Maybe you can even show him your place. We'll be barbecuing late in the afternoon, when the boys come in."

"Sounds good to me."

"Why don't you give Chloe and Martha a call and see if they can join us for the barbecue—say around four?"

"You want me to invite them?"

"If you don't mind. I'm having dinner with friends in a few minutes. I was just on my way out the door."

"Okay. I'll call Chloe." Then he had a thought. "Edward, I forgot." He slapped his forehead. "I could put your whole family in danger. I'd better not come. Whether that terrorist succeeds in his larger mission, I think he still wants revenge for his fallen comrades."

"Well, I've got faith in your agent," Edward told him. "You can't stay by yourself all the time."

"But this terrorist may think taking out your whole family was a just revenge. Or he may not care about collateral damage."

"We've got the rent-a-cop back at the gate. He can't get in."

For a minute, this assuaged Rob. Then he thought of a new angle. "Edward, he could come by sea, dock his boat at the city pier, and walk up here on the beach."

"Well, we've got till tomorrow. Let's see what happens, okay?"

"Are you sure?"

"I'm sure."

Rob said, "I'll leave the party before it gets dark."

"If you insist. But I agree you're likely to be safer during the day."

After he hung up, Rob went back and forth in his mind about whether he ought to go. Finally, he decided that the guy who was after him had no advance notice of his plans and wouldn't be able to plant a bomb without the agent noticing it. They would be on Edward's patio. No one could sneak in carrying a gun without the agent catching him. It ought to be pretty safe.

He put off calling Chloe, afraid he would succumb to the desire to invite her over to play chess. Instead, he microwaved his dinner and then vacuumed the house in preparation for its potential buyer. After cleaning the bathrooms, he decided to dust. He needed to have his usual cleaning lady come in, but he would wait until this business with his potential killer was cleared up. He didn't want her involved in any way.

Finally, at about nine P.M., Rob phoned Chloe.

"Rob," she said softly. He could hear her close a door.

"Can you talk a minute?" he asked cautiously.

"Of course. What do you need?"

"Edward's having a barbecue for the Fourth tomorrow. His son is coming down from Salt Lake. He wants to know if you and your mother can come around four."

She responded immediately. "Yes, of course. Is there anything I can bring?"

"You'll have to call him in the morning and ask him. He's out for the evening."

"No more incidents?"

"No. I'm being properly looked after. So far, our man hasn't made an appearance. The tanker's far enough out to sea that if it explodes, the worst that can happen is a massive oil slick. And a lot of that would be burned by fire."

He was dying of curiosity about her day. "How was sailing?"

"It was a beautiful day for it."

"Oh." He wanted more information but couldn't think of what to say. Finally, he asked, "Is Luke coming up for the Fourth?"

"That depends," she said. "Do you think Edward would mind?"

That didn't sound good. Maybe she was trying to get Edward to interest the man in spiritual matters. But why wasn't that good? He told himself that he wanted Chloe to be happy. "Edward's son and grandchildren will be here for the weekend, but I'm sure that will be fine. I'll let him know."

"Oh." The single syllable sounded disappointed. "Edward might not have time for Luke. But I'd still like for them to meet."

"I see."

"I'm not sure if Luke will really be interested in this spiritual search of mine," she rushed to say. "I just thought I'd give it a try. I've decided I can't risk the sense of loss my mother has felt since she lost my father. If I marry, it will have to be forever."

Rob hung up a few moments later with a hollow feeling in his chest. He'd enjoyed his spiritual search with Chloe. He wasn't ready to admit a third person into their quest.

Why? After a while, he was forced to admit that he liked the intimacy it created between them. An intimacy he hadn't shared with anyone. Ever. To be truthful, he hungered for it. And now it looked as though she were going to share that intimacy with someone else. Someone who had broken her heart, no less. Someone who didn't deserve her.

Feeling deeply disturbed, he went in search of the Book of Mormon Edward had given him. Didn't he need to be sealed to Pamela so he could be sealed to Robbie? But such a sealing would mean nothing because she was an adulteress. What was he to do? He must talk to Edward about this.

If he were honest, he would have to say that thoughts of Chloe were becoming more than a balm. They were becoming like honey on warm, new-baked bread. Comfortable, sweet, substantial. But if he wanted Robbie, was there a place for another woman in his life?

~

Edward's son Anthony was tall and broad-shouldered. He looked to be in his mid-forties with blond hair and a good tan that his open shirt showed off—he was a natural outdoorsman. For the first time, Rob wondered where Anthony's wife was. She hadn't ac-companied them. Then he noticed the man wore no wedding ring.

"Anthony, this is my good friend, Rob Stevens. Rob, Anthony."

The two men shook hands and sat down. Edward's deck had been decorated for the celebration with red-, white-, and blue-striped furniture, and the glassed-in patio sat right up against the rocks over the ocean.

"So you're interested in selling your house?" Anthony asked.

"Yes. The sooner the better. There's nothing wrong with the house or the development. It's just that I want to relocate inland."

Anthony smiled sympathetically. "I hope you don't mind, but Dad told me about your son. I'm sorry. What an awful thing to happen. I'd want to move, too. In fact, coming down here is kind of an escape for me. My wife died a couple of years ago. I don't like spending holidays alone with the boys. It'd be handy to have a place close to Dad so we wouldn't have to impose on him all the time."

A fellow widower. Rob shrugged. "It's rough. There's no doubt about it."

"Yeah, I understand you lost your wife, too. Mine died of ovarian cancer. The boys were just coming into their teens. It's been quite a journey."

"That's one way of looking at it, I suppose." Rob was surprised how comfortable he felt with this man.

"What's your business, Rob?"

"Smart phone circuit boards. I've got a plant in Indonesia. I understand you're a lawyer."

"Yeah. Pretty demanding career for a widower."

They talked business for a while. Edward brought them out some lemonade.

"So where's your Homeland Security agent stashing himself?" Edward asked. "I don't see him anywhere."

"I've got no idea. Probably out in the parking lot covering the house. I just go on faith that he's there somewhere."

"Homeland Security agent?" Anthony asked. "Dad, you didn't say anything about that."

"I figured I'd leave Rob some of his own story to tell."

Rob related the events of the past week and a half.

"So we're expecting an explosion of an oil tanker at sea? And then this guy is going to stick around for revenge on you? That's truly bizarre. I'm glad you called in Homeland."

"I'm the bait in a trap," Rob said. "I just wish this guy would make his next move so we can catch him."

Anthony shook his head. "It'd be hard to know what to wish for. It must be like waiting for the other shoe to drop."

Rob said, "I sure hope I'm not endangering your family by being with you today."

"Like I said already, I've got faith in your agent. Let's try to forget about it for a little while," Edward said.

Rob shook his head. "It's impossible. The only time I seem to be able to forget about it is when I'm worrying about something else or reading the Book of Mormon."

"You're reading the Book of Mormon?" Anthony asked, interest sparking in his eyes.

"Yes. I'm clear through Mosiah. I'm a lapsed Mormon. Since high school. I've never read it before."

"And how's it coming?" Edward asked.

"It's about the only thing that's bringing me any peace right now."

"I'm glad it's doing that."

"Yes. I find myself hoping it's true. I really want to be sealed to my family."

"I can understand that," Anthony said. "That's the only thing that's kept me going until recently. The fact that I'm sealed to Gretchen."

"What do you mean 'until recently'?" Edward inquired. "Has something happened that I don't know about?"

"I've met someone, Dad."

"So you're thinking of marrying again, and you've never said anything to me?"

"Well, nothing's for sure yet. But the boys love her."

"But you've been sealed!" Rob found himself protesting. Then he said, "I'm sorry. I don't know what I was thinking. It's none of my business."

There was an uncomfortable silence.

Finally, Rob said, "Well, what about coming over to see my place now? It would be safe. There's someone watching it."

"Yeah. That'd be great. The boys won't be in from surfing until it's time to eat."

Anthony loved the house. "How soon do you want to sell?"

"Well, I should probably wait until they catch this guy. If by any chance he gets me first, the house would go to Ginger, my sister. I'd want her to have a place to stay."

"Oh, does she live with you?"

Rob explained about Ginger and her rehab.

"I'm sorry to hear that. Boy, you sure have your share of problems right now."

"Hopefully, HS will have this guy soon. They've put an army on it."

"Why don't you call me when things get settled down? We can talk about price and so on then. I'm definitely interested."

By the time Chloe, Luke, and Martha arrived, two tall, thin teenaged boys had joined the party. Even though they were two years apart, at thirteen and fifteen they were virtually indistinguishable. Both had their father's blond hair, green eyes, and tan. Their names were Jeff and Joey.

Chloe appeared festive in white capri pants and a royal blue T-shirt. Martha had gone all out and appeared to have had her hair done, as well as her talon-like fingernails, which were red, white, and blue. Her floor-length gored skirt was topped with a gauzy, off-the-shoulder red blouse, and she had tied a cobalt scarf around her neck. Rob was beginning to believe she was one in a million. Just like Chloe, who was looking him over.

"You seem to be all right," she said.

"Yes, and you have a sunburn."

She laughed. "My own fault. I forgot the sunblock." Then, "Everyone, this is Luke, a friend of mine."

Her friend was dressed in knee-length yellow shorts and a white Ralph Lauren polo shirt. He began the round of handshaking.

Martha, Chloe, and Luke were introduced to Anthony and the boys.

Anthony said, "Dad tells me you're a best-selling author."

She looked a bit embarrassed. "Yes, I suppose I am. At least, I write books."

"And you've lived all over the world?"

Rob wondered if Edward had invited Chloe in an attempt to be matchmaker for his son. It appeared he'd given her quite a buildup. Anthony was looking at her with definite interest. Rob found himself annoyed.

"Chloe's my guardian angel," he said. He wished he could shock Anthony and Luke with Chloe and Rosemary's antiterrorist exploits, but he settled for the tamer action. "She saved my life the other night."

"Chloe, child!" her mother exclaimed. "You didn't tell me about this!"

"How so?" Anthony asked.

Chloe said, "It was nothing. Rob likes to exaggerate. He was walking me home from his house when we saw a guy doing something to Rob's car. The guy drove off on his motorcycle."

"Oh, you were there?" Anthony asked. "You both could have been killed if he'd had a gun."

"He did—and missed," she said simply. "By the way, Rob, where is your HS agent?"

"Safely hidden somewhere close by. Edward seems to think we're safe, but now, with you and the kids here . . ."

"But I'm your guardian angel." She laughed. There was an impish look in her eyes when she looked at him, and he felt his annoyance with Anthony and Luke fade.

They had steaks grilled on the barbeque, potato salad, and corn on the cob. While Luke tried to ingratiate himself with Martha, Rob entertained the teenagers by showing them all the bells and whistles on his smart phone.

"Boy, I love some of the apps you've got! I didn't know they existed!" Joey said.

Jeff exclaimed. "Dad, I've got to have one of these. This is almost as cool as the iPhone you won't let me have."

"As soon as you get straight A's," Anthony told his son.

The boys, having been primed by their grandfather, asked Chloe to tell them about her favorite place to live.

"Definitely Cinque Terre. I would move there in a second if I could persuade my mother to come along."

"Where in the world is Cinque Terre? I've never heard of it," Anthony asked.

"It's only recently become a tourist destination. It's actually five villages along a really rugged patch of Italian coastline. Now you can approach it by a slow little train from Florence, but until recently, you could only get there by water. It's gorgeous and, so far, unspoiled."

"Wait a minute," Anthony exclaimed. "Are you the Chloe Greene who wrote that whodunit that took place in Lucca?"

"Yes. Several years ago."

"I read it in the hospital when Gretchen was sick. I remember how much I enjoyed it. It was a great balm to read something so enthralling that it took me away from my troubles."

Rob felt his annoyance return. Why had he never realized the extent of Chloe's fame?

"What did you like the most about Lucca?" Rob asked her, hoping he didn't sound like a Johnny-come-lately.

"Oh, lots of things. It's like a village or a small city. You have to park outside the city walls and go through this spooky tunnel to get inside. The whole place simply breathes Puccini and silk—its two claims to fame. Plus without the cars and without a lot of tourists, it's a gem of a town—little narrow streets. Apartments with window boxes. And enormous churches. But by far my favorite things were the nightly Puccini concerts. I never missed one."

"Who's Puccini?" young Jeff asked.

"The composer of the most sublime opera ever sung. There's no evidence of it, but I think I have Italian blood in my veins."

"No, honey bunch," her mother said. "You've got Texans that go back to the Alamo and Jewish intellectuals from Eastern Europe. No Catholics whatsoever."

"Which opera?" Joey asked.

To Rob's surprise, Chloe cleared her throat, and began Musetta's comic song from *La Bohème*, acting so well that you could envision her vanity and swishing skirts as she teased first one man and then the other.

Anthony's eyes were on her. Had he forgotten about his special friend in Salt Lake City?

"Where did you come by such a lovely voice?"

"Daddy was an opera fanatic. He insisted I take voice lessons. But I just sing for fun."

It occurred to Rob that Chloe would have had plenty of time to meet many men from all over the world during her career. Was she promiscuous? No. He couldn't possibly taint her with that word. The woman he was coming to understand would treat a sexual relationship as something almost holy. Despite her resemblance to a character in a famous nude painting, she, like that Venus on the half-shell, seemed ethereal and pure.

Suddenly, he needed to establish some common ground with her. "She doesn't just write mysteries. She has written a novel, which I'm reading, about Prague coming into the post-Communist era. She makes good use of her anthropology degree in it."

Chloe laughed again. Rob had never seen her so happy. Was it Anthony or Luke? Or did he himself just have a depressing effect on her? He had to admit that none of their encounters had been under terribly jolly circumstances.

Just then, his cell phone rang. He excused himself and walked to a corner of the patio.

"Rob, this is Brooke Sampson. Have I called at a bad time?"

"No," he said. He heard the party going on behind his back. No one would miss him.

"So what can you tell me about Ginger? I'm ashamed I've kind of lost track of her since Pamela died."

"I didn't know you and Pamela ever saw Ginger."

"Oh, we didn't. But Pamela kept me updated on her. Your sister really didn't want anything to do with the two of us, you know. Everything we knew about her was through you."

"Really? Weren't you good friends once?"

"Yes. That was the odd thing. Ginger just withdrew from everyone. Is she still that way?"

"Very much so. I suppose you know she's an alcoholic?"

"Yes. I figured as much. What's wrong with her now?"

"She's trying to dry out. But she's putting up quite a fight. Her therapist and I have decided that there must have been a trauma in her past. Do you know anything that could help?"

"You're going behind her back?"

"Yes. It's the only way. She won't talk."

"Well, I'm afraid I can't help you. And if Ginger doesn't want to talk, I think you should leave her alone."

"But she's drinking herself to death."

"It's her life."

Rob wondered why the woman had bothered to call him if she cared so little for Ginger.

"Where is she staying, anyway?" Brooke asked.

For some reason, Rob didn't want to tell her. Maybe because she seemed so uncaring.

"I'm afraid I can't tell you that," he said, vaguely ashamed of his spitefulness.

"Oh, well, I don't suppose they'd let me see her anyway. It was just an idle thought. Call it my attempt at a good deed for the day."

"No. I'm sure they wouldn't let you in. But thanks for your call."

"I'd still like to go ahead and meet you tomorrow. There are probably some things you should know about Rick. You know, her old boyfriend?"

"Great. Where would you like to meet?"

"How about the Dana Point Marina? One o'clock?"

He hung up and joined the party just in time to see Luke sidle up to Chloe, put his arm around her, and whisper something in her ear.

She whispered back fiercely, but he could hear her. "This beach? Are you crazy? Don't you have any shred of memory about the last time we walked here?"

Jeff was talking about something called EFY and how it was to-tally awesome. A pang hit Rob as he looked at the young surfer. Robbie would never be that age. He would never surf, never have a smart phone, never go to Europe. A wave of grief swept Rob. This was the first of many holidays he would spend without his son.

Then Chloe was at his elbow, her eyes questioning.

"More bad news?" she asked, as the boys regaled their grandfather with tales of their latest backpacking trek.

He shook his head. "Not really. That was Brooke Sampson, one of Ginger's former friends. I'm meeting her tomorrow."

"Was she any help?"

"She has something to tell me about Rick that she thinks might be helpful." Then, because he couldn't keep himself from doing it, he asked, "Join me for lunch first?"

"Sure. I'd love it."

"Ginger was the one who ended the relationship, she says. Probably because of whatever it was that drove her to drink. But Rick might know what that was. I'm beginning to think that Ginger was closer to him than to anyone else."

"I guess you should try to talk to him," Chloe agreed.

Rob felt consoled by her nearness and her concern. He pulled her hand into the crook of his elbow and held it there. She didn't seem to mind.

"Hey, you two! What plots are you hatching?" Anthony teased, breaking in on their reverie.

"We're planning on running away to Cinque Terre and leaving all this madness behind," Rob said, forcing a grin.

"I've got a better idea," said Edward. "Why don't you two join us for church this Sunday?"

Chloe and Rob looked at one another. "Why not?" Chloe said.

"I'm game," Rob agreed, "if you don't mind a random HS agent tagging along."

"Tell him he'll need a tie," Edward said with a laugh.

And so the day passed, and it was only when they were watching fireworks that Rob realized he had forgotten to leave at dark and that there had been no visible sign of a tanker blowing up out at sea. Had the terrorist failed?

If so, he would be out for revenge, big time.

Rob observed Luke, Chloe, and Martha watching the bursts of spangled color in the sky. He really didn't know what he was going to do. It was becoming clearer and clearer to him that he couldn't possibly watch Chloe marry Luke. Yet how could he choose Chloe over Robbie?

CHAPTER TWENTY-FIVE

When all the guests were gone, Rob cornered Edward in his kitchen, grabbed a towel, and began drying dishes as he presented him with his dilemma. "If I become worthy to go to the temple," he said, "I'm certain you're aware that I want to be sealed to Robbie."

"Of course."

"So, Edward, I'm torn. I'm falling in love with Chloe, as you may have noticed."

"Relax, son. Don't worry about that Luke character. He had his chance and blew it. I don't know why in the world she brought him today."

"You were hoping to interest Anthony in her. Admit it."

"Well, I wasn't sure how stuck you were on Pamela. I thought a little present-day rivalry might change your mind."

"What do you mean?"

"If Chloe joins the Church, which I think will eventually

happen, given her purity of spirit, I wanted you to seriously consider the possibility of marrying her in the temple."

"Don't you see that I'd already thought of that?"

"Well, then." Edward stopped washing dishes and turned to face him. "What's the problem?"

"If I have to choose between being sealed to my son and being sealed to Chloe, I have to choose Robbie."

Edward took the towel from him, dried his hands, and led him back outside onto the porch. Anthony and his boys were driving over to Dana Point for the big fireworks show that would begin at ten.

"You've got something mixed up here. Why don't you explain your reasoning?"

"Well, Pamela is Robbie's mother. But she wasn't a good wife— she cheated on me for nine years. I don't want to be sealed to her, but don't I have to be, if I am going to be sealed to Robbie?"

"No, Rob. Robbie wasn't born into a forever marriage. You were never sealed to Pamela. That means you can be married to someone else—hopefully our little firecracker, Chloe—and have Robbie sealed into your eternal family."

Rob felt a tremendous load lift from his chest. He could now put Pamela and her deceit behind him forever. And, if Chloe decided, in her own time, that she could choose The Church of Jesus Christ of Latter-day Saints, then that would mean she could be Rob's wife and Robbie's mother forever.

Bouncing up, he said, "Let's go finish those dishes."

"Don't let the euphoria cause you to let your guard down. There's still someone out there who apparently wants you very dead," Edward reminded him.

"What are you?" Rob asked with a grin. "A spoilsport?"

Despite the fact that it was now July, the fog hung on worse than ever, and the sky was merely pale pink. Chloe felt uncomfortable being with Luke after all the possessiveness he had shown during the day. Grateful for her mother's presence, she maintained a safe distance between Luke's patio chair and hers. His touch disturbed her. It had made her uncomfortable in front of Rob. And that disturbed her. Rob knew about Luke. He had Pamela. And yet, hadn't she caught herself wishing several times that day that Luke's being there would bother him? Make him jealous? The thought made her squirm. *I'm using Luke, and it's not fair to him.*

"Thanks for coming up here today so we could spend the holiday with Mother. I know you would rather have been on your boat."

Luke looked at Martha. "I'd say you're welcome, but I'm not at all sure you appreciated it, did you, Martha?"

"I'd just as soon you walked out of our lives again, Luke," Martha said.

"Mother! Will you stop being so impossible?" Chloe asked, forcing a laugh. "Luke will think you don't like him."

"I'd like him a lot more if he weren't trying to attach himself to you," Martha said.

"Please just give me a chance, Martha," Luke said. "I've been honest. I know I've messed up. But I'm going to do my best to prove I've changed. I never stopped loving Chloe."

"Well, you had a peculiar way of showing it. And I've watched her suffer because of it. I don't intend to watch it happen again."

"You won't have to, because she's not going to suffer. I'm committed for the long haul. I've told Chloe I'll move my business wherever she is."

"And don't I have something to say about all of this?" Chloe asked, irritated anew at his presumption. "You're talking about me as though I weren't here. As though my opinion is of no consequence." She paused and looked at both of them. "Well, I can tell you this, I'm the one who's going to make the decision about what to do with my life. Mother, I know you mean well, and Luke, I know you do, too, but it's *my* life."

Chloe's mother rose. "Well, I can see that I might as well go in the house."

Hating for her mother to leave them alone and yet disliking the tension, Chloe said, "I won't be long, Mother."

As soon as she had gone, Luke said, "You weren't kidding, were you? You're not ready to come back to me yet. Am I going to have to win your approval in a joust with Rob or something?"

"Rob has nothing to do with it. And I'd already thought of Mother's objections. I'm plenty wary on my own, Luke. You know that."

"Then why are you even seeing me?" he asked, his eyes searching hers.

"To see if there's anything left that's strong enough to make me think I could trust you again."

"So you think it's possible?"

"I once loved you with all my heart, Luke. I held nothing back. You were the first and the last. It's not a matter of choice. I simply haven't been able to love since. There's only one thing I know that can heal me enough to love you again."

"What's that?" he asked, his eyes turning eager.

"The love of God. It's the only thing that brings me peace." She said this softly, almost pleadingly.

"And this is where the Mormon church comes in?"

"Yes. I want to be sealed to my husband forever in one of their temples. You couldn't even manage a relationship before, not to mention a forever marriage."

"But you're not even a member!"

"I'm working on it."

"And you want me to be a member, too?"

"I want to share this with my husband, whoever that may be."

A look of soberness veiled Luke's former enthusiasm. "You know I couldn't become a member just for you. It's a huge commitment—a whole change of lifestyle. It wouldn't be right if I couldn't commit myself wholeheartedly."

"I know that. I hope you can share these things with me, Luke. Seriously, it's the only way things could work again between us."

He drew a breath. "Well, if it means that much to you, I'll certainly try it. Though I must say it would be a stretch."

"Maybe not as much of one as you think. Rob is very accepting of it."

"Rob? He is? He's been studying it?" Luke seemed a little frantic.

"He's already a member." She felt slightly guilty for enlisting his obvious jealousy in her cause. But when Luke began studying the Church, he would see for himself that it was worthy of investigation. She hoped.

"When can I begin?"

"Well, there are missionaries. They can probably teach you in San Diego. But I would like you to speak to Edward first. He's the one who paved the way for me. I wouldn't have to be there if you felt like it was putting too much pressure on you."

"But I *want* you to be there. I want to share this with you."

"Okay. I'll see about Monday after Edward's kids are gone, if that would be all right with you."

"I'll make sure it's all right. How soon will you know?"

"I'll call you after I've spoken to Edward."

Luke pulled out his wallet and extracted a business card. "Here's my cell number."

"Thanks."

They sat in silence for a few moments listening to the surf, watching the shrouded sunset. Then Luke said, "There's something that's been driving me crazy all day." He took her hand. "Chloe, may I kiss you?"

She instinctively recoiled. "Not yet, Luke."

Disappointment deepened the blue of his eyes. "Have you turned to ice?"

"No. I just don't want to awaken those feelings yet, because I'm *not* made of ice." She looked at him earnestly, willing him to understand. Whatever her head told her, she feared her attraction to Luke was the fatal kind. *Would it always be there?*

"I hope you change your mind soon."

He caressed her cheek and thus awakened the memory of Rob doing the same thing. Is that how it was going to be? Luke running a poor second, because she couldn't have Rob? She hoped not. She sincerely hoped not.

On Friday, Rob woke wearily. Then his conversation with Edward came back to him, and he remembered he was having lunch with Chloe. Christensen had informed him last night that there had been no explosion, just as Rob had suspected. What's more, one of the idiots Chloe and Rosemary had captured had broken down under questioning. He had told them where the bomb was, "because it doesn't make any difference now." He swore there was no one left to detonate it.

That left everyone puzzled. If it wasn't one of the terrorists who had been fiddling with his car and let off that shot the other night, who in the world was it? Did he have yet another enemy?

He knew it was irrational, but his mind flew to Rick Niebolt. He was the only one who hadn't been in touch. He was Ginger's old boyfriend and someone she might want to protect. Perhaps they had committed some crime together? His mind went back to the hit-and-run scenario. Perhaps that was what Brooke wanted to speak to him about.

Heaving himself out of bed, he realized it felt great not to have Islamic extremists after him anymore. It would be much easier to tackle Niebolt. And it was almost heaven without a bodyguard. Christensen had been very happy to close the case. There was no oil slick in the Pacific, either. Rob knew the agent still suspected him of breaking and entering into the terrorist hive and carrying out the Taser job. Thank heaven for Edward's rock-solid alibi. It didn't hurt that he was a Mormon. Homeland Security, the FBI, and the CIA were partial to Mormons because of their high moral standards, Edward had told him later.

After showering, Rob dressed and ate a bowl of Honey Nut Cheerios. Robbie's favorite. He should probably switch to something else, but he couldn't bring himself to do it. It was like his morning salute to his son.

Laptop in hand, he disarmed the alarm and went out the door, remembering to rearm it. Never had he suspected he would so rely on it. Starting up the rented Audi, he wondered how long it would be before his Porsche was ready. For the first time, he drove to his new office. When he opened his e-mail, he was pleased to see that a nonviolent Islamic cleric was trying to talk down the group that had been holding his Jakarta operation hostage. If he was unsuccessful, the Indonesians had decided to remove the insurgents by force. Once that took place, Rob needed only to train another manager, and all the employees were anxious to resume work. Another problem solved.

There remained only Niebolt, whom he planned to tackle after his lunch with Chloe and his talk with Brooke.

Hope. Could it possibly be that Chloe and Robbie could both be his?

Chloe saw Rob standing by the railing across from the Fisherman's Cave. He looked awfully good to her, standing there in his khakis with his yellow polo knit shirt and his light brown hair gleaming in the sun. She could barely restrain herself from embracing him in her relief that he was still alive.

His eyes were soft as he grabbed for her hands. "It's so good to see you."

She threw restraint to the winds and gave him a hug. He was solid and comfortable, and he hugged her back.

"I have a feeling that you're going to find out all the answers from this Brooke woman today. Then you will finally be safe. It must be such a relief." She disengaged herself from his arms and looked into his eyes that were still warm and caring. Much *too* warm. She took a step back. They headed down the stairs towards the marina for a walk before lunch. Chloe was suddenly conscious of every detail. Rob's proximity, the damp fog that was cooling her uncomfortably blushing cheeks, the slight breeze off the water, the vista of yachts whose masts disappeared into the mist. And the gulls. How often she had wished she were a seagull, free to fly and swoop down and fly again. It was the freedom from being earthbound that she had sought in her travels.

"Are you absolutely sure it was Niebolt who was after you?" she couldn't help asking.

"Who else could it be?"

"But why?" Chloe wondered.

"When the police pick him up, I predict Ginger will crack. Especially because I think Brooke is going to give me the key."

Chloe went over the evidence in her mind. She supposed he was right. There didn't seem to be any other option.

"I want Ginger to face whatever it is and overcome it," Rob said.

They had reached the boardwalk beside the marina and began walking along it. The big white boats with their blue canvas covers floated side by side. Chloe found herself wishing she and Rob could just hijack one of them and take off over the horizon, leaving Niebolt, Ginger, and Luke behind. Sailing had always seemed so heavenly and enchanting to her. She loved the variations of the sea, water, cloud, and sky. It was hard to believe there could be evil in such a world.

"I talked to Edward yesterday," Rob said. "He told me something very interesting."

"What was that?" Chloe wondered at the abrupt, seemingly random change in the conversation.

"I don't have to be sealed to Pamela in order to be sealed to Robbie, Chloe."

He looked at her, his chocolatey brown eyes warm and caring.

She was confused. "But I thought you wanted to be sealed to Pamela."

"Our marriage was never great, and I found out the other day that she'd been cheating on me with an old boyfriend since Robbie was born. You would never do that in a million years, would you? Whether you choose me or choose Luke, I know you'll be faithful."

While she was trying to take in his words and their implications, Rob's cell phone rang.

What is he telling me? Why is there suddenly so much love in his face?

The phone kept ringing, but he just kept looking at her, and she felt they were absolutely alone in the world. Then he slowly reached into his pocket and took out the phone, reading the caller ID.

"Brooke Sampson," he said. "I'd better take this. I'm sorry. I'll put it on speaker."

"Rob, I'm waiting for you down by the gate to Pier 17. Who's that you're with?"

"Chloe Greene. I thought our appointment wasn't until one. We were going to have lunch first."

"Well, sorry to interrupt, but I have something to do later. I was going to see if we could move it up."

Exasperated, Rob rolled his eyes at Chloe as he answered, "Let me just take Chloe up to the restaurant so she can get in line to be seated. I'll be with you in a minute or so."

"Yeah, that's fine. I have a long story to tell you. That's why I insisted on the in-person meeting."

"Okay. How will I know you?"

"I've got bright red hair, and I'm wearing a yellow tunic."

"Got it."

"Okay. See you."

"Right."

He hung up and shrugged at Chloe. "I've got too much to say to you to do it in a hurry. Would you mind going into the restaurant and waiting for me? I don't know if she'll talk in front of a stranger."

Chloe nodded. "This could be the break you're waiting for to nail Niebolt. I'll watch from the restaurant."

As she sat at the window of the Fisherman's Cave, Chloe could smell the lobster and crab cooking. Her heart was singing. She had worked it all out. Robbie could be sealed to another mother. To her, in fact. Could Rob have been on the point of proposing? She became lost in dreams of the San Diego temple with its magical spires, herself in a wedding dress of clean, elegant lines, with a mantilla over her hair styled in a simple French twist . . . *her hair? She must be dreaming!* It wasn't at all hard to imagine Rob in a tuxedo. She would have a bouquet of lilies of the valley.

There. That must be Brooke Sampson. Red hair. Yellow tunic. She hoped their conversation would be short.

What was happening? The woman was walking closely behind Rob toward one of the short piers. She had one arm around him, and the other was stuck against the middle of his back. He was walking haltingly, reluctantly.

In a flash, Chloe realized what she was seeing. Standing, she craned her neck for a better view. Then she ran out of the restaurant.

Brooke Sampson has a gun against Rob's spine! She must be leading him to a boat. Was she the criminal who had been trying to kill him? Once she got out onto the water, she could kill him and dump him into the ocean!

Chloe's first impulse was to run outside and stop the woman. A voice spoke urgently to her mind. *Call the police!*

Dialing 911 on her cell phone, she spoke desperately to the dispatcher, "Have you got anyone near the Dana Point Marina? A woman is forcing my fiancé onto a boat with a gun at his back. She's tried to kill him before!"

"I'll get someone over there right away, but it might not be soon enough," the dispatcher said. Her voice was dry and matter-of-fact. "Try to follow the woman and get the name of the boat. Keep this line open. The police are on their way. Does your fiancé have a cell phone?"

"Yes!" Chloe failed to see that this was relevant. Rob could hardly take calls. Clutching the phone to her ear, Chloe sprinted out of the restaurant and down the wooden steps to the pier. In her haste, she tripped when her sandal caught the stair, and she fell on her face. Kindly pedestrians stopped to help her, penning her in.

"Are you hurt?"

"No, thank you, I've got to run. Sorry. Thank you."

When she oriented herself, she saw that Brooke had entered the gate to a pier that seemed impossibly far away. Pain shot through Chloe's knee, and she was reduced to a hobble. *I'm not going to make it! But I have to! I just have to!*

Despite increasing pain, she dragged her nearly useless leg, making her way down the boardwalk. When she arrived at Brooke's pier, she was just in time to see Rob being forced aboard a yacht called the *Dana Queen*. He was yelling at the top of his lungs. She could barely hear.

"Naomi! Naomi!"

She tried to speak into her phone but found it had smashed in her hand when she fell. She listened for sirens but heard nothing.

Chloe threw herself fruitlessly at the gate to the pier. The lock was shiny and solid, but she was praying for a miracle. With tears streaming down her sweaty face, she watched the *Dana Queen* pull out of its slip and into the harbor.

CHAPTER TWENTY-SIX

R ob clamped his jaw as the woman in yellow punched his spine with what could only be a gun. *So I was wrong about Niebolt. But Brooke? What was her part in all of this?* He wasted time by speculating when he should have been trying to think of a way to escape. There was none with Brooke's gun prodding him painfully down the boardwalk.

"Down to that next gate. My husband's got it open and is waiting for us."

Rob headed toward the gate, his heart pounding. Walking out on the pier, he preceded the woman as she headed for a small, sleek, white fishing yacht. Still at gunpoint, he climbed up the ladder onto the boat, hopelessness swamping him. He was as good as dead. Behind him, he heard some commotion. Then something struck the back of his head and all was blackness.

Rob was coming to in the tiny cabin of the boat. No one was with him. He pulled out the cell phone and dialed 911.

"This is Rob Stevens. I've just been kidnapped and taken out on a boat from the Dana Point Marina. My captors have a gun. They want me dead. In case they get me, they are Brooke Sampson and her husband. They are responsible not only for the attempts on my life but for some as yet undisclosed . . ."

Brooke entered the cabin and swatted his cell phone away from him. Calling out "Bill, he's awake," she covered him with her gun.

The man he now recognized vaguely as the delivery man/ bomber at his office took the gun away from her and aimed it at him. Rob spun away just as the bullet whizzed by. It ricocheted off the metal hull of the boat and flew back to hit Brooke in the arm. She screamed.

"Don't do it in here, you idiot. Take him out on deck."

"First, why don't you tell me what this is about?" Rob asked. "I deserve to know why I'm going to die."

Brooke grimaced. "Well, since you are definitely going to die this time, there's no harm in telling you."

Clutching her arm from which bright red blood was spurting— *dare he hope the bullet had severed an artery?*—she preceded them out of the small cabin. Bill was a very large man and he hauled Rob easily out to the deck by his collar.

"My husband had a little accident one night," Brooke said, looking at her arm. "He's prone to them."

Rob was dismayed to see that the fog was even thicker out to sea than it had been in the harbor. No one would ever find them in this. His future, or lack of one, seemed to be sealed. But, strong as Bill Sampson was, Rob had stayed in shape since his football years. The fight wasn't over yet.

"Anyway, your sister was there. She saw it. She would have reported it, too, but Bill managed to convince her she was to blame."

"What kind of an accident?" Rob asked, trying to gain time.

Brooke shrugged. "A practical joke gone wrong. Bill is a real joker. He spiked the punch at a party we were at and a bunch of people got drunk. One of Ginger's Mormon friends was there, and Ginger thought she was too uptight. Needed some loosening up. So she got her friend to drink the punch, knowing it'd been spiked. Ginger and I were the only other people besides Bill who knew about the spiked punch. For some reason neither of us could understand at the time, it killed her. We set it up to look like a suicide."

Chloe's Mormon friend! The one who had supposedly committed suicide!

"I didn't know until years later—after I married Bill—that he thought it would be fun to see what happened if he gave the Mormon girl a few drugs along with the alcohol. Unfortunately, he underestimated the strength of the drugs and alcohol together. That's really what killed her."

"So why did Ginger think she was responsible?"

Brooke shrugged. "Ginger was the one who got her to drink the punch in the first place. We made a pact not to tell anyone. But if Ginger talks, there is sure to be an exhumation. Traces of the drugs will be found, and the whole evening will be put under a microscope. We can't risk that happening, can we?"

Rob sighed. Poor Ginger. Getting someone drunk wasn't a punishable offense. But he could see why she would feel guilty for the girl's death. Especially since she was a lapsed Mormon herself.

"Ginger had no intention of telling me, you know. She was prepared to drink herself to death."

"That's a chance we couldn't take. Homicide isn't something to be taken lightly."

"Neither is first-degree murder, which is apparently what you have planned for me. And I've called your names into 911. Plus my friends know all about you. You won't get away with this, even if you kill me."

"Oh, we just plan to have you disappear. No one will be able to prove a thing."

"Except the 911 dispatcher I called."

An ugly look crossed Brooke's face. "We've got this all planned. We're heading for Mexico. And do you know what? As long as we're confessing, I have to tell you that I really hated your wife. She was a pretentious hypocrite. Did you know she was carrying on behind your back with Rick for close to ten years? They even had a business together. But you deserved it. I don't think you ever gave that woman a glance. I mean, she was flagrant! And you didn't even care enough to notice. I only kept up with her to keep tabs on Ginger. Now you're going to join Pamela. Won't that be nice?"

Rob sensed it was time to make his move. "You'd better put that gun down and tie a tourniquet on your wife's arm, Bill. That's arterial blood. See how it's spurting?"

Brooke looked at her arm in alarm. Bill lost his focus for a few seconds. Rob sent up a hasty prayer and tackled him straight to the deck, where he banged Bill's head repeatedly against the hardwood. The gun spun out of the man's hands and lodged under the bow. It was too far away for him to grab easily, but Bill wasn't. Unconscious, he weighed a good half ton, but Rob managed to haul him over to the edge of the yacht. Then, grabbing Bill's ankles, he tipped him overboard with a couple of herculean thrusts, just as Brooke came up behind him with the gun.

One down, one to go. Brooke was not going to last long, bleeding like that.

"Okay, Rob. Find something for a tourniquet and tie my arm, or I'll shoot you through the head this instant!"

Pulling the bandanna handkerchief he always carried out of his back pocket, he began to tie it as requested. Then suddenly he let go and simultaneously pushed Brooke to the deck.

She let off a shot as she fell. Twisting instinctively, he avoided the bullet. But he had underestimated this dying woman. The next shot was to his chest. Then the gun fell, and she collapsed, her eyes staring wide.

He was scarcely conscious when he heard the distant rotors of a helicopter. *The fog. They'll never find me in the fog.*

CHAPTER TWENTY-SEVEN

Rob is dying. The Coast Guard had needed to use the GPS signal from his cell phone to get to the boat, and it had taken too long. Chloe sat in the surgical waiting room, staring at the complicated bandage on her knee.

They had given him two transfusions before surgery to repair his lung and artery, but they had told her they weren't hopeful of the outcome. They couldn't keep up with the blood loss, and he had already lost way too much.

Luke stood next to her, his hand caressing her shoulder, trying to offer comfort. Dry-eyed after hours of weeping, Chloe simply stared at the bandage that was holding her knee cap in place until she could have surgery to repair the torn ligaments. *I failed. Dear God, how could you let me fall? I could have caught them. Are you there at all? Do you even care?*

Luke knelt on the floor in front of her. "Chloe, don't give up now. We need to pray. We need to have faith."

Her mother on the other side of her was murmuring to herself over and over about déjà vu, sounding like a madwoman.

"You do it, Luke. I'm afraid I'm fresh out of faith."

Luke bowed his head, "God, wherever you are, please help Rob and the doctors. We need a miracle here. Help. Amen."

Suddenly, Edward was there. Pulling her up out of the plastic chair, he engulfed her with a hug. He whispered, "Everything's going to work out according to plan, Chloe. No death is ever the end."

Anger broke through Chloe's consciousness. "I will not let this happen! I will not let Rob die!" Grabbing her crutches, she hobbled down the hall to the nurse's station. "I'm a universal donor!" she cried. "Take my blood! Take as much as you want. Just save Rob! We're going to get married. In the temple. For eternity. Nothing is going to stop that! Nothing!"

The nurse looked at her with such a blank face that Chloe wanted to hit her. "Do something!" she demanded.

Edward came up behind her then and put a hand on her shoulder. Shaking it off, she almost didn't hear him say, "The doctor just came out."

Trying to turn too fast with her crutches, Chloe fell. Edward helped her up. "Here now, take it easy. He wants to talk to you."

Fear gripped her. It was bad news. She knew it was bad news.

"We managed to get a stent into the torn artery," the man in the green scrubs told her gently. "But like I told you, he's lost a lot of blood, so we're continuing to transfuse. I wish I could say for sure that he will make it, but at least he's no longer losing blood. We'll just hope what he's getting now isn't too little, too late."

"How about his lung?" Chloe asked.

"He's doing fine with one lung for the moment. We've got him on a respirator. If he wakes up, we'll worry about the lung then.

That's where the bullet's lodged. But we don't need to introduce the trauma of another surgery right now."

"How soon will we know if he's going to be all right?"

"If he makes it through the night, things will look very positive in the morning," the doctor said. He flashed a tired smile.

"Thank you, doctor. Thank you." Chloe put her hands to her eyes and wept.

She spent the night with her head on Luke's lap. He stroked her hair until she couldn't feel the pain in her knee any longer, until she was too tired to hold on to her fear. The last thing she remembered before she fell asleep was Luke's voice saying, "Man, the fog is really rolling in out there. Doesn't God realize it's July?"

In the morning, Chloe woke to see Luke dozing uncomfortably above her. Her mother was gone. *Has Rob died and my mother left because she couldn't bear to tell me?*

Forgetting her crutches and heedless of the pain in her knee, she limped her way through the busy halls screaming, "Rob, Rob, where have they taken you? Where's the morgue in this place?"

⌒ン

Rob felt himself being shaken awake after what seemed like days. He wasn't dead unless Ginger was, too, and paradise looked like a hospital.

"Rob! You've got to wake up! They just took out your respirator. You're going to live!"

Light was pouring through the windows. In part of his slow-moving mind, he registered that the fog had finally lifted.

"Ginger. You're here." He took in the sight of his sister's frightened face, her rumpled clothing, and her messy hair. His throat hurt. She'd been talking about a respirator.

"Yes. But not for long. I had to get away!"

"Ginger. The Sampsons are dead. They confessed to murdering that girl at Stanford before they shot me."

"They told you that?"

Even though it was difficult, he continued. "Yes. Now you can get sober and quit talking about suicide. You didn't kill anyone."

Ginger, already pale, looked as though she might faint.

"Look, Sis, encouraging someone to drink is bad, but it's not criminal. What's criminal is that you've been covering for Bill Sampson all these years."

Tears coursed down his sister's cheeks, and he felt her self-condemnation.

"Bill Sampson? You don't understand. That girl died! She died because she drank that punch. I killed her!"

Rob tried to lift his arms, but he was too weak to offer Ginger the hug she needed so badly. "Is that what they told you, Brooke and Bill? That she died from the punch?"

"Yes!"

"She didn't. She died of a drug overdose. Administered by Bill. Brooke told me. She also told me they kept you in line by telling you that you were in it with them. But now the truth is out."

His sister looked confused, and his strength was waning. How they had found the boat and managed to save him from a mortal wound he couldn't imagine.

He made one more effort. He had to stop her from going to the police. He was the only witness to the truth. "If you want to confess to purge your soul of your tiny part in all of this, I suppose you can, but it would just muddy the waters. Let things be. I can tell the police what Brooke told me, and I don't think they'll bother you at all. The Sampsons' desperation speaks for itself."

His sister appeared completely bewildered. "Then I'm not a murderer?"

"No." Rob looked into her teary eyes and tried to imagine how she must be feeling. He couldn't.

Ginger just shook her head. "I can't believe it. After all these years."

Listening, he heard someone screaming his name in the hallway, demanding to know the way to the morgue.

Chloe! She doesn't know I'm alive!

He gripped his sister's hand with puny strength. "That's my Chloe out there, raising Cain. Will you please go out and tell her I'm alive?"

"The girl out in the waiting room sleeping in the lap of the most handsome hunk of man I've ever seen? Sorry, Bro. I don't think she's yours."

For a moment he felt a qualm, but then belligerence surged up inside of him. "Get her in here right now!"

"She was lying in his lap, and he was stroking her hair."

"I don't care! She probably thinks I'm dead or she would never allow such a thing."

"You've got a heck of a nerve, thinking you can compete with that specimen!"

Rob pushed away all doubts. Life was precarious. He couldn't waste a moment of it. "Get her!" he commanded.

"Only family is allowed in ICU," Ginger said, a ghost of a grin crossing her face.

"Tell anyone who questions you that she's my fiancée!"

"I've tried that, Rob, but it doesn't work," Chloe whispered hoarsely from the doorway. He could hear the smile in her voice. "This is as far as I'm allowed to go."

"I'm the invalid here, and I say that you'd better get yourself in here and explain why you've been draping yourself all over that male model and letting him stroke your hair. Not to mention raising the dead in the morgue with your screaming."

Chloe looked both ways and then limped in beside his bed. Rob hardly registered Ginger's exit.

Laying her hand over his, she said, "That male model said the prayer that saved your life, so you'd better play nice."

Then she stooped down and kissed him on the lips. Whatever was wrong with him hadn't affected his heart. It had just received such a shot of that warm honey-sweetness that he knew for certain his recovery had accelerated one hundred percent.

"You're mine?" he asked solemnly.

"All yours," she assured him.

"Then get out of here before you get caught and tell Luke that saving my life does not give him the right to stroke that gorgeous Botticelli hair of yours."

"So we're back to Botticelli, are we?" Her look mocked him.

He sobered. "He's inescapable, I'm afraid. Remember, the first time I saw you, you came out of the mist, rising from the foam."

"But I wasn't naked," she told him.

He decided it was best that he keep silent after that and just kiss the woman. He loved her body and soul, and her kiss was telling him that poor Luke had just lost the most important thing in his life.

ABOUT THE AUTHOR

G. G. Vandagriff studied writing at Stanford University and later received her master's degree from George Washington University. She worked for five years in the financial field before her children were born. After that she taught part-time in several different colleges. She was very happy when the day came that she could finally concentrate on her first love: creative writing. *Foggy with a Chance of Murder* is her tenth novel. G. G. received the 2009 Whitney Award for Best Historical Fiction for her novel *The Last Waltz: A Novel of Love and War.*

Now living in Provo, Utah, G. G. and her husband, David, are the parents of three children and the grandparents of two. Besides her number one favorite pastime of playing in the tent with her grandchildren where they make up stories, she loves to travel. Also high on her list of favorite things is communicating with her readers through her blog, ggvandagriffblog.com, and her various websites: ggvandagriff.com, last-waltz.com, deliverance-depression.com, and arthurianomen.com.